Changing Scenes
of Life

Judy Ford

Bernie
Fazakerley
Publications

Changing Scenes of Life.

Published by Bernie Fazakerley Publications

ISBN-10: 1-911083-09-2
ISBN-13: 978-1-911083-09-2

DEDICATION

To the Spinal Injuries Association and everyone living with
spinal cord injuries.

CONTENTS

ACKNOWLEDGEMENTS

For information about living with spinal injuries:
Spinal Injuries Association:
http://www.spinal.co.uk/page/living-with-sci

For information about ovarian cancer:
Cancer Research UK: http://www.cancerresearchuk.org/

Rowan Williams' address at Wycliffe and Trinity
theological colleges in Toronto:
http://rowanwilliams.archbishopofcanterbury.org/articles.
php/1428/archbishop-in-canada-church-needs-to-listen-
properly-to-the-bible#sthash.uPuX3Zx0.dpuf

"You'll Never Walk Alone": words from the Rodgers and
Hammerstein musical Carousel.
Copyright © 1945 by Richard Rodgers & Oscar
Hammerstein II
Copyright renewed. International Copyright Secured. All
Rights Reserved.
Used by Permission of Williams Music, A Division of
Rodgers & Hammerstein: An Imagem Company.

"When I am an old woman": poem by Jenny Joseph. In
Jenny Joseph Selected Poems, Bloodaxe Books, 1992.

"The Mystery of the Invisible Thief": Enid Blyton, Hodder
& Stoughton, London, 1950.

"The Very Hungry Caterpillar": Eric Carle, World
Publishing Company, 1969.

Every effort has been made to trace copyright holders.
The publishers will be glad to rectify in future editions any
errors or omissions brought to their attention.

1 TELL ME THE OLD, OLD STORY

'Hello? I'm Bethan Abbott, from *Inspirational Lives*. I'm here to talk to Detective Chief Inspector Jonah Porter.'

The young television researcher spoke anxiously into the intercom by the front door of a large house in the suburbs of Oxford.

'That's right,' came a rather indistinct male voice, 'push the door and come in.'

Bethan obediently pushed the green-painted door and stepped cautiously inside. As her eyes became accustomed to relative darkness after the bright sunshine, she saw, emerging from a room to the left, a man in an electric wheelchair. She immediately recognised him as the police detective who had won fame and admiration for returning to work successfully after suffering a gunshot wound that had left him almost completely paralysed.

'Chief Inspector Porter?'

'Jonah, please. Now if you don't mind closing the door behind you …'

Bethan did as she was asked.

'Come through here: this is my study. We can talk without being interrupted here.'

With a slight movement of his left index finger on a

joystick, Jonah manoeuvred the chair round and retreated back into the room from which he had come. Bethan followed.

'Sit down.' Jonah inclined his head towards an armchair. 'Now, can I get you anything? Tea? Coffee? Or do you only drink water, like so many of you young people nowadays?'

'No thanks, I'm fine. There's no need …' Bethan trailed off, unsure of the correct answer. How could he produce the offered beverages, given his disability? But would it be patronising to decline his hospitality for that reason? She was saved from further embarrassment by the arrival in the room of a woman in her late fifties with short grey hair, who put her head round the door and announced in a strong Liverpool accent, 'Hi! I'm Bernie. I'm just about to make a brew, would you like one?'

'Miss Abbott?' Jonah looked up at her enquiringly. 'We always have a cup of tea in the middle of the afternoon – won't you join us?'

'Yes. Thanks. And call me Bethan, please.'

'Right. Won't be long.' Bernie's head disappeared and Bethan made an effort to gather her thoughts. She opened her bag and got out a notepad and a pen.

'Now Chief Inspect – Jonah,' she corrected herself, 'I think my colleague explained to you the format of the *Inspirational Lives* series? It's a new programme to fill our Sunday afternoon religious spot. The idea is that one of our presenters interviews someone whose life could be seen as an inspiration to others: people who have achieved great things or come through difficult situations or succeeded against the odds. They talk about their lives and what inspires *them*; and they choose their favourite hymns, which we get our choir to sing for them.'

'A sort of religious "Desert Island discs",' commented Jonah with a smile.

'Yes – something like that. Now,' Bethan consulted her notes. 'First, I'd just like to check some basic facts. You've been paralysed since being shot in the back of the neck eight years ago – is that right?'

'Apart from three fingers, that's right,' agreed Jonah, illustrating the point by wiggling his left thumb, index and middle finger. 'But it's amazing what you can do with three fingers – plus voice recognition, of course. And I've been lucky to have lots of help from people around me – designing this chair, for example. I can go almost anywhere in it, and this screen gives me built-in internet access and videoconferencing and if there's anything I can't deal with myself I can summon help in an instant!'

He pressed a button on the arm of his chair and a few seconds later the screen lit up showing a picture of Bernie's face. 'You rang, milord?'

'Just giving Bethan a demo of my emergency support system; but while you're on, how about bringing her a piece of that ginger cake that Lucy made yesterday?'

'Already on the tray. Now, if you've quite finished playing games, maybe I could be permitted to fill the teapot!'

The screen went blank and Jonah looked up at Bethan's face, which displayed an expression of mild amusement. She hastily rearranged her features and returned to business.

'Perhaps you could start by describing what happened. I mean, how were you shot?'

'Nothing much to say, really. Our garden backed on to a golf course. Not here, of course – we had a house over Reading way in those days.'

'Was it your disability that meant you had to move?' Bethan asked, keen to understand the impact on Jonah's life of his sudden injury.

'Oh no – that was years later. We made all sorts of modifications to that house – a lift, an automatic front door and intercom system (like the one we have here), all sorts of things. The house wasn't a problem at all; but after my wife died it just made more sense to move in here with

Our Bernie and co.'

Bethan opened her mouth to ask another question, but Jonah continued with his story.

'Anyway, someone must have walked across the golf course and waited until I was in the garden on my own and then shot me from behind. Clearly pre-meditated, but I've no idea what the motive could have been.'

'And the perpetrator has never been brought to justice – does that make you feel bitter?'

'No, I wouldn't say "bitter" – more just puzzled, I suppose. What did I do to make someone hate me enough to try to kill me? What were they expecting to achieve by it?'

'So no resentment that you are effectively serving a life sentence while the person who shot you has got away scot free?'

Jonah smiled and shook his head. 'I'm not sure that I agree with this idea that every victim of crime is serving a life sentence. Plenty of people have life-changing events that aren't the result of a crime. The way I see it is that it's up to me to make the most I can of my life whatever the circumstances, and brooding on the injustice of it all doesn't help. Every policeman feels frustrated when a case can't be solved, but I can't feel resentment against someone when I don't know who they are or why they did it.'

'Do you think you were targeted *because* you were a policeman?'

'That's what we've always assumed, but who knows? The only concrete suspects were connected with a gang rape case, which was due to come to trial a couple of weeks after I was shot. We'd caught two of the group and they were remanded in custody, but we knew that there were others whom we couldn't identify. My evidence was crucial to getting a conviction, so the theory is that the other gang members were trying to prevent me giving it. In the event, my written reports and records of interviews with the suspects were sufficient to send them down; so if that *was* the motive for shooting me, it didn't succeed.'

While he was speaking, the door opened and Bernie reappeared with a tray containing a small jug of milk, a basin of sugar cubes, a cup and saucer and a plate, all in matching bone china. On the plate lay a single slice of ginger cake. Also on the tray were a large teapot in a knitted cosy and a plastic cup with a lid and a long straw. She put the tray down on a coffee table in the centre of the room and turned to Bethan, waiting for Jonah to finish speaking, before addressing her.

'Milk?'

'Yes please.'

Bernie poured some milk into the china cup and topped it up from the teapot. Then she repeated the process with the plastic cup, replaced the lid firmly and put it on a small tray attached to Jonah's chair, adjusting it carefully to check that he could reach to drink from the straw.

'Only one cup?' he asked, looking pointedly in the direction of the coffee table and then up at Bernie's face.

'Things to do,' Bernie replied, heading for the door. 'Call me if you need anything.'

'She's very protective of my independence,' Jonah explained as the door closed behind her. 'She's afraid that if she stays you'll start speaking to her about me, instead of addressing me direct – the "Does he take sugar?" phenomenon.'

'And does that happen a lot?'

'Well, in my work I'm generally the one asking the questions,' Jonah smiled. 'But, yes, sometimes people do still find it difficult to know how to talk to someone in a wheelchair. Shopping tends to be the worst – in fact I do most of my shopping online these days.'

'How does it make you feel?'

'It doesn't bother me – certainly not as much as it bothers Our Bernie! I know it's not malicious and I'm quite capable of speaking up for myself and getting noticed. People are understandably nervous about speaking to someone with disabilities because they're afraid of saying the wrong thing and maybe upsetting or embarrassing them.

'Take trying on shoes, for example,' Jonah went on, warming to his subject. 'It's unreasonable of me to expect the shop assistant to know how to go about putting shoes on to someone who can't move his feet. And what do I say if they ask me whether they feel comfortable when I haven't been able to feel my feet for eight years? Actually, in that situation the most useful input is going to be from a carer who's had the dubious privilege of looking after my feet and can say things like "I think they're going to rub that patch of damaged skin on your right big toe".'

Bethan smiled. 'So, do you have any advice for people who might be anxious about how to approach someone with a disability?'

'I suppose only the obvious – ask them how they'd like to be treated. Then it's up to them to tell you enough about their needs for you to get it right. But ask them direct – don't start out by addressing the carer, as if you assume that anyone in a wheelchair is incapable of speaking for themselves.'

Jonah paused and smiled to himself as he recollected past experiences. 'It used to drive Margaret – that's my wife – mad. It got so's I didn't like going to places with her in case she launched into her lecture on the evils of infantilising the disabled! Our Bernie's more subtle – she just doesn't answer anyone if they ask her questions that she thinks they ought to have asked me.' He chuckled. 'Now there's a thing! "Our Bernie" and "subtle" in the same sentence – I doubt if that's ever happened before!'

'Why do you keep calling her "Our Bernie"?'

'Everyone calls her "Our Bernie" – in recognition of her linguistic roots.'

'Meaning?' asked Bethan, puzzled.

'You must surely have noticed,' Jonah was smiling broadly, "that she speaks a dialect of English known technically, I believe, as "Dead Scouse"!'

Bethan still wasn't sure that she understood, but decided not to pursue this line.

'Tell me about your wife.' she prompted. 'It must have been a dreadful shock to her when you were injured.'

'Yes,' Jonah agreed, 'and all the worse for her because she also had the boys to worry about. Well, I say "boys" but Nathan had just finished his first year at Oxford and Reuben was married and working as a junior doctor in County Durham. So they were young men really, but still completely shocked at what had happened. I think that, as far as they were concerned, it felt as if my life – or any life worth living – had ended.'

'And didn't you feel like that yourself at all?'

'Well, if I'm honest, there were times when I was pretty down – and probably in those early weeks, the times when I wasn't may have been more due to not really being able to believe that it was happening to me – but, no, I think that Margaret (and other friends) managed to keep me believing that I still mattered and could make a contribution. She was a real pillar of strength, particularly during those first few weeks.'

'So it must have seemed like a particularly cruel blow when she died?' Bethan suggested gently.

'Yes – and no.' Jonah paused to think. 'Yes, of course I'd come to rely on her a lot. She was my main carer when I wasn't at work. And she was my best friend and the one person whom I never needed to worry about saying the wrong thing to. But, I actually think that it might have been more difficult to have lost her if I'd still been able-bodied.' He paused again, trying to find the right words to explain.

'Before I was shot, Margaret and I were very much a couple. We had friends, but none of them were particularly close. We each had demanding jobs and when we came home we liked it to be just the two of us. One of the benefits of becoming disabled was that we both had to learn to accept help from other people – and it was amazing how many people wanted to help. By the time that Margaret died, we'd gathered around us a wonderful group of friends who were there to support me through her last illness and beyond. It was like having a new family – although,' he added hastily, 'of course some of them, my mother and sister, the boys and so on, were already actual family members.'

Bethan nodded. 'I think I understand. Now, would it be OK for you to tell me some more about your wife? How you met – that sort of thing? And do you have a hymn that you particularly associate with her memory?'

'By all means. Sit back and eat your cake and I'll recount the story of our romance.'

Bethan looked at the single piece of cake, doubtfully. 'What about you?'

'I fear not,' Jonah said ruefully. 'Got to watch my weight, I'm afraid. Can't burn off the calories the way I used to, and I've got to think about the people who have to lift and carry me. Go on – tuck in! Lucy will be disappointed if you spurn her confection.'

Bethan smiled, picked up the cake and bit into it.

2 THOU GOD OF TRUTH AND LOVE

'Regarding a hymn to represent my wife,' Jonah went on. 'I'd like to choose *Thou God of truth and Love*. It started out as a love poem from Charles Wesley to his wife.'

'Really?' Bethan noted this down. 'I'll get that checked out. It's just the sort of titbit of information that our viewers may be interested in.'

'But the reason I'm choosing it,' Jonah went on, 'is the second verse, which goes:

'Why hast thou cast our lot in this same age and place,
'And why together brought to see each other's face?

'It was such an amazing conjunction of circumstances that brought about our meeting that it's hard not to imagine that it was part of some grand plan. We met in the A&E department one Friday night – she was doing her postgraduate medical training and I was a humble police constable. She had come up to Oxford from Bolton and I was still living with my parents in Kidlington. I escorted a couple of drunks to A&E after they'd got into a fight and injured themselves. Margaret patched me up when one of them turned on me in the waiting area.

'It could so easily never have happened. Margaret could have gone to train at a different medical school. My parents could have moved down to Kent a couple of years earlier than they did and I might have gone with them. Margaret might not have been on duty that night. If I'd been more experienced, I wouldn't have allowed myself to be caught off-guard and I wouldn't have needed medical attention.

'So we were very lucky to have met at all on that fateful Friday night back in November 1979.'

****

'There, I think the nosebleed has stopped now,' Margaret peered closely at Jonah's face, assessing the damage. 'But I'm, afraid you'll probably have a couple of black eyes in the morning. How does your head feel?'

Jonah turned his head from side to side experimentally. 'OK.' He lied bravely, hoping that the attractive young doctor standing before him had not noticed him wince. He struggled to focus on her face, which had deep brown eyes surrounded by dark lashes and dark hair tied back by a bright green ribbon, just visible behind the nape of her neck. Her lips were a glossy deep red and her eye shadow was a green colour that matched the hair ribbon.

'*I* believe you,' she said, smiling. 'Thousands wouldn't. But, to be on the safe side, I'd go straight home now, if I were you – no more chasing criminals tonight. '

'My shift is supposed to end in about half an hour anyway,' Jonah agreed. Then he added hopefully, 'What time do you go off duty?'

Margaret looked at her watch. 'About twenty minutes ago!'

'Can I drive you home?'

Margaret looked amused. 'That's very kind of you, but I have my own transport thank you.' Then, seeing his evident disappointment, she went on. 'But if you care to come with me, I could fix up a restoring mug of cocoa for you.'

'Sounds good. Where do you live?'

'Is your car outside?'

Jonah nodded, wincing again as he discovered that the movement made his head throb.

'Tell you what – I'll get my things and meet you there with my vehicle. Then you can follow me home.'

Jonah waited impatiently in his car, looking out for Margaret to appear. Eventually he was startled by a tap on the nearside window. He leaned over and wound it down to allow the motorcyclist who had drawn up next to him to peer in. 'Ready to go?' enquired Margaret, smiling at his surprised expression as he recognised her. 'I'd offer you a lift, but I don't have a spare helmet.'

As the motorcycle moved away Jonah noticed her hair hanging down beneath the helmet in a long, thick plait fastened at the bottom with another green ribbon.

A few minutes later, they were entering the house, which she shared with a group of postgraduate students, and heading upstairs to her room. Margaret put the key into the lock and tried unsuccessfully to turn it. Eventually she tried the handle and the door swung open.

'That's odd,' she murmured 'I could have sworn I'd locked it.'

They went in and Margaret waved her hand towards a battered sofa. "Sit down there while I pop down to the kitchen and -,' She broke off suddenly, staring at the mantelpiece.

'What's the matter?' asked Jonah, puzzled.

'I had a photo there – on the mantelpiece – and it's gone. Someone must have been in while I was out and taken it.'

'Was it valuable? Is anything else missing?' Jonah was suddenly alert and reaching for his pocket book.

'No – not valuable at all. It was just a holiday snap. Only it was the last holiday that we went on with my Nan before she died.' Margaret sat down on the sofa and stared at the floor, thinking hard.

'Aren't you going to check whether anything else has been taken?' Jonah urged.

'Maybe later, but I don't think there will be anything. This isn't the first time things have gone missing. Over the last few weeks, practically all of us have lost something. It's never anything particularly valuable, just little personal things that you wouldn't want to lose.'

'Such as?'

'Well, there was the fountain pen that my Nan bought me when I started at the grammar school. It wasn't anything special, but I kept using it because it reminded me of her. And one of the lads downstairs lost his old school tie, of all ridiculous things! Then there were a couple of personalised mugs, and,' Margaret giggled, 'Derek Holder had this dead naff pair of Union Jack underpants, which he claimed disappeared from the washing machine.'

'Did you report any of these thefts?'

'No!' Margaret sounded scornful. 'Who would have taken them seriously? Even *we* didn't take them seriously. At first, we just kept telling each other that we must be misremembering where we'd left them and they'd turn up sooner or later. But none of them *have* turned up and it isn't pleasant to think that one of us must be taking things.'

'So what are you going to do about it? I couldn't live in a house where I knew there was someone just waiting to sneak into my room to take my things.'

'You're right,' Margaret agreed. 'And you've put your finger on it – this theft is different from the others. All the other things disappeared from the communal area – the living room or the kitchen. It's much more sinister to think that someone may have a key to my room.'

'You ought to change the lock.'

'I'm not sure the landlord would be happy with that. Anyway, the chances are that I just forgot to lock the door when I went out. No,' Margaret spoke decisively now. 'I think we ought to investigate this ourselves and see if we can't work out who it is.'

'And when you use the term "we"?' Jonah sounded sceptical and slightly amused.

'You and me, of course! I can tell you all about the suspects and what's gone missing and when, and then we can use the process of elimination to work out who could have taken everything.'

'If you want a police investigation you ought to go through the proper channels – and I'm not in CID, y'know.'

'I told you – if we went through the "proper channels" as you call it they'd just laugh. Besides – it would be so awkward having the police questioning everyone. Oh, go on! It'll be fun.'

'Oh all right.' Jonah still sounded reluctant, torn between a feeling that it was his professional duty to refuse to get involved and a desire to take the opportunity of seeing more of this attractive, albeit somewhat intimidating, young woman. 'But not tonight.' He said firmly. 'It's high time we both turned in. How about tomorrow? I'm not on duty this weekend, so I could come round whenever it suits you.'

'Perfect! Come first thing. I can do breakfast for you if you like.'

Jonah shook his head ruefully. 'I think my parents would worry if I told them I was going round to a girl's for breakfast. I'll come about nine – if that's OK.'

The following day Jonah was there promptly at nine. In fact, in his anxiety not to be late, he arrived twenty-five minutes early and spent an anxious time parked a few streets away waiting until he dared to approach the house. He rang the bell and was surprised that the door was opened almost immediately by Margaret, who must have been waiting in the hall for him to arrive.

They stood staring at one another for a few moments. Without his uniform, Jonah looked younger, Margaret thought. Twenty perhaps? Surely, he couldn't be still in his teens, could he? Of course, he had admitted that he was still living with his parents. She smiled to herself, remembering how her father used to say that you can tell that you are getting old when the policemen start looking younger. His brown hair, just long enough for Margaret to discern a gentle wave, was scrupulously combed. As predicted, dark bruising had appeared on either side of his nose and his eye sockets were puffy. It would be a while before she would be able to see what his face was really like. The eyes themselves – were they blue or grey?

Margaret too looked different today. Most of her hair was loose, with a purple ribbon tying back the front and sides to keep her face clear. It cascaded down her back almost to her waist. Her eye shadow was a pale lilac colour while her lips and nails were deep purple to match the hair ribbon. Her eyes were bright and she looked fresh and alert – no longer the tired junior doctor at the end of a busy shift.

They recollected themselves and made their way upstairs to her room where two mugs and a kettle were standing on top of a chest of drawers ready to make tea. Margaret flicked a switch to put the kettle on and then drew Jonah across to a large desk beneath the window.

'Here you are – I've made a start,' she said, showing him some sheets of paper. 'This is a list of everyone who lives in the house; and this is a list of the things that have gone missing and when. So now,' she moved the papers aside to reveal an A3 sheet marked out in a square grid, 'we can look at when each theft took place and check that against where everyone was at the time – or at least note down whether or not they were definitely somewhere else – and with luck there'll only be one or two of them who could have taken all the things.'

Jonah was sceptical. 'Or else we'll find that nobody can quite remember where they were a week ago last Thursday, or whatever. And in any case – why would they tell us, if they could?' Then, seeing the look of dissatisfaction on Margaret's face, he went on. 'Look – why don't you start by telling me who all these people are? I don't know anything about the set up here – things like: do people regularly borrow things without asking? What are the rules about sharing the washing machine? What relationships are going on between people?'

The kettle boiled and Margaret made tea. Then they sat down together with an A4 pad and a pen. There was only one chair of a suitable height for the desk, so they sat together on the sofa. Margaret put her list of residents on the rather inadequate coffee table in front of them and started to go through them one by one, while Jonah took notes.

'Downstairs we have three men, because the university doesn't consider it safe to house women on the ground floor.'

'But this isn't a university building, is it?' queried Jonah.

'No, it's privately owned, but to be on the list of Approved Lodgings it has to meet certain standards. The landlord doesn't take any undergraduates here: it's strictly postgrads and professional people. I've been here since I was a postgraduate medical student. Most of the others are students – except for Paul and Jane upstairs, who are postdocs.'

'OK. So, you were starting downstairs. Who are these three men in your life? I hope they are all either spoken for or else elderly, balding and generally unattractive. And if I get a whiff of an idea that you fancy one of them, I will immediately become convinced that he must be the culprit!'

'I'm so glad I thought of bringing in someone from outside to look into this,' Margaret observed with dry humour. 'It's so good to have a completely unbiased view.'

Their eyes met and they laughed together. Suddenly it seemed as if they had been friends forever.

'Let's see,' Margaret mused. 'There's Karl Meissner. He's from West Germany – Stuttgart I think. He's been living here longer than anyone else, apart from me. This is his third year. He's doing a DPhil in Physics.'

'DPhil?'

'Doctor of Philosophy – it's a postgraduate degree.'

'Any of his stuff gone missing?'

'No-o,' Margaret paused to think. 'No, nothing; but then he doesn't tend to leave any of his things lying around in the communal areas. He doesn't have any of his own cooking things, for example. He just uses the crockery and cutlery that come with the house. So there isn't as much opportunity for his stuff to be taken.'

'So your photo was unusual – being taken from your room, I mean?'

'Yes – I told you that it was a first. I suppose I must have forgotten to lock the door and the thief took advantage.'

'OK. So, back to this Meissner character: what's he like? Does he have a girlfriend? What does he do in his spare time?'

'I don't really know him very well – he keeps himself to himself and seems to spend most of his time working. Maybe he has a girlfriend back home.'

'I'll put him down as "suspicious foreigner".'

'In the spirit of keeping an open mind until you have all the facts?'

'Precisely! Until I have confirmation of this hypothetical German girlfriend I shall have to keep my mind open to the possibility that he has stayed living in this house for so long solely in order to be close to you.'

'Moving swiftly on,' Margaret giggled, "in the other front bedroom, we have Derek Holder. He's a fourth year chemist. Chemistry students do their finals after three years and then a fourth year doing a research project. So they count as postgraduates even though they haven't actually finished their degree yet.'

'Sounds complicated,' observed Jonah.

'Yes, but that's Oxford for you. If you're one of the oldest universities in Europe, you're expected to have eccentric rules. And why choose a simple and logical course structure when there is a complicated, illogical one available?'

'So, presumably this Derek fellow has only been living here for a few weeks – if he was only eligible this year?"

'Well, actually, he moved in just after the end of Trinity term.'

'So he didn't go home for the long vacation?'

'No. He and Julie – that's another fourth year chemist – both moved in, in July. They were going out together then, but they split up over the summer.'

'And presumably she moved out?'

'No. she's still here. Her room's on this floor – diagonally across from mine.'

'Any idea what caused the rift?'

Margaret shook her head. 'I just assumed that, after living under the same roof for a few weeks, they realised that they didn't care for each other as much as they thought.'

'And no idea who dumped whom?'

'No. As far as I could tell, it was by mutual agreement.'

'Or maybe she decided that she couldn't bear his choice of undergarments.'

'You've lost me.'

'This *is* the proud possessor of the famous union jack underpants we're talking about, isn't it?'

'Yes. So you *were* paying attention after all.'

'Of course. Anyway it's down here in black and white,' Jonah indicated the list of stolen items. 'So this Derek may be a spurned lover who would be tempted to turn to you on the rebound. That definitely elevates him to the top of the suspect list!'

'Jonah!' Margaret said reproachfully, 'You really aren't taking this seriously at all are you?'

'On the contrary, I'm deadly serious. The thought that some spotty chemistry student with poor dress sense may be about to throw himself at your feet is an extremely serious matter indeed!'

'Then there's Simon Coulter,' Margaret said firmly. 'He's in the third year of a Maths DPhil. He lived in college in the first year and moved in here just over a year ago. He spends a lot of time in his room, so I suppose he'd have more than average opportunity to pinch things while other people are out. Karl and Derek are out working in the labs most days. Before you ask,' she went on, seeing Jonah opening his mouth to speak, 'He has never made any attempt to get off with me – or with any of the other lasses, as far as I know – and I'm not aware of him having a girlfriend.'

'And his room is presumably the one at the back?' asked Jonah, 'seeing as the other men had the two front rooms?'

'That's right.'

'With its door right opposite the door to the living room?'

'Yes – fancy you noticing that.'

'I'm a policeman. We're trained to be observant.'

'So you're saying that it would be easy for him to watch out for when things were left unattended and sneak in and take them.'

'Precisely! Which ought to move him to the top of the suspect list – except that you are determined to portray him as pure as the driven snow. But,' Jonah mused, 'perhaps it's a case of "the lady doth protest too much" – are you quite sure that you don't have designs on his body which you are cunningly concealing from me?'

Margaret laughed out loud. 'Not unless he lands up on the operating table! I'm hoping to become a surgeon, so naturally I would jump at any opportunity to carve him up – in the interests of his continuing health, of course.'

'OK. Let's leave him for the time being and proceed, metaphorically, upstairs. You said that it's "Men Only" on the ground floor, but presumably any surplus males could be housed upstairs?'

'Yes – but we don't have any. So there are four women on the 1st floor and then Paul and Jane in the second floor flat.'

'They're a married couple, I take it?'

'Not exactly. The flat has two bedrooms, but we all assume that they're what my mother would describe as "living in sin". They're postdocs working on some big research project about the importance of invertebrate species in tropical rainforests. They're not here at the moment. They went off on a field trip about three weeks ago and aren't due back until a week on Friday. So that means,' Margaret went on, consulting her list of missing items, 'that the only thing *they* could have taken is my pen, which went the day before they left.'

'It looks as if we can rule them out,' agreed Jonah. 'So that just leaves us with the girls on the first floor.'

'Well there's me–,' began Margaret.

'Dr Margaret Hulme, Senior House Officer,' interrupted Jonah. 'Another example of my powers of observation,' he went on, 'which, I believe,' he added, 'makes you a Junior Doctor.'

'That's right. Hence *I'm* the one who has to stay on beyond the end of my shift to patch up policemen who get into fights in A&E!'

'Boyfriend?' Jonah enquired. 'I ask merely in order to further this enquiry and not so as to be able to beat to a pulp any man presuming to court you – though that would, of course, be nice!'

Margaret laughed. 'Don't worry! My love life is a metaphorical desert – which is probably just as well considering your recent record when it comes to fist fighting.'

'Excellent!' said Jonah with satisfaction, noting down the information. 'Obviously we assume that you are not guilty, but we'd better keep you on the list for completeness. Now – who else is there?'

'Mandy Molyneux and Lesley Fanshaw are both doing

PGCEs -'

'PGCEs?'

'Postgraduate Certificate in Education,' Margaret translated. 'They've finished their degrees and now they're training to be teachers. Mandy did music and Lesley did, um, history I think. They both have boyfriends who are in their final year, which I suspect had some influence on their decision to stay on. I don't mean that that's why they decided to do a PGCE, but that's why they stayed in Oxford rather than going somewhere else.'

'And these boyfriends aren't eligible to live here because they're still undergraduates?'

'That's right. Mandy's is in the year below her, and Lesley's is a Modern Languages student who did a year abroad.'

'And how would you rate their opportunities for pinching things?'

'Well, they were both in and out of the room when my pen went AWOL, but more generally I'd have said that their course keeps them out of the house a lot during the day, so, probably quite limited.'

'OK, we can look at that in more detail later. Now, by a tremendous feat of deduction, I conclude that the only remaining person in the house is Julie, the erstwhile companion of the odious Derek with the unspeakable underpants. Julie Potts, according to your list. Is there anything else I ought to know about her?'

'I don't think so. She's a bit jumpy sometimes. I know she got very anxious over her final exams and was prescribed sleeping pills. Obviously it's a bit awkward for her and Derek to be still living in the same house, but they just seem to try to avoid one another as much as possible.'

'And neither of them have formed new attachments?'

'Not as far as I know.'

'Right. So now let's have a look at this list of missing items.'

Margaret looked at her watch. 'How long have you got?

I mean – is your mum expecting you home to lunch or anything?'

'I told my parents that I'd probably be out all day – I hope that wasn't presumptuous. If you want me to leave sooner just say the word. I just thought this Miss Marple stuff might take some time.'

'No. I was hoping you'd stay. I was just wondering whether we had to hurry to meet a deadline. Is tinned stuff OK for lunch? It's about all I've got in at the moment. You can choose between tinned meatballs, corned beef or, if you're feeling adventurous you could risk allowing me to make a meat and potato pie using a tin of stewed steak.'

'They all sound fine to me – certainly as good as the police canteen.'

A couple of hours later they were sitting companionably at the large kitchen table eating Margaret's 'home-made' meat and potato pie accompanied by tinned carrots. At the other end of table, the two student teachers munched on bread and cheese and chatted about lesson plans and the absurdities of the allocation of teaching practice schools. Margaret introduced them to Jonah, but did not tell them what his profession was or why he was there. They displayed no curiosity and made no effort to include Margaret and Jonah in their conversation.

Karl, the taciturn German, wandered in, nodded by way of greeting at the two little groups around the table and then made himself a cup of strong black coffee and disappeared back to his room with it. None of the other residents of the house was in evidence.

'So,' Margaret asked teasingly, 'You're still living with your parents. When are you going to take the plunge and move into a place of your own?'

'Eleven weeks today.'

'Really? Where are you going?'

'Don't know yet.'

'So how come you're so definite about the date? Have they given you an ultimatum?'

'In a way. My Dad's a Baptist pastor. He's been invited to go down to Kent to look after the church where he grew up, and that's the day that they're due to make the move. It's all very fortuitous really: it means that they'll be close to my Gran, who's recently widowed and not too well herself.'

'But it leaves you homeless?'

'Well, you could hardly expect the new pastor to let me stay on in the manse, could you?'

'What sort of place are you looking for?'

Jonah shrugged. 'Somewhere cheap.' Then, seeing that Margaret expected more, he went on. 'Maybe a flat, but probably just a room – like this – to keep the cost down. I want to be able save up to buy somewhere for myself eventually – a house, with a garden, so I can grow things.'

'You like growing things?'

'Yes – the manse has a big garden. I grew lots of vegetables and soft fruit this year, but ...'

'You can't expect the new pastor to let you stay on using the garden.' Margaret finished for him.

'Precisely. I've got my name down for an allotment, but there's a waiting list. I hope I get one before spring, or next year will be wasted.'

'Maybe you'll find somewhere with a garden that you could cultivate,' suggested Margaret. 'I bet lots of landlords would be only too happy to let the tenants keep things tidy outside. There's a bit of garden out the back here,' she went on, 'but nobody does anything with it. Someone comes round and mows the lawn sometimes but, apart from that, it's just growing wild. Now,' she stood up and collected their empty plates together to take them to the sink. 'For afters, you have a choice of tinned peaches and tinned peaches.'

'Hmm! A difficult decision, but ... on balance I think I'll plump for the tinned peaches, please.'

****

'So that's how it all started,' said Bethan, scribbling

22

frantically in her notebook. 'And did you ever find out who it was that was stealing things?'

'We did indeed,' Jonah replied, 'But a couple of weeks later it all became a whole lot more dramatic and exciting.'

****

'Jonah! Telephone!'

At the sound of his mother's voice, Jonah hastily finished fastening his uniform shirt and hurried downstairs, tucking it into his trousers as he went.

'It's a woman,' his mother whispered when he reached the hall. 'Said her name was Margaret Hulme.'

'Hello Margaret, what's up?' Jonah was puzzled at this summons so early on a Sunday morning, especially since Margaret knew that he was on duty that day.

'Jonah? Thank goodness!' Margaret sounded uncharacteristically agitated. 'Can you come over – now, at once?'

'Why? I'm on duty in less than an hour.'

'It's Simon – I mean, we've just found Simon – I mean Simon's body. He's dead! Lying on his bed with a plastic bag over his head.' The words, tentative at first, came out in a rush now. 'Nobody had seen him since Friday evening and we started to wonder whether anything could have happened to him. So, we went round the back and had a look in through his window – and there he was! We managed to break open the door and I examined him, but he was dead as a doornail. We've called 999 and they said the police would be over soon – and an ambulance – but I'd like you here too. Can you come?'

'Yes, of course, I'll be right over.'

Jonah put down the telephone receiver and grabbed his uniform tunic and helmet.

'Got to go, emergency!' He called over his shoulder as he pulled the front door closed behind him.

When he reached the house there was an ambulance outside and two uniformed men were being admitted by a rather white-faced young man, whom Jonah recognised as

Derek Holder.

'In here!' Margaret called from the doorway of Simon's room. The ambulance men pushed their way past Derek, who stood in the hall unsure what to do next. Jonah followed them into the house and gently steered Derek into the living room.

'Sit down in there and make yourself a cup of tea,' he instructed him. 'We'll let you know if you're needed.'

Derek nodded gratefully and sank into a chair.

'I'll put the kettle on,' Mandy Molyneux volunteered, glad of an excuse to abandon her fruitless efforts to calm a small dark-haired girl who was sitting on a two-seater settee weeping hysterically. Jonah had not met her before, but assumed that it must be Julie Potts. Another two-seater settee was occupied by a couple whom Jonah recognised as Paul Wilson and Jane Whittaker, the inhabitants of the top floor flat, whom he had met one evening while visiting Margaret. They were holding hands and looking around as if unable to believe what had happened. Karl Meissner stood impassively, staring out of the window.

'The ambulance crew have confirmed that he's dead,' Margaret said as she joined them in the living room. 'But he can't be moved until the police and the pathologist have seen him.'

The doorbell rang and Jonah turned to see two plain-clothes police officers, whom he vaguely recognised but couldn't put a name to, entering at the open door.

'Detective Inspector Paige,' the first of the men introduced himself. He was around forty years old, above average height and sturdily built with yellow-blond hair and pale blue eyes. 'And this is Detective Sergeant Johns.' His colleague followed him into the hall and Jonah saw that he was shorter and slighter, with red hair of the shade that invites the nickname 'carrots'.

'And you are?' the inspector enquired of Jonah.

'Constable Jonah Porter, sir.'

'Well now, Constable Porter, what have we got here?'

Jonah pulled himself together and tried to speak professionally. 'The deceased is a postgraduate student called Simon Coulter. This is a shared house and he had the ground floor room over there. The other occupants of the house became worried about him and looked in through the window to check he was OK – which he wasn't. They forced the door and came in to find him dead.'

'I see.' Inspector Paige nodded, looking around, noting the damage inflicted on the door.

'I've told them all to wait in here,' Jonah went on, pointing to the living room.

'Good man.' The detectives entered Simon's room. Jonah followed them, keeping a discrete distance.

'It looks as if he suffocated,' one of the ambulance men volunteered. 'Apparently this plastic bag was over his head when they found him, with this elastic band holding it on. They took it off to check that he was dead – not that there could be much doubt. The pathologist will confirm it, but I'd say he could have been dead for more than 24 hours.'

'And do you have any idea what the significance of all these might be?' Paige pointed at an apparently motley collection of items arranged carefully around the body on the bed: a mug bearing the name 'Amanda', a rather battered fountain pen, a striped tie, a copy of the Oxford Book of English Verse, a mug with a picture of a kitten on it, a photograph of a family group on the beach next to Blackpool's south pier, a postcard of Brittany, a seal pup soft toy, and a pair of union jack underpants. 'Are they supposed to tell us something?'

'Sir?' Jonah spoke hesitantly, unsure whether he was supposed to be taking part in the proceedings. 'I can tell you what they are.'

'Can you indeed? Pray enlighten me.'

'They're all the things that have gone missing from people in this house over the last two months. The pen and the photo belong to Margaret – that's Dr Hulme – the mugs belong to Julie Potts and Mandy Molyneux, the seal is Mandy's too, the–'

'Hold it there,' ordered Paige, holding up his hand. 'Before you go on, tell me how you managed to acquire this mine of information so soon after arriving on the scene.'

Jonah blushed, unsure how to explain his involvement in the situation. 'We,' he said hesitantly, 'Margaret – that is to say Dr Hulme – and I, have been trying to work out who's been taking things. We made a list of everything that had been taken, and when, and tried to match up who, from in the house, could have done it.'

'I see. So you're telling me that all these objects here,' Paige gestured towards the bed, 'are property stolen from someone living in this house?'

'Yes, sir.'

'So what's the theory then?' asked Sergeant Johns, speaking for the first time. 'Did this fellow steal the things and then kill himself in a fit of remorse?'

Paige looked towards Jonah, raising his eyebrows interrogatively. 'What do *you* think, constable?'

'We worked out that Simon couldn't have done it. He wasn't here when some of the things went missing. Of course, until now, we couldn't be sure that we hadn't included some things that had just got mislaid and weren't part of the pattern after all; but he definitely couldn't have taken all of these.'

'And did you identify who the real thief was?'

'We narrowed it down, sir but, with a lot of the things, people weren't sure exactly when they'd disappeared; and even when we knew that, it wasn't easy to be sure where everyone was at the time.' Jonah paused. 'Look, I think you ought to talk to Margaret. She knows these people, and she can show you the table we made -'

'Very well. Let's have her in – or better still, is there anywhere else we can go to talk? This room is going to get very crowded with pathologists and forensics people soon.' Paige always felt a reluctance to linger in a room containing a corpse. Although he was nearing twenty years' experience in the police force, the presence of a dead body still made him uncomfortable.

'Margaret's room?' Jonah suggested. 'Our notes are all up there anyway.'

'Good idea. Go and get Dr Hulme – but just say that we've got some questions for her. Don't let the others know that we're interested in the thefts. Are they aware that you were investigating them?'

'No – it was just between the two of us.'

'Good.' Paige turned to Sergeant Johns. 'You'd better stay down here and direct operations. Try to keep all the witnesses together in there. Don't let them go wandering around the house. While you're about it, get some basic information from them – names, home addresses, where they were from Friday evening up to this morning, all the usual stuff. And make sure that someone takes photographs of the body with all those things around it – you never know, there may be some significance in the way they've been arranged.'

A few minutes later Jonah and Margaret were sitting on the sofa in her room facing Inspector Paige, who occupied the upright chair, which he had moved from the desk. Margaret placed a large sheet of paper on the small coffee table that stood between them.

'This grid summarises what we found out,' she said. 'Across the top we've listed all the people in the house and down the side there's a list of all the things that were taken.'

'And the crosses in the squares mean?'

'We tried to find out where everyone was when each thing disappeared.' Margaret explained. 'A cross means that person couldn't have taken that thing – for example, Paul and Jane have a lot of crosses against their names because they were abroad for a month.'

'I see.' Paige peered closely at the paper in front of him. 'It looks to me as if you have three suspects left: MH, LF and JP.'

'But, if you're assuming that the thief also had something to do with Simon's death,' Margaret interjected, 'you also have to rule out Lesley – that's LF. She went home for the weekend on Friday evening and won't be back until tonight. Simon was definitely alive on Friday after Lesley left.'

'You're sure of that?'

'Yes – because of the washing. He filled the washing machine quite late – after ten I should think – and Karl complained that the noise would keep him awake and he had an early start in the labs in the morning, but Simon said he *had* to have some of the stuff because he was going out on Saturday night. It was the washing,' she went on, 'that made us think there was something wrong this morning.'

'Oh?'

'Well, after making such a fuss about how it *had* to be done on Friday night, we all thought it was a bit odd that Simon didn't bother to empty the machine in the morning. When it got to lunchtime on Saturday, several people were getting quite annoyed with him, because they wanted to do their own washing. In the end, Derek got all Simon's things out and piled them up on top of the machine. It was when they were still there this morning that we started to wonder if something was wrong.'

'And you did – what?'

'First we banged on his door. Then someone – Mandy I think – had the bright idea that we might be able to see whether he was there by going round into the back garden and looking through the window.'

'Weren't the curtains drawn?'

'Yes, but there was quite a big gap so we could see in – and there he was!'

'So then you came back in and forced the door?'

28

'Yes. Karl found a spade in the garden shed and used that. The key was in the lock on the inside, so we assumed he must have done it himself. I took the plastic bag off his head to check for certain that he was dead – but I knew already.'

'Was the window locked?'

'I didn't look to see. It was closed, but the catch may not have been fastened.'

'Who else came into the room?'

'Just me and Karl. Julie went into hysterics as soon as she heard about what we saw through the window and Mandy took her into the living room out of the way. Derek stayed in the hall. Paul and Jane didn't come down until later.'

'I see. And is that everyone accounted for? You said that one girl has gone home. Is anyone else away for the weekend?'

'No – we're all here.'

'So-o,' Paige looked at the paper again. 'It looks as if we are left with JP and MH as our chief suspects – assuming that the thief was also involved in this death. And their full names are?' He paused, noticing that Jonah and Margaret exchanged glances before replying.

'Julie Potts and Margaret Hulme.' They said together, with Jonah adding 'sir' before dropping his eyes and staring studiously at his feet. There was silence for a few moments. Paige looked from one to the other then addressed Margaret in a mock-serious tone.

'I don't suppose you feel like clearing this whole thing up by confessing to everything, so that we can all get off to our Sunday lunch?'

'Sorry, no.' Margaret tried to speak lightly, despite feeling rather shaken. 'I have my professional registration to think of – theft and murder are the sort of thing that might well get me struck off.'

'And if you were guilty of the thefts,' Paige observed, watching Jonah closely, 'why would you have brought the constable here in to investigate them? What do you think, Porter?'

'I think,' Jonah paused, trying to work out what he *did* think. 'I think that, if it is the same person who stole all the things and then killed Simon (assuming that it isn't suicide), they must have some sort of mental illness, because it doesn't make logical sense stealing a whole lot of things that aren't worth anything and then killing someone because they found out. It would be much more sensible just to admit to taking the things and claim it was all a joke. And I suppose, in that case, whoever it was *might* be so full of themselves that they thought that nobody would ever catch them, and it might have added to the thrill to know that someone was investigating.'

Paige nodded. 'I'm impressed. Go on.'

'Or,' Jonah went on, 'I've heard that sometimes people who commit crimes through mental illness subconsciously *want* to be found out – it's a form of attention-seeking – so that might be another reason for drawing attention to the thefts and getting me involved. Not that I think for a moment that Margaret did any of it,' he added hastily, suddenly realising what he had just said.

'Well now, Porter,' Paige said, with the faintest hint of a smile on his face, 'As I said, I'm impressed. You're thinking like a detective. But a word of advice: unless you have ambitions to end up as an old bachelor like me, possibly you ought to be a bit more circumspect about accusing your girlfriends of murder to their faces. In my experience a lot of women take offence at that sort of thing.'

'But he's quite right to point out those things,' Margaret leapt to Jonah's defence. 'And we agreed from the start that I was to be treated exactly the same as everyone else in the house.'

For a few moments, Paige sat looking from Jonah to Margaret as if sizing them up. Then he got briskly to his feet.

'We'd better get on.' He declared. 'Now Dr Hulme, as a doctor you'll understand about confidentiality. You mustn't talk to anyone about what we've discussed here – particularly, I don't want any of your housemates knowing that we think there may be a connection between the thefts and this death. Let them carry on assuming that it's suicide. Have you got that?'

'Yes. I understand.'

'And if anyone asks why you were singled out for interview first, it's because you were the first doctor on the scene and examined the body. Now I'd better go and talk to them.'

'Before you do, sir,' Jonah put in nervously. 'I think you might want to see these. It's the notes I took about the thefts. There's information about everyone living here. It might save you some time.'

'Good man!' Paige looked at the notes with approval. 'These look very clear and comprehensive.'

'Of course Jonah was the brains behind our investigation,' Margaret told him. 'He worked everything out. I just supplied the data.'

'Of course,' Paige agreed, carefully avoiding eye contact with either of them. 'Now, while I read these, Porter, you go down and tell Johns that I'd like everyone to go to their own room and stay there until I call them for questioning. We'll interview them one at a time in the living room.'

'Yes sir. Er – sir?'

'Yes. What is it?'

'Well, I shouldn't really be here, sir. I'm supposed to be providing a visible police presence to deter crime on the Blackbird Leys estate this morning.'

'Don't worry about that. I want you here. I'm sure Blackbird Leys can manage with a visible police absence just this once. And,' he went on seeing the look of anxiety on Jonah's face, 'I'll square it with your sergeant if anyone notices.'

'Thank you, sir. I'll go and give Johns your message

now, sir.'

He and Margaret left the room and started downstairs.

'Why did you tell him that working out who might have taken the things was all down to me? It was your idea!' Jonah whispered.

'*I'm* not the one hoping to have a glittering career in the police force,' Margaret whispered back. 'You've made a good first impression. Now you need to milk it for all it's worth.'

'I don't see …,' Jonah tailed off as they reached the door of the living room. They went in and Jonah delivered his message to Sergeant Johns, who immediately addressed the assembled company.

'Right, now: you've all given me your details, but Inspector Paige would like to speak to each of you individually. So now, please, go back to your rooms until you're called for.'

Everyone left, except for the tall German. 'How long is this likely to take?' he asked. 'I would like to get back to the laboratory.'

'We'll be as quick as we can, sir,' Johns assured him. 'You can be first, if that would help.'

'Thank you. That would be most helpful. I shall wait here?'

'Yes. Inspector Paige will be here soon.'

Sure enough, the inspector came in at that moment. He gestured to Karl to sit down in a chair, while he and Johns sat on a settee opposite. Jonah sat on the other settee.

'Constable Porter will take notes,' Paige explained. 'Please try to relax. Nobody is under suspicion. We're just trying to get a clear picture of what happened.'

'I understand.'

'You were one of the group of people who looked through the window to see whether Coulter was alright?'

'That is correct. I think I was probably the only one tall enough to see clearly that there was something wrong.'

'I see. And then you broke the door open?'

'Yes. I used a spade from the garden. Once the door was open Margaret went in first to see if there was anything she could do.'

'And did anyone else go into the room?'

'No, the others waited outside.'

'Did you notice whether or not the window was locked?'

'It was not. I managed to raise it slightly from the outside – I was thinking of getting in that way – but I could not get a good grip and decided to try the door.'

'Thank you. Now tell me: how well did you know Simon Coulter?'

'I would not say that I knew him well.'

'But over, what? – fourteen months? – you must have formed some idea of the sort of person he was?'

'Perhaps. I did not really think about it.'

'And did you notice any change in his mood recently. Would you say he seemed depressed, for example?'

'No. He seemed quite his usual self. If anything he was rather, let me see,' Karl paused, looking for the right words. 'He seemed rather pleased with himself, I would say – even more than usual.'

'So you wouldn't have expected him to take his own life?'

'No.'

'Would you say he was popular?' Johns made his first contribution to the conversation.

'No – I would not say that.'

'Are you suggesting that he was *un*popular?' Paige pressed him, getting a sense that Karl knew more that he was saying.

Karl hesitated. It appeared that he was not sure whether or not to expand on what he had already said. Then he appeared to make up his mind and spoke again.

'I do not know how other people felt about him, but to me he did not seem to be a nice person.'

'Anything in particular?' Paige asked encouragingly.

'Let me give you an example of what I mean. It was your talk of suicide that reminded me of it. Like most postgraduates he gave tutorials to undergraduates. Last summer, just after taking his final examinations, one of these students jumped to his death from the top of the engineering building. Speaking about it afterwards, Simon did not appear at all concerned about the death of this young man. In fact, he said to me that he had told the student in question that he might as well give up the idea of doing a DPhil because he had no chance of getting a first class degree. There was something about the way he said it that was, I do not know, creepy, I suppose you might say. I got the impression that he was rather pleased – proud even – to think that he might have contributed towards making the young man take his own life.'

There was a long silence while the three police officers digested this statement.

'Thank you, you've been very helpful.' Paige said at last. 'You can go now. If we need to speak to you again we'll be in touch.'

It took the remainder of the morning to complete the interviews. None of the housemates admitted to having been close to Simon Coulter and none appeared very distressed at the fact of his death. Julie Potts was still rather tearful, but it was clear that her distress had more to do with the shock of a violent death having taken place in her home than any sense of bereavement. She told them that Simon had made cruel remarks about her when Derek had finished their relationship – and Derek confirmed this.

When asked what had caused them to split up, Derek simply said that living in the same house together made him realise that they were not compatible after all. The famous underpants had been a gift from Julie. He did not like them and only wore them on occasions when he had run out of clean underwear. He had assumed that they had been taken as a joke and expected that they would turn up when the perpetrator got bored with waiting for him to react.

Mandy knew an ex-girlfriend of Simon's who had dumped him after he proposed some, unspecified, 'kinky' behaviour. Mandy did not think that he had been violent, but had gained the impression that Simon's demands had been distinctly 'weird'. The stolen mug bearing her name had been a present from her fiancé and she was upset to think that anyone from the house had taken it, knowing its sentimental value to her.

Neither Paul nor Jane admitted to knowing any of the inhabitants of the lower floors well, but Jane recalled having been called down from the flat over the summer when Julie suffered a panic attack and was unable to leave her room for five days. It was round about the time when she split up from Derek. All the other girls were away, as it happened, and Karl had summoned her to talk to Julie woman-to-woman. No, she didn't know whether Simon Coulter had anything to do with Julie's problem, but she had noticed that he seemed completely unmoved by her distress.

Jonah could hardly believe it when, that afternoon, he found himself sitting round a table in Paige's office with sandwiches and mugs of coffee, going through the notes that he had taken during the interviews. More surprising still, Paige appeared to treat him as an equal member of the team.

'So, to summarise,' Paige said, 'we have a series of petty thefts and a suspicious death. The body was naked when found, with a plastic bag over its head. The time of death is uncertain at present, but was probably Friday night. The door was locked on the inside and the window was closed, but not fastened, so it would have been possible for someone to kill the victim and leave by the window. Unfortunately the ground under the window is a mass of footprints because of the little expedition this morning to peer in through the window. Whose idea was it to do that, by the way?'

Jonah consulted his notes. 'Mandy Molyneux suggested it and Karl Meissner led the party, which also included Mandy, Margaret and Julie.'

Paige nodded then continued, 'The stolen items were arranged around the body as if intended to draw attention to some link between the thefts and the death. The dead man could not have been responsible for all of the thefts, so the working assumption is that the thief murdered him, possibly because he was threatening to expose them, and left the items round the body – either in order to implicate Coulter in the thefts or as some sort of symbolic gesture. The consensus among those who knew him seems to be that Coulter was an unpleasant character, which suggests that he might well be capable of blackmail.'

'But if you're talking about the thefts, surely they were too trivial for serious blackmail?' Johns argued. 'We've already agreed that the thief would be able to simply laugh them off as a joke.'

'A good point – what do you think, Porter?'

'Well,' Jonah thought rapidly, conscious of Paige's eye on him and keen to make a good impression on the senior detective. 'The thief might have a past history that would make these petty thefts more significant – if they were already on probation, for example. Or,' he went on, another thought occurring to him, 'or even *petty* theft might be important because honesty was essential for their career – as a teacher, for example.'

'Or a doctor,' observed Paige quietly.

'Yes, but sticking with teachers for the moment,' Jonah went on excitedly. 'Mandy and Lesley were training to be teachers and they were great friends by all accounts. What if they were in it together?'

'You mean,' put in Johns, 'Lesley stole the things and then Mandy did the murder while Lesley was away and couldn't be suspected?'

'But what motive did they have?' asked Paige. 'If it was a conspiracy then we can't fall back on the "mad people don't behave logically" argument.'

For a few moments they sat in silence.

'Never mind,' Paige said at last. 'No point in speculating. We'd better do background checks on all the residents – see if any of them *does* have a past history that might make them vulnerable to blackmail or potentially violent. The pathology report won't come through until tomorrow. That ought to give us a more accurate idea of the time of death and I hope it will also throw some light on the question of how someone persuaded a fit young man to take off a his clothes, lie down on the bed and put a plastic bag over his head – all without disturbing the other residents of the house.'

'Even though they were most likely all being kept awake by the sound of the washing machine,' murmured Jonah thoughtfully, remembering Margaret's account of the dispute with Karl.

'As you say,' Paige agreed with a smile, 'even though they were being kept awake by the washing machine. Of course, I do have my own theory,' he went on, mischievously. 'I think the whole business is a plot by the lovely doctor to seduce young Porter here! Anyone can see she fancies him. First she tries to get him interested with a few petty thefts – gives her an excuse to keep inviting him round to the house. But she's not sure that she's got his full attention, so in the end she resorts to murder!'

Jonah blushed bright red, but had the good sense to remain silent. Johns hurriedly broke in, to cover his embarrassment. 'We'll get started on those background checks right away, sir. Porter – I suggest that we split them between us. You take the ground floor and the top flat, and I'll cover the girls on the first floor.'

He got up and made for the door. Jonah followed him. Once out in the corridor, Johns said in a low voice. 'Don't mind him. It's just his way. It means he likes you.'

****

Jonah paused to take a long draught of his tea. Bethan

37

looked up from her frantically scribbled notes.

'It's all very dramatic. I wonder if we might try to do a reconstruction – or,' Bethan paused to think, 'maybe some still pictures. Do you have any photographs of you and your wife at that time? Something of her on the motorcycle would be good, for example.'

Jonah nodded. 'We can look some out for you.'

'Thanks. Now, please – go on. You still haven't told me who dunnit.'

****

'So now,' Margaret leaned her head comfortably on Jonah's shoulder as they sat together on the sagging sofa in her room three days later. 'You've made the arrest and charged your murderer, but I'm still not sure what it was all about. Tell me what was really going on and how you worked it out.'

'It was all very straightforward really,' Jonah said, putting his arm round Margaret's shoulders. 'Once the pathologist's report came through, we had a pretty good idea how it was done, which helped a lot. He'd been drugged before he was killed – diazepam it said in the report.'

'Valium,' Margaret translated. 'That's the same as–'

'Which of course makes is very lucky for you,' Jonah went on, ignoring the interruption, 'that the time of death was late Friday night or the early hours of Saturday morning.'

'Oh, aye?'

'If you hadn't been on duty doing another late shift in A&E you would almost certainly have been under suspicion, as someone who had access to drugs for sedating your victim.'

'Under very strict control, I might add,' Margaret pointed out. 'With detailed records kept in the hospital pharmacy.'

'Very true – and there were no discrepancies in the records, as it turns out.'

'You checked?'

'Of course – as a matter of routine, not because anyone seriously thought you were responsible.'

'I should think not!'

'Anyway – to get back to the pathology report – he probably hadn't been given enough of the drug to send him completely unconscious, and certainly not enough to kill him, but enough to make him compliant with being gagged so he couldn't shout out; and he'd been handcuffed hand and foot to the bed so he couldn't resist being suffocated. Probably that was done with a cushion over his face and then the plastic bag was put on after death to make it look like suicide.'

'But hang on,' Margaret interrupted, 'what do you mean, "handcuffed to the bed"? Where did the handcuffs come from?'

'We found them in the bottom of the wardrobe. Mandy told us that she'd heard that Simon's sexual proclivities were somewhat strange. It turns out that included a liking for bondage.'

'You mean he used to handcuff people and then have sex with them?'

'So it would appear.'

'My mother always did say they were queer folk down South! But go on, how did you find out who *was* the murderer?'

'Lesley was also out of the frame,' Jonah went on, starting to enjoy his role as narrator, 'being in Taunton with her parents all weekend. But anyone else in the house could have done it. *However,*' he paused dramatically, 'when we discovered that Julie's sleeping pills were the same as the sedative that Simon had been given; and her GP admitted that she'd continued to prescribe them for her well after her exams were over because of her anxiety and depression, following the breakup of her relationship with Derek, all the evidence seemed to point towards her.'

'And,' Margaret put in, 'she was the one person who

could have taken all the stolen items *and* committed the murder.'

'Precisely! Inspector Paige brought her in for questioning and she admitted everything. It was a terribly sad story really. All she ever wanted was a bit of love and affection.'

'She went a strange way about getting them.'

'Not rational behaviour I admit, but maybe understandable. She seems to have had a pretty dismal childhood. Her parents were in the diplomatic service and she was sent to boarding school from the age of six. Conditions there were pretty grim by all accounts and she grew up feeling that nobody really loved or cared for her. She had an older brother who appears to have been the apple of their parents' eye, while Julie could do nothing right. Even her scholarship to Oxford was seen as a failure, because apparently she *ought* to have followed the family tradition of going to Cambridge. Applying to Oxford was seen as an unforgivable gesture of rebellion, whereas she was actually just trying to avoid following in the footsteps of her oh so perfect brother, who would have still been there when she went up.'

'Poor kid.'

'Anyway, she finally thought that she'd found true love when she hitched up with Derek – and I think he thought so too, at first. But he couldn't cope with her constant need for affection and for reassurance that he cared for her, and in the end he decided the only answer was to make a clean break.'

'He must feel awful about it now.'

'Yes – but he wasn't to know. Anyway, she was back to feeling that nobody cared about her; she was the only person in the world who had nobody to love them. She started taking things that were symbols of other people's relationships – your pen and photo that reminded you of your Nan, the mug and soft toy that Mandy's boyfriend gave her, the postcard that Lesley's sister sent her and the book that was a present from her Dad.'

'And the underpants that she'd given to Derek.'

'She got her GP to prescribe diazepam because she was getting panic attacks and having trouble sleeping. But she didn't take it – she hoarded it, possibly with the intention of taking her own life with an overdose. Then, somehow, Simon found out that she was the thief and threatened to tell her college. He convinced her that if the college authorities heard about it she would be sent down.'

'And of course, she believed him – being already so low and not having anyone else to turn to.'

'Precisely. So she saw no alternative but to give in to his demands.'

'So he was blackmailing her?'

'Yes – I would describe it as that, although the payment he asked for wasn't money. You remember I told you he was into sexual bondage?'

'He threatened to get her sent down if she didn't have sex with him?'

'That's right. You remember Mandy's cuddly toy seal was taken on Tuesday 13th and Simon was killed on the following Friday? Well he came to Julie on the Wednesday and told her he knew what she'd done and explained what he wanted from her to keep his mouth shut. She was to come to his room each night between eleven and midnight. If she didn't come or if she screamed out or made any fuss, he would tell all.'

'How horrible!'

'She put up with it for two nights and then, on Friday, she somehow managed to get some of her sleeping pills into his drink, which knocked him out enough for her to put the handcuffs on him and suffocate him with a pillow. Then she arranged all the stolen things, which he'd forced her to give to him "for safe keeping", around his naked body, removed the handcuffs, put the plastic bag over his head, fastened it with an elastic band and got out through the window. She pulled it down after her and hoped that people would think Simon had killed himself.'

'Poor girl! What do you think will happen to her?'

'With a good lawyer – and her parents ought to be able to afford one for her – she may well get off with manslaughter due to diminished responsibility.'

'And poor Derek! He must be feeling awful.'

'Not so much of the "poor Derek" – merely thinking about you sleeping under the same roof is bad enough without all these declarations of sympathy which might so easily lead you to do something that I would regret!'

Margaret laughed. 'Which reminds me,' she said, 'I was going to ask – have you found anywhere to live yet?'

'No – I haven't had time to look.'

'That's good, because I was thinking – there's a spare room here now, on the ground floor, so we could do with another man. The rent is very reasonable, and you might even be able to do something with the garden.'

'Sounds good.' Jonah smiled broadly. 'So long as you realise that, if I'm living here, your flirtation with poor Derek is going to have to stop!'

'I was more concerned about your head being turned by seeing Lesley and Mandy in their skimpy negligées of a morning.'

'I promise to avert my eyes.' Jonah hugged Margaret closer. 'And now I have some more news for you. Thanks to your fraudulent declaration to Inspector Paige regarding my detective skills, he's organised to get me transferred to CID in the New Year.'

'That's wonderful! I knew you were making a good impression. Congratulations!'

****

'So you have your wife to thank for starting your career as a detective,' said Bethan with satisfaction. 'That'll make a good storyline.'

'I have my wife to thank for a lot of the good things that have happened in my life,' Jonah agreed with a smile.

****

Thou God of truth and love,
We seek thy perfect way,
Ready thy choice to approve,
Thy providence to obey:
Enter into thy wise design,
And sweetly lose our will in thine.

Why hast thou cast our lot
In the same age and place?
And why together brought
To see each other's face?
To join with loving sympathy,
And mix our friendly souls in thee?

Didst thou not make us one,
That we might one remain,
Together travel on,
And bear each other's pain;
Till all thy utmost goodness prove,
And rise renewed in perfect love?

Then let us ever bear
The blessed end in view,
And join, with mutual care,
To fight our passage through;
And kindly help each other on,
Till all receive the starry crown.

O may thy Spirit seal
Our souls unto that day,
With all thy fullness fill,
And then transport away!
Away to our eternal rest,
Away to our Redeemer's breast!

Charles Wesley (1707-1788)

43

3 YOU'LL NEVER WALK ALONE

'Jonah, have you ...? Oh sorry! I hadn't realised you had a visitor.' The door burst open and a young woman entered, stopped as she noticed Bethan, and then turned to go. Her hair was blond and curly, making a halo around her face. As a child, she would certainly have been first choice for an angel in the school nativity play.

'No, don't go Lucy. Come in and be introduced. This is Bethan Abbott. She's interviewing me about how I manage to cope with adversity. I think she ought to meet you.'

'Of course! Your chance to become a TV star – I'd completely forgotten.' The newcomer turned to Bethan and held out her hand. 'I'm Lucy Paige. You'll have met my mother, Bernie Fazakerley.'

'Lucy,' Jonah told Bethan seriously, 'is a very important person in the story of my life. In fact, I'm not sure how things would have turned out, without her – and Our Bernie.'

'Don't be silly!' Lucy blushed. 'We didn't do anything special – just what you'd expect in the circumstances.' She looked directly at Bethan and spoke earnestly.

'Jonah was very good to me – to both of us, but specially to me. He used to just turn up every year on my

44

birthday, with some wonderful present – not expensive, but always just the right thing. And then, after a few hours, he'd go off again. It was like having my own private Father Christmas. He always made me feel as if I was the most important person in the world while he was there. So *of course* we wanted to help when he needed it.'

'It was like this,' Jonah put in. 'I worked with Richard Paige – that's Lucy's father – when he was a Detective Inspector and I was a raw Detective Constable. He was my boss and my mentor, but I was transferred to another team and we lost touch. He died as a result of an accident while he was on duty – that was eighteen years ago now – and I went to his funeral.'

****

Detective Inspector Peter Johns led Jonah through the clusters of funeral guests partaking of light refreshments in the Church Hall.

'Richard's wife kept her maiden name,' he was saying, 'because of her work. So she's still Dr Bernadette Fazakerley, but everyone calls her Bernie.' He touched Bernie gently on the elbow to attract her attention 'Bernie, let me introduce Chief Inspector Jonah Porter. He used to work with me and Richard.'

Detective Superintendent Richard Paige's widow looked Jonah up and down.

'Pleased to meet you,' she said politely. 'It's amazing how many of Richard's colleagues have come to see him off. I had no idea he was so popular.'

'I owe him a lot. He took me on when I first joined the CID. He taught me all I know.'

'I doubt that,' Bernie gave Jonah a wry smile. 'Aren't you the officer who was responsible for clearing up that big fraud case? The one involving the banker with the odd name –what was it? Something weird and Welsh. Richard would never have been any good with something like that – his command of even simple arithmetic was absolutely dire. A bent banker would easily have been able to run rings around him.'

'Merlin Price-Davies,' Jonah answered, struggling to collect his thoughts.

'That's the one. It makes you expect someone in a druid costume with long hair and a beard, but he turned out to be just some banker in a pinstriped suit who's probably never been out of the Home Counties. I gather it was quite a coup to get a conviction. You will obviously go far.'

'Oh, I don't know about that!' Jonah gave a deprecating laugh. 'It wasn't all down to me. Anyway, I didn't come here to talk about my achievements. I wanted to tell you how sorry I was to hear about Richard's death and to say how much I owe to him.'

'And to see what sort of woman would marry him after all these years?' Bernie suggested.

'Since you mention it – I confess I *was* curious to meet you. Richard had been such a very confirmed bachelor – very much married to the job – and we were all rather taken aback to hear that he'd taken the plunge into matrimony at what you have to admit was a fairly advanced age. I mean – it would have to be someone rather special.'

'Or maybe he was just desperate to ensure that he would be cared for in his declining years.'

'I'm quite sure that was not even a part of his considerations.'

'You're probably right. He was generally quite astute, and if that had been his motivation, I'm sure that he could have found someone more suited to the role. I make no pretence of having a caring or sympathetic nature. So, if you are wondering why he married me, join the club – *I* certainly wouldn't have been foolish enough to sign up to living with me on a permanent basis!'

Jonah was unsure how to follow this. 'Someone told me you were a don,' he said, trying to keep the conversation going.

'That's right. I'm Applied Mathematics Tutor at St Luke's College.'

'It must be the busiest time of the year for you, with all the new students starting. I hope you're allowed some time off, under the circumstances.'

'Well done!' Bernie looked Jonah in the eyes and smiled up at him. 'You didn't say it. I'm impressed.'

'Say what?'

'Usually at this point in the conversation, people give a little laugh and say, "I was never any good at Maths at school." And then they start looking for an opportunity to get away and talk to someone more interesting.'

'Ah! But *I* was always very good at Maths at school.'

'And at everything else, I'm sure,' put in Peter with just the slightest touch of resentment in his voice, 'and doesn't he know it!'

'I must say,' Jonah went on, ignoring Peter's interjection, 'you aren't my idea of a typical Oxford don.'

'You mean,' grinned Bernie, 'I don't sound as if I went to Roedean or Cheltenham Ladies College, and you're wondering how I ever came to be allowed into the Oxbridge establishment. Richard always used to say-' Bernie stopped speaking and Jonah became aware that she was looking distractedly over his shoulder towards the door.

'Look, I'm sorry,' she went on, 'Richard's mother is just leaving: I must see her off. Thank you for coming. Maybe we can speak again later.'

Bernie hurried off across the room, weaving between the guests with mutters of apology. Jonah watched her pensively.

'Richard always used to say,' continued Peter, 'that when she was interviewed for her fellowship the panel asked at the end, "and now do you have any questions for us?" and she said,' he paused before resuming in an exaggerated Liverpool accent, '"Are youse giving me this job or what?" and none of them had the courage to say "no"!'

Jonah turned back to face Peter. 'How is she, d'you think? No tears. Putting a brave face on it d'you reckon?'

'Our Bernie doesn't show her emotions, but don't think for a moment she doesn't feel Richard's death very much.' Peter's answer came with a vehemence that surprised them both. 'She and Angela are very close – I think that's what's keeping her going at the moment, and of course she's been keeping busy with the funeral and everything.'

'Angela?' Jonah realised that he was expected to recognise the name.

'My wife.'

'Of course! I remember now. And what about the children – you had two, didn't you – a boy and a girl?'

'Hannah's at university studying to be a nurse and Edward's in lower sixth. We were afraid that he was going off the rails, but Bernie took an interest in him and persuaded him that he could indulge in his obsession with computers by doing a computer science degree. He finally knuckled down and actually did quite well in his GCSEs after all, which is a great relief to us all. I must say I don't envy Bernie having it all still to come – and on her own too.'

'What do you mean? She and Richard didn't have any kids, did they?'

'Not yet. But … look, I don't think I ought to be telling you this.' Peter lowered his voice. 'Yes: Bernie's expecting – and racked with guilt that she didn't tell Richard before he died. She didn't know how he would take it. I don't think either of them had thought about the possibility; what with her being the wrong side of forty and him, well...'

'Getting on for sixty, I suppose.' Jonah looked thoughtful. Then he took Peter's arm and moved closer. 'Let me know when the baby's born – I'd like to … send a card or something.'

That was how it started. Lucy duly arrived about six months later and a few days afterwards Jonah called at Bernie's house with a card and a mobile for keeping the baby amused in its cot. From then on every year he would arrive, unannounced, at some point during her birthday and present her with a neatly wrapped parcel, which she never failed to greet with joyful appreciation, declaring, 'Jonah always brings the best presents.'

Although he always came looking immaculate in his smart suit and tie, Jonah never baulked at joining in with whatever activity Lucy suggested, whether it was football on the lawn, climbing the big oak tree in the back garden to inspect her new tree house or digging in her own patch of garden. On her ninth birthday, Peter captured the scene on videotape: a birthday tea in the sunny garden with enthusiastic singing before Lucy blew out the candles in one breath; then afterwards a boisterous game in which she climbed repeatedly into the tree house and leapt down into Jonah's waiting arms, while Bernie protested that this was no way to treat a guest.

Then a month later, came the news: Bernie and Lucy heard it reported on the radio while they were cooking their evening meal. The police officer who had been shot at his South Oxfordshire home that afternoon was named as Detective Chief Inspector Jonah Porter. He was reported to be in a stable condition in hospital. Investigations into the identity of the gunman were ongoing.

Bernie and Lucy looked at each other in silence. Then Lucy said in a small voice, 'Will he be alright?'

'I don't know. We'll have to wait and see what happens.'

'Can't you find out? Isn't there something we can do?'

'Later. I'll ring his wife after you're in bed. But you'll have to be patient. She may not want to talk to me. She doesn't know us.'

About three weeks later, Bernie was on her way to the

specialist spinal unit, some twenty miles from her home in Headington, to visit Jonah for the first time. She had not wanted to intrude on the family in the first days of their grief or to steal precious moments of visiting time from them. She could not get out of her head the possibility that he might only have limited time left. However, Margaret had been insistent that Jonah would be pleased to see a fresh face and that the family was starting to struggle to fit constant vigil at his bedside with their other commitments and to find things to talk about when they were there.

So, here she was, on her way, unsure what to expect but knowing that it would be a difficult meeting. Margaret had prepared her with the basic facts: the bullet had caused damage to the spinal cord, but it was uncertain how bad it was; surgery had stabilised the spine, but it would be some time before he could remove the neck brace protecting it. The injury had left Jonah almost completely paralysed, but there was some hope that, once the inflammation died down, the nerves in the spinal cord might recover to a limited extent. At present, movement was confined to the index finger of his left hand.

On the positive side, his mind was as active as ever and his greatest frustration was being unable to hold a book or turn a page. Except when he had visitors, his only mental stimulation was the television and he was doggedly trying to master the remote control with his single working digit.

Bernie parked the car and studied Margaret's instructions for finding Jonah's ward. The nurse at the nursing station broke into a smile when she mentioned Jonah's name and led the way to a side room. Bernie paused for a moment to brace herself before walking briskly in and announcing her arrival in her broad Scouse accent.

'Your wife tells me that you're bored with your visitors and need someone more interesting to cheer you up. I asked around all the interesting people that I know and none of them could make it, so you'll just have to put up with me!'

'Bernie!' Jonah looked up and smiled broadly. He looked pale and somehow smaller than Bernie remembered him. 'It's really good of you to come. I'm sure you have lots of far more important things to do.'

'Nonsense! I had to come. Lucy's been pestering me constantly to find out how you are, ever since we heard. She'll be green with envy when she discovers I've been here – which reminds me.' Bernie fished in a plastic carrier bag and brought out a bunch of sweet peas. 'These are from Lucy – she grew them herself. I told her I'd see that you got them.'

'They're lovely. Tell Lucy I like them very much. How is she?'

'Very well – apart from worrying about you!' Bernie looked around vaguely, wondering what to do with the flowers.

'Put them in the sink for now.' Jonah gestured with his head. 'One of the nurses will put them in water later.'

Bernie deposited the flowers and then sat down on the chair next to the bed. 'Now, if it's not too painful, please, tell me what happened – and do you have any idea why?'

'It all seems so absurd!' Jonah replied. 'One moment I was dead-heading the roses and the next I was face down in the rose bed and unable to move. If it hadn't been for Mrs Cameron from next door happening to look out of her landing window, I could have been there for hours, because Margaret was at work.'

'And do you have any idea who did it?'

'No. I've been racking my brains to think who might have a grudge against me. I can only assume it was some criminal who blames me for putting him inside, but we've been through all the likely suspects – especially any who were released fairly recently – and none of them seem to fit, or else they have cast-iron alibis. Mrs Cameron says that she thinks she caught a glimpse of a figure behind the fence at the bottom of the garden, which is where they reckon the bullet must have been fired from. She says it was bright yellow – maybe someone in a yellow cagoule. They found footprints behind the fence, right by where one of the palings had been loosened at the bottom so that it could be rotated round to give a view of the garden and a space through which to fire the gun.'

Jonah became animated as he recounted the investigation so far. 'The footprints were size 11 wellington boots, but the odd thing is that they were, so the experts in such things tell me, not as deep as you would have expected, which suggests that whoever was there was surprisingly light for his size. There were several golfers out on the course that afternoon, but none of them had seen anything – especially not someone in a yellow cagoule!'

'Which', Bernie observed, 'could very easily have been taken off and secreted about the attacker's person, if it *was* a cagoule.'

'My very thought.' agreed Jonah. 'I couldn't help thinking when they told me about it that the only reason for wearing bright yellow to commit a crime was because you *wanted* it to be seen.'

'So they don't have any suspects?'

'No. They've checked out everyone with a firearms licence within a fifty-mile radius. None of them has had a gun lost or stolen and none has a motive for shooting me. And, as I said, we've been through every case of mine back to the year dot, but we haven't even found anyone with size eleven feet!'

'And there really haven't been any other leads?'

'No. They're trying to find the gun, but no luck there, and no luck either in tracing the wellington boots.'

'And really, nobody saw *anything*?'

'There's a line of bushes a few feet away from the backs of the gardens, to prevent balls crashing into people's greenhouses and things. It almost amounts to a hedge. So it's not surprising that the golfers didn't see anyone lurking behind our fence. And there are any number of public footpaths crossing the golf course, so they wouldn't have taken any notice of anyone wandering about before the shot came.'

'But afterwards – didn't they see anyone running away?'

'It looks as if our villain was a cool customer – probably strolled away before anyone realised what had happened. The only thing is: how did he conceal the weapon? Ballistics reckon it was a rifle, which means he'd need a long bag or case of some sort to carry it in. You'd think someone might have noticed him, either before or after the shooting.'

'Maybe in a golf bag? I don't know much about guns, but would a rifle be the same sort of length as a golf club?'

'Now there's a thought! You could have something there. I should think it would be quite easy to hide a gun in among a set of golf clubs – from a distance anyway. I'll get them to re-check the statements. The trouble is everyone expects to see golfers on a golf course, so if anyone did see someone it probably wouldn't register with them. I doubt if anything will come of it.'

'But the police won't give up?'

'Oh no! The force is always particularly keen to catch someone who attacks one of our own. They've put Thompson on the case. He's very experienced and thorough, but …'

'It must be frustrating not to be able to get out there yourself and make sure they haven't missed anything!'

'Precisely! But never mind. Now tell me what you and Lucy have been getting up to since her birthday. Did you get to the FA cup final?'

'We did indeed – and very good it was too, although the result wasn't exactly what we were hoping for.'

'Really? I thought you were Liverpool supporters.'

'So we are – but if Liverpool isn't playing then any Merseysider is going to favour Everton over one of your poncey Southern sides! What do *they* know about football?'

'Evidently enough to give Everton a thrashing.' Jonah observed drily.

'Anyway,' Bernie went on, ignoring this remark, 'the whole of my dad's side of the family are Everton supporters: how d'you think I got the tickets? Good old cousin Joey!'

It didn't seem long before a nurse put her head round the door to announce that visiting time was over. Bernie got up to go.

'Come again soon – and bring Lucy with you.'

'I will.' Bernie paused briefly at the door and then hurried out, conscious of tears pricking at the back of her eyes.

On her way back to the car, she noticed a sign, 'Chapel and multi-faith prayer room'. She slipped inside and gazed around in what seemed, after the bright corridor, to be semi-darkness. As she became accustomed to the light, she saw a rather bare room, with a table at the front bearing a wooden cross and two candles in brass candlesticks, several rows of chairs and a modern-looking stained glass window depicting a rainbow. On the back wall was a notice board with pieces of paper pinned up, which she identified as prayer requests. Beneath it was a table with some books, a pile of slips of paper and two ballpoint pens.

She sat down in a chair in the second row and gave up trying to fight back the tears.

'Would you like one of these?'

It was some minutes later; Bernie looked up and saw a man in a clerical collar sitting two chairs away from her holding out a box of tissues, which he placed on the chair between them. She took one and blew her nose.

'Is there anything I can do?' the chaplain asked gently.

'No.' Bernie sounded desolate. 'I've just been to see a friend of mine. He's almost certainly paralysed for life. And there's nothing anyone can do!' They sat for several more minutes in silence.

Then Bernie went on. 'I hadn't realised I cared so much about him. Up until today, I'd only actually met him on eleven occasions altogether. You wouldn't think you could get so fond of someone in that time, would you?'

'Eleven is a very precise number. You seem to have been counting carefully.'

'No – it's easy,' Bernie explained. 'He came to my husband's funeral and when my daughter was born and then to each of her birthdays. She's nine now, so that makes eleven.'

More silence.

'And now I've got to go back to Lucy and prepare her to come to see him. Death she understands, but I don't know how she'll cope with the idea of permanent disability.'

'Do you have to tell her right away that it *is* permanent?'

'Oh yes! I've always been completely honest with her about everything. She has to be told exactly as it is. And you can be sure, if I don't tell it to her straight, she'll ask and then it'll look as if I was trying to conceal something from her.'

'And your friend – does he know? How is he taking it?'

'He knows alright – and he's taking it with amazing bravery, but that's only what I'd expect. He's a very brave person – and a very kind one.' Bernie thought for a few moments, 'but underneath – I don't know. Can anyone really be that brave? He must be absolutely terrified.'

'Would you like me to go and see him?'

'I don't know. We've never spoken about that sort of thing – I mean, for all I know he's violently opposed to all religion and would resent you talking to him – especially he might resent the idea of me sending you to give him spiritual guidance, or whatever you call it.'

'I know how to be discrete,' the chaplain smiled. 'We see all sorts of people here and it's surprising how many of them are pleased to see us. And I don't need to let on that you had anything to do with it. What's his name?'

'Jonah Porter – he's a policeman. He was shot in the back of the neck a few weeks ago. It was on the news.'

'Jonah! Well, I think maybe it could be that I've had more meetings with him than you have. His vicar asked me to keep an eye on him, and to be honest it's been good to have the excuse to spend time with him. You're quite right – he is a remarkable man.'

'Well,' Bernie got up. 'I'd better be going. Lucy will be out of school and wondering where I am. Thank you for listening.'

'That's what I'm here for. And can I mention to Jonah that I've spoken with you?'

Bernie nodded. 'Yes – but don't tell him, well, I mean … I don't want him to think that … Look – it must be bad enough for him as it is without thinking that he's making us unhappy too. Do you understand?'

'Don't worry. I'll tread carefully, but I think you ought not to be too keen to hide your feelings from him. It might make it easier for him to show his own if other people aren't afraid to let him know how much his injury is hurting them. Think about it.'

****

'Now Lucy, make yourself useful and refill the teapot while I fill Bethan in on your role in my rehabilitation. Oh! And persuade your Mam to come and join us will you?'

Lucy picked up the teapot and turned to go, pausing to catch Bethan's eye briefly, 'Don't believe everything he says,' she said with a smile. 'He tends to exaggerate my contribution. I don't do anything much really.'

Jonah watched Lucy's exit and then turned to Bethan.

'I didn't have to wait long: Lucy insisted on coming to see me the very next day.

****

'So you've come to help with our problem patient, have you?' A black nurse smiled up as she finished smoothing down the sheets, after propping Jonah up in bed ready for visiting time, and greeted Lucy, who had burst into the room and now stood staring uncertainly at the unfamiliar scene. She spoke in a soft West Indian accent: 'and what's your name, young lady?'

'Lucy Paige.'

'Ah! Lucy. You're a bit of a gardener, I hear.' The nurse indicated the sweet peas, now displayed prominently on the bedside locker. 'I'm Nurse Jeanette and it's my job to keep this young man comfortable and make sure he behaves himself!'

'Can I really help?' Lucy looked earnestly into Jeanette's eyes. 'I'd really like to!'

'Now I don't see any reason why not. Tell you what,' Jeanette bent down so that her face was level with Lucy's. 'There is one very important thing you can do for me.'

'What?'

'Well you see, Lucy, Jonah here hasn't been eating properly. Every day, I come in and cut up his food and feed it to him; and every day he tells me he can't face more than a few mouthfuls. Something tells me that maybe if *you* was to give it to him he'd find he could eat more. What do you say? Shall we give it a go?'

'Yes please! I'd like that.'

'OK then. I'll go and get you all some tea and toast and you see what you can do for me.' She winked conspiratorially at Lucy. 'I'll be back in two ticks.'

Lucy held out a large white envelope towards Jonah. 'I made this for you.'

'That's very kind of you. Open it up and show me.'

Lucy tore open the envelope and took out a card adorned with colour photographs of various flowers, cut out from a gardening catalogue.

'That's lovely. Is there anything inside? Hold it up so I can read.'

Lucy obediently opened the card and held it in front of Jonah's face.

'A bit further away – that's right.' Jonah strained to

focus on the words, which Lucy had written in her best joined up writing. 'To Jonah, with all my love,' he read out. '*All* your love?' he queried. 'Don't you think you ought to keep some back for your Mum?'

'Oh Jonah!' Lucy cried scornfully. 'Don't you know about love?'

'What about it?'

'The more you give it away, the more you have.' Lucy replied triumphantly. 'So if I give you all my love I've got even more left for my Mam! Don't you know *anything?*'

She giggled and then climbed up on the bed and threw her arms round him.

'Careful! Lucy,' Bernie warned. 'Don't be too rough with Jonah's neck – it isn't healed up yet.'

Lucy slithered back to the floor and looked Jonah in the eye. 'My mam says that you can only move one finger – is that true?'

'Well now Lucy, it was, but have a look at this.' Jonah indicated his left hand with his eyes. He waggled his index finger. Lucy watched intently. Then the middle finger moved slightly as well. Lucy continued to stare, entranced. Finally, with a great effort, Jonah moved his thumb inwards and brought his index finger down to meet it. Lucy looked up with a broad grin on her face and their eyes met.

'You're getting better!' she whispered in awe. 'Does this mean you going to get *really* better?'

'I don't think so. The doctors are all being very careful and restrained and saying how important it is not to get false hopes. They seem to think that the most I'm likely to get is full movement in that hand – or possibly the whole arm.'

Lucy nodded seriously. Then an idea occurred to her and she grasped Jonah's hand and moved it on to his chest. Then she took the open card and placed it between his thumb and forefinger. He gripped them together and was delighted to see that he was able to hold the card firmly.

'There you are!' Lucy declared triumphantly. 'You didn't need me to hold it after all.'

'So I didn't' he agreed. 'Well, well, well.'

'And,' Lucy went on, removing the card from his grip and inserting her own small hand in its place. 'You can hold my hand!'

Jonah smiled and squeezed Lucy's hand as hard as he could with his three working digits. For several minutes nobody spoke.

'Lucy has a theory about your featherweight wellington boot wearer,' Bernie broke in, afraid that they might all start getting emotional. 'Do you want to hear it?'

'Really? I'm glad someone has got a theory about all this – the CID guys don't seem to be making any headway at all. Go on, Lucy, let's hear it!'

'*I* think,' Lucy said eagerly, 'that it might be like in "The Mystery of the Invisible Thief".'

Jonah looked puzzled.

'Enid Blyton,' Bernie explained. 'The Five Find-outers and Dog. Surely, you must have read them when you were a child? Although,' she went on with a smile, 'I can't quite picture you as a child; I think you must have come into the world fully-formed, aged about thirty!'

'Yes,' Jonah pondered briefly. 'I did read all the Enid Blyton books when I was Lucy's age. Five find-outers? That was Fatty and Bets and co. wasn't it?'

'That's right,' confirmed Bernie. 'Really, I'm surprised at you. You've got two boys: didn't you read to them when they were younger? I'm having a great time now that I've got an excuse to go back to all my old favourites for Lucy's benefit.'

'Sad to say,' Jonah admitted in a tone of remorse, 'I never seemed to have time for that sort of thing. I must have been a pretty poor father really. It comes with the job, I suppose.'

'Peter reads to me lots,' Lucy remarked thoughtfully.

'He says it helps him relax and then he solves crimes *better.*'

'Peter—,' began Jonah, intending to express the opinion that Peter could certainly do with something to improve his crime-solving abilities.

'I think,' cut in Bernie firmly, giving Jonah a warning look, having guessed accurately the purport of what he was going to say, 'that Peter is spending a lot of time with you, Lucy, to assuage his guilt over not spending as much time with his own kids as he thinks he ought to have done, when they were your age.'

'So, Jonah,' Lucy looked at him mischievously, 'would you like to ass- assuage *your* guilt by spending lots of time with me too?'

'That rather begs the question whether *you* would want to spend time with *me*, doesn't it?'

'But to get back to the question of the Wellington boot prints …' prompted Bernie.

'Yes,' Lucy addressed the company seriously. 'In "The Mystery of the Invisible Thief", the thief was a man with very small hands and feet but he made everyone *think* that the thief must be a big man by putting on big gloves and shoes and leaving lots of hand prints and footprints. So couldn't the person who shot you have been someone wearing boots that were too big for them – to make you *think* that they were bigger than they were?'

'Now that,' said Jonah, 'is about the most sensible thing I've heard anyone say about this case so far. I'll have a word with-,' he broke off as Jeannette re-entered carrying a tray. She put it down and beckoned to Lucy to come over to the sink.

'Let me show you how to wash your hands properly. See these special long handles on the taps? They're so you can turn them on and off with your elbows, so you don't have to touch them with your hands. … That's right! … Now some soap, and rub your hands really well all over… the backs as well … and between your fingers – like this. Well done! Now dry them with these paper towels.

Excellent! Now we're ready to go.'

Jeanette returned to the tray and poured milk and tea into a plastic cup. She screwed on a lid and Lucy could see a long straw poking out of the top. Jeanette placed the cup on the tray table and moved it so that the straw was within Jonah's reach.

'Here you are, young man! Just how you like it – a dash of milk and no sugar. Now Lucy, see this toast?' Jeanette handed Lucy a plate containing two slices of buttered toast. 'You can either cut it up into bite-sized pieces with this knife and pop them in his mouth –.'

'Like the host at mass.' Lucy suggested brightly.

'– or you can hold the whole slice up so that he can bite off a piece himself. There are two cups here, so you and your Mum can both help yourselves to tea and here's a chocolate biscuit as a reward if you manage to get him to eat up all the toast!'

Jeanette moved towards the door. 'I'll leave you to it. Do your best – he needs to build up his strength. Remember – just little pieces and plenty of sips of tea in between and call me if he chokes.'

Jonah looked embarrassed. 'She will keep fussing,' he complained. 'It's not as if I can burn up many calories lying here all day.'

He did, however, yield to Lucy's persistent gentle demands to take 'one more bite' and managed to finish both slices of toast. She reached for the chocolate biscuit.

'Now you've earned your reward. Do you want me to break it up in bits or hold it for you to bite?'

Jonah smiled, 'I think nurse Jeanette meant it as a reward for you, Lucy.'

'Share it! Please, Jonah!' Lucy looked pleadingly into Jonah's eyes.

'OK. Go on.'

Lucy broke the biscuit in half and held one half up to Jonah's mouth so that he could bite off a portion. While he was chewing, she ate a piece from the other half. Soon both halves were consumed.

When Jeanette returned a few minutes later, she gazed around with an exaggerated expression of amazement on her face. 'What is all this I see? Both slices of toast gone? Where are you hiding it?' She made a show of peering under the bed and behind the curtains before turning to Lucy.

'Tell me Lucy, did he really eat it all?'

Lucy nodded, grinning, 'Every bit – and half of the biscuit!'

'Half a biscuit too!' repeated Jeanette, her eyes wide. 'Now Lucy, I wish I had your skill with this patient. We could do with you at meal times to bring him to order and get him to eat up properly!'

'I could come.' Lucy jumped up excitedly. 'We could come over and help at meal times, couldn't we, Mam?' She took Bernie's hands in hers and looked anxiously into her face. 'We could, couldn't we?'

'What time do you serve your meals?' Bernie asked cautiously.

'Lunch is at twelve thirty and dinner is at six, but I didn't mean –'

'Please, Mam!'

'Lucy would be in school at lunch time, but I don't see why we couldn't come at dinner time – if we really wouldn't be in the way.' Bernie turned to Jonah, 'but how do you feel about it? Would you like Lucy to come in to feed you?'

'I'd like that very much, but it's a long way for you to come.'

'No it isn't!' Lucy looked round at each of the adults in turn. 'Please!'

'OK. I'm happy to give it a go.' Bernie was secretly pleased, but tried not to sound too eager. She turned to Jeanette. 'How about dinner tomorrow?'

'That would be just great! I'm on duty again tomorrow, so I'll meet you at ten to six and get you set up. Just press the buzzer by the door to the ward and I'll come and let you in.' She crouched down to address Lucy. 'You and me are going to make a great team! This young man' she gestured with her head towards Jonah, 'just won't be able to resist our combined charms!'

****

'And that,' Jonah said, 'is how the conspiracy started, to feed me up and get me back into shape.'

'Lucy came every evening for about three months, I should think. It was great for me. It wasn't anything like as humiliating to be spoon-fed by a nine-year-old girl than by an adult, and Lucy was delighted to be in a position to tell a grownup to eat up his greens! I managed to convince myself that she really did enjoy every minute, as she said she did, but looking back, it must have been a very traumatic time for her.'

****

'If I pray really, really hard for Jonah,' Lucy asked her mother as they drove home after visiting Jonah that first time. 'Do you think he'll get well again – I mean back to how he was before he was shot?'

'I wouldn't rule it out completely,' Bernie answered cautiously, 'but I very much doubt it.' She paused to gather her thoughts. 'You see, Lucy, I don't think God likes to keep stepping in and tweaking his creation every time we ask him to – the Laws of Nature are there to make life predictable; if miracles happened all the time we wouldn't know where we were.'

Lucy frowned, clearly not satisfied.

'Look, let's take an example,' Bernie started to warm to her argument. 'The weather forecast uses mathematical modelling to predict the weather over a few days ahead. It takes into account current conditions (air pressure, humidity, wind speed and direction, etc.) and works out what is likely to happen in the future. If God answered prayers by doing whatever we ask for: firstly he'd have to grant some people's wishes and not others because there would often be people asking for contradictory things – farmers wanting rain to make the crops grow and organisers of barbecues and garden parties wanting it to be fine – and secondly, how could the weather forecasters make any predictions if they had to take into account not just the physical conditions but all the prayers that people were making, and second-guessing how God was going to respond to them?'

'But this is much more important than the weather.' Lucy persisted. 'Why won't God make him better? Or why didn't he stop it happening?'

'It's all to do with free-will. Someone *chose* to hurt Jonah – not God, a human being who hated him so much that they wanted him dead – and if God came along and fixed things every time someone did something bad, it would effectively be impossible for anyone to choose to do bad things. If, for example, the person who stole your bike the other day knew that it would miraculously appear back in the bike shed a bit later, it would be pointless to steal it in the first place.'

'Wouldn't that be a good thing?'

'Well, I suppose it would be nice to know that nobody would ever steal anything, because they couldn't keep it if they did – but that wouldn't make the people who would *like* to steal any better. They wouldn't be leaving your bike alone because it was wrong to steal it, only because stealing it was impossible. That's what we mean by free-will – being able to choose whether to do the right thing or the wrong thing and having to live with the consequences of your choices.'

'But it's not fair!' Lucy was still unconvinced. 'Jonah didn't do *anything* wrong.'

'I know it's hard. And that's why I said I wouldn't completely rule out divine intervention – as a one-off very, very occasionally – but if it happened frequently then people like whoever shot Jonah would know that, however hard they tried, they couldn't really hurt people. And that would undermine their free-will.'

There was silence for a few minutes while Lucy digested this idea.

'I think that the main way that God answers our prayers,' Bernie resumed, 'is by changing people – helping the people that we're praying for to cope with their problems, and helping the people around them to be better friends to them.'

'I'm going to pray that God will make me into a really, really good friend for Jonah,' Lucy said earnestly.

'I think you already are, love,' observed Bernie, feeling very proud of her daughter. 'And I'm going to pray to be a good friend to him too. Tell you what – why don't we call in at St Cyprian's on the way home and light a candle each for him?'

Lucy nodded and seemed to brighten up. It wasn't until bedtime that she resumed the conversation.

'I do love Jonah so much!' she whispered as Bernie made to leave after tucking her in. 'How can he bear it – just lying there like that?' Tears started to run down her cheeks.

'I know, love. It doesn't seem fair, does it?' Bernie knelt down beside the bed and put her arms round Lucy. 'It's very, very sad; and it makes me feel very angry too; and I think it's OK to feel like that. I remember when our Angie died, our Peter seemed to be shouting and crying in turns for about a month before he started to work out how to survive without her.'

Lucy nodded. 'I don't really remember,' she admitted, 'but I *do* remember being frightened, because I'd never seen a grown up cry before. I thought something really, really awful must have happened.'

'It had. They'd been married for nearly twenty-five years. Suddenly being without her must have been like having one of his arms cut off.'

'But now, he's got you – so it's like having a new arm put back on!'

65

'No.' Bernie shook her head emphatically and held Lucy tighter. 'I'm more like a rather badly-fitting prosthetic limb that helps the patient to function but keeps rubbing the stump and making the skin sore!'

'Oh Mam!' Lucy was indignant. 'I bet that isn't what our Peter would say.'

'I dare say he'd be more polite about it, but we both know that I'll never be a replacement for Angie – and he'd never forgive himself if I was. But what I was trying to say was that when something happens, like Jonah being shot, it's OK to be upset and angry, but in the end we generally find a way to muddle through.'

Lucy nodded obediently, but was unable to stop the tears flowing.

'Do you think that Jonah would rather be dead?' she asked at last.

'No, I'm sure he wouldn't. At least,' Bernie's natural honesty compelled her to think this one through more carefully. 'I suppose maybe sometimes it may all get a bit too much and it might cross his mind, but he's very brave and I don't think he'd allow himself to feel like that for long. The main thing for *us* to do is to make sure he knows how much we care about him and value having him around – so he won't start thinking he's being a burden.'

Lucy nodded and smiled again, but still could not hold the tears back.

'Lucy, love?' Bernie asked gently. 'You do realise that Jonah isn't going to stay there in that hospital bed forever? Nurse Jeannette tells me that it won't be long before they'll be getting him out in a wheelchair – just as soon as they're sure that his neck won't get damaged by the movement. There's a garden in the hospital grounds that's specially designed for patients with spinal injuries to get around in. And these days there are all sorts of clever devices to help disabled people to do things for themselves. It's not like in "What Katy Did" and "Pollyanna" and all those improving stories from the Victorian era, where you have invalids languishing in semi-darkened rooms!'

Lucy brightened up. 'Will I be able to push him?'

'I expect so – sometimes – but I think they're hoping that he'll have an electric wheelchair that he can learn to control himself.'

'Oh!' Lucy looked slightly disappointed. 'I suppose that'll be much better,' she conceded.

'Which means that you can concentrate on walking alongside and making conversation and pointing out the flowers to him. Now,' Bernie said firmly, getting up to go, 'Try to get to sleep. You've got a busy day tomorrow – what with your new nursing job and all.'

****

'Anyway,' Jonah continued, 'the next day when Lucy came to give me my dinner, there I was out of bed, propped up in a special chair to support my back. Bed rest is apparently very bad for you in lots of ways – gives you skin ulcers and urinary tract infections and messes up the circulation and, in the longer term, makes you develop brittle bones. So I was hoisted out of bed every afternoon to start getting used to being upright again.'

'And at that point, what sort of future did you imagine you were going to have?' asked Bethan. 'I mean – what had the medical staff told you?'

'I'm not sure,' Jonah thought for a moment. 'I think they tried to be honest – and of course Margaret had a pretty good idea what chances there were likely to be of any sort of recovery, so I don't think I was ever under any illusion that things would ever get back to normal. I do remember the nurses and physios talking about how they'd soon be getting me out in the fresh air and how important it was to take things slowly and not to get depressed when it took a long time to learn how to do things that I'd never even had to think about before. '

'Can you give an example?'

'Well, there was the TV remote. You have no idea how difficult it is to use with just one finger – and how easily it slips out of reach! But after one of the OTs strapped it to my wrist, I managed to master it,' he gave a small laugh, 'after about a week of trying!'

****

'Well now!' Jeannette exclaimed coming into Jonah's room to collect his dinner tray. 'You two look very comfortable there.'

Lucy and Jonah looked up from the book that Lucy was holding for Jonah to read aloud. She was squeezed up next to him in his chair, her head resting against his shoulder while his head leant gently on hers.

'And what is it you're reading? It looks as if it must be something good!'

Lucy slid from the chair and brought the book over. Jeannette looked at it.

'My, my!' she exclaimed. 'Pollyanna! I loved that book when I was a little girl in Jamaica. It used to make me cry.'

Lucy smiled. 'Did you play the Glad Game, Nurse Jeannette?'

'No, I can't say I did.'

'Lucy played it for about a fortnight,' said Bernie, joining in the conversation from a chair in the corner of the room, where she had been working on her laptop. 'And didn't we know it! It drove us up the wall. You have no idea how tiresome it is having someone being perpetually cheerful and telling you to be glad about everything. In the end I told her that if she didn't stop it she might well have to find something to be glad about in being a victim of domestic violence!'

Jonah laughed, but looked puzzled. 'But where does a game come in? Enlighten me, please.'

'That's in the next chapter,' Lucy explained. 'Whatever happens to you, you have to try to think of something to be glad about it.'

'That's right,' put in Jeannette. 'So when the Ladies' Aid sent Pollyanna a pair of crutches, instead of the doll that she was hoping for, her father told her that she could be glad that she didn't need them!'

'But,' said Bernie drily, 'Not even Pollyanna could find anything to be glad about in being injured in a road accident and being told she'd never walk again.'

For a moment, there was an uncomfortable silence. Then Jonah smiled. 'Well I think that I can do better than your Pollyanna,' he said, 'because I can tell you that I'm *very* glad that I was born left-handed.'

'Oh Jonah! I do love you!' Lucy hugged Jonah and kissed him on the cheek.

Bernie rolled her eyes and looked at the ceiling. 'She's at it again,' she said in a tone of mock resignation. 'Don't encourage her!'

They all laughed.

'This all sounds very jolly!' Margaret entered the room and looked around. 'Mind if I join you?'

Her shoulder length hair was dyed a reddish brown colour with creamy stripes. Her nails were painted the same brown, which also matched the cowboy boots that she wore beneath a knee-length flowing skirt. She carried a bright red crash helmet under her arm. Lucy stared at the unexpected apparition; she had never met Margaret before.

'We were just leaving.' Bernie closed her laptop and put it in its case. 'Come along Lucy.'

'No – don't go,' Margaret urged. 'We always seem to pass like ships in the night. I'd rather you stayed, so I can start to get to know you.'

'Well – if you're sure we won't be intruding.' Bernie was still hesitant about taking up valuable visiting time when Jonah and his wife could have been alone together.

'Did you come on a motor bike?' Lucy asked, looking at the helmet.

'I did indeed! It's very handy for getting through the traffic – and more fun than a car too.'

'We all thought she'd grow out of it,' Jonah said, 'but after thirty years we're starting to think that it's a vain hope!'

'So, Lucy,' Margaret went on, ignoring her husband's remark, 'Jeanette tells me that you want to be a doctor?'

Lucy nodded. 'Yes. I'd like to be a pathologist.'

'A pathologist?' Margaret was taken aback. 'You mean looking at dead people? Wouldn't you rather be a surgeon like me – making people better?'

'Well,' said Lucy, considering the matter, 'I would like to do that, but forensic pathology would be really interesting – like being a detective. And I'd be a bit nervous about cutting up *live* people – in case I made a mistake.'

'Mistakes on dead people can be serious too,' Jonah pointed out. 'I remember once: we were all set to prosecute a mother for battering her baby to death. *Our* pathologist was adamant that the injuries must have been inflicted deliberately, but the defence came up with another expert who showed that the baby had a genetic condition that meant that even quite gentle handling could cause bruising and broken bones. If everyone had just relied on the first doctor's opinion an innocent person might have gone to prison for a long time.'

Lucy reflected on this statement. 'I suppose,' she said at last, 'at least with dead people you *can* always get someone else to have a look. If a surgeon makes a mistake, it might be too late to put it right.'

'Now that's a very good point,' Margaret agreed, 'but we really don't make that many mistakes you know. And think about how good it feels when things go right. This morning, for example, I've been to the ward to see a lad who came in last week after an argument with a chainsaw. We thought he was going to lose his arm, but we repaired the damage as best we could and now it's looking as if he's only going to lose a bit of function in the elbow joint.'

'Mike says that he always double-checks anything that the police are going to use as evidence.' Lucy went on, still thinking about the responsibilities of forensic pathologists. 'He likes to be sure that it isn't his fault if someone goes to jail when they don't deserve it.'

'Mike?'

'Michael Carson,' Bernie explained. 'He's a friend of Peter's. He gave Lucy a tour of his labs and since then she's been dead keen on forensic pathology.'

'Well, Lucy,' Jonah said, 'we certainly need the best forensic pathologists we can get. I hope you'll come and work on my patch once you're qualified.'

For a moment there was silence, while the thought crossed both Bernie's and Margaret's minds that Jonah appeared to have forgotten that, given his current situation, he was unlikely to be going back to police work.

'Talking of getting to know you,' Bernie said brightly, keen to move the conversation on to another topic. 'I've been wondering for some time whether it's Bawlton or Burri.' She pronounced the names of the Pennine towns of Bolton and Bury using the vowel sounds of East Lancashire.

Jonah looked puzzled, but Margaret knew immediately what Bernie was getting at.

'Horwich.' She answered, 'but Bolton was a good guess.'

'At least I didn't accuse you of hailing from Yorkshire!'

'Funny you should say that; only a few days ago a patient told me I sounded like Alan Bennett.'

'These ignorant southerners!' Bernie joked. 'They think "The North" is the same all over: all flat caps and clogs and cobbled streets!'

'You're right,' Margaret agreed, grinning as she caught Bernie's eye. 'I think they expect me to live on tripe and black pudding.'

'To hear them talk, you'd think civilisation ended at Watford Junction!'

'Of course, it's not their fault really,' Margaret conceded graciously. 'They can't help it, poor dears. They're frightened to go to see for themselves.'

'I suppose you're right,' Bernie mused, pretending to

consider this assertion seriously. 'We mustn't be too hard on them.'

'Hold on there!' Jonah intervened at last, well aware that he was being gently teased. 'Don't us poor southerners get a chance to have a say in all this?'

'Now there's a thought!' Margaret continued to talk across Jonah to Bernie. 'Do you think we ought to let him speak?'

'I'm not sure,' Bernie frowned in mock concentration. 'Would there be any point? I mean – what would a southerner know about anything?'

'I think you're both being very mean to Jonah!' Lucy burst in, unable to contain herself any longer. 'Stop it!'

'Sorry, love,' Bernie suddenly became serious. 'We were only pulling his leg.'

'Don't you worry,' Jonah reassured her. 'I'm used to being hen-pecked.'

Lucy looked round at each adult in turn; unsure at first, then eventually satisfied that everyone was still friends.

'And now,' Bernie said, getting up. 'We really must be going.'

Lucy looked sulky and seemed about to protest, but Jonah spoke first.

'Off you go, Lucy. I've had more than my fair share of you today; it's time you went home. Thank you for feeding me – and for sharing your book with me. Will you leave it here? I don't want you getting ahead of me.'

Lucy put the book down on the bedside cupboard. 'I'll come again tomorrow and we can read some more,' she promised. 'We will, won't we?' she asked her mother anxiously.

Bernie nodded. 'Of course. We've got to make sure your patient isn't allowed to starve himself!'

They went out, followed closely by Jeanette.

Margaret picked up the book and looked at it. 'Pollyanna!' she exclaimed. 'Has Lucy got you reading this sentimental, sanctimonious …?'

'I'm rather enjoying it,' Jonah interrupted. 'I seem to have missed out – everyone else appears to have read it in childhood. Lucy is repairing the deficiency for me.'

'My grandmother forced it on me,' admitted Margaret. 'But I don't imagine even she would have expected a boy to read something so obviously intended as improving literature for little girls. I suppose Lucy fancies herself as a little Pollyanna going through the world spreading sweetness and light.'

'Quite probably,' agreed Jonah. 'Would that be such a bad thing?'

'No, of course not.' Margaret conceded. 'Oh! I'm sorry. I didn't mean to be critical. I know how much you enjoy her visits. I just … I just worry in case she's very disappointed if she doesn't get the happy ending that she's hoping for. She seems such a nice lass and I'd hate for her to be upset.'

'You and me both.' Jonah agreed.

****

'You would have thought,' Jonah said to Bethan, 'that Lucy would soon have got tired of coming to see me. I'm sure that, when I was nine, I had much more interesting things to do than visiting a boring old man in a wheelchair! But she persisted, and even when Bernie wasn't able to bring her, she persuaded her stepfather, Peter, to drive her over – with an interesting result.'

****

'You'll like Nurse Jeanette,' Lucy said earnestly to Peter as they waked from the hospital car park. 'She reminds me of Auntie Angie.'

Peter winced inwardly, not having any desire to meet someone who might be expected to remind him of his dead wife. 'Why's that?' he asked, trying to sound natural, but imagining that Lucy must be able to detect the edginess in his voice.

'Well, of course the obvious thing is that she's black – and she talks like Angie. That's because she was born in

73

Jamaica too. Her parents brought her over here when she was only a bit older than me, so she doesn't remember it all that well. I showed her the scrapbook that Angie gave me, with pictures of her and her brothers in Jamaica, and she was very interested. I wish I could remember more of the stories Angie told me – I'm sure Nurse Jeanette would like to hear them. I always did.' Lucy prattled on. 'She's awfully kind. She looks after Jonah really, really well – and she lets me help with everything. She said I'd make a good nurse, but I told her I'd rather be a doctor.'

They reached the ward and pressed the buzzer to be allowed in.

'Good evening!' Jeanette greeted them with a wide smile, 'and you must be Peter. I've been looking forward to meeting you - Lucy's told me so much about you.'

Peter mumbled something inaudible in reply. Seeing his embarrassment, Jeanette led them briskly to Jonah's room.

'Here you are, young Lucy! Your patient is all ready for his dinner, so I'll leave you to it. Don't forget to wash your hands.'

Lucy marched eagerly over to the sink. Peter and Jonah exchanged rather stilted greetings. Their relationship so far had been as professional colleagues, rather than friends. To Peter it did not seem right somehow for Jonah's vulnerability to be exposed so graphically in front of him. Jonah too felt regret that Peter was about to witness the spectacle of his being hand-fed like a baby. It was so much better with Lucy than when the nurses fed him, but he still could not get out of his head a feeling that it was somehow degrading not even to be able to feed himself. It was not something that he yet felt comfortable doing in public – or in front of a fellow police officer.

Jeanette, noticing their awkwardness, addressed Peter, 'This is likely to take some time; why don't you come to the Day Room and have a cup of tea while you're waiting?'

Peter looked at her gratefully. 'Yes – that would be nice.' Then, to Lucy: 'see you later then. Don't get up to mischief!'

'You won't be disturbed here,' Jeanette said, as she ushered Peter into a room containing half a dozen plastic-upholstered high-backed arm chairs, two low tables bearing an assortment of magazines, a bookcase holding a selection of worn paperbacks, and a television screen. It reminded Peter of a dentist's waiting room.

'The patients are all having their dinner,' she went on. 'Feel free to put the TV on if you'd like to watch. I'll have to go now – it's always very busy on this ward at mealtimes because so many of the patients need help. Young Lucy has been a godsend, I don't mind telling you; just as an extra pair of hands, never mind the way she seems to be able to handle young Jonah better than any of us!'

Peter could not help smiling at the term 'young Jonah', reflecting that the nurse must be much of an age with her patient. 'He never did take kindly to following orders,' he agreed.

'So, I'll love you and leave you,' Jeanette continued. 'I'll send someone in with a cup of tea in a minute.'

Peter settled down with his tea and started thumbing through one of the magazines. About forty minutes later Jeanette returned carrying two more steaming mugs.

'I've brought you another cup of tea,' she said, sitting down heavily in the chair next to Peter's. 'And this time, if you don't mind, I'll join you. I simply must take the weight off my feet for a few minutes before visiting time kicks off!'

'Thanks.'

For a few seconds they sat in silence.

'You must be very proud of young Lucy,' Jeanette remarked.

'I certainly would be if she was my daughter,' Peter agreed. 'But I'm afraid I can't claim any credit for her.'

'You've played a big part in her upbringing, by all accounts,' countered Jeanette, 'I'd say that entitles you to a good deal of credit for how she's turning out.'

More silence.

'Lucy tells me your son is settled in Jamaica now.' Jeanette made another attempt at starting a conversation. 'She showed me some of the wedding photos. It quite took me back to my childhood.'

Peter did not answer, so she continued.

'I haven't been back since my grandmother's funeral in seventy-five. I kept planning to go, but somehow something always cropped up to prevent me. And now, I couldn't leave my mother for that long. So I guess I'll probably never make it.' She sighed. Then, brightening up, 'Your son's wedding looked like a very joyful occasion.'

'Yes,' Peter agreed, feeling that some sort of answer was required.

'But, of course,' Jeanette continued cautiously, 'He must have missed his mother being there.'

'Yes. He went out there to find his roots after she died. It was hard on him, being so young, and not being able to understand …' Peter's voice trailed off.

'Not understanding why it happened?' Jeanette's voice was soft and gentle.

'You see, we'd never experienced any real racial abuse before – silly name-calling in the playground of course, but nothing worse than I used to get for being ginger. So, it was completely unexpected. And the worst part of it is,' Peter paused, and then continued, unsure why he was saying things, to this comparative stranger, which he had never voiced before, 'that, being white, I'm sort of complicit in it.'

Jeanette opened her mouth to protest, but Peter continued. 'I don't mean that all white people are racists. I just mean that, as part of the white majority – and, as a police officer, part of the establishment – I'm part of a society that hasn't done enough to prevent those things happening.'

'I'm sure that isn't how your kids saw it.'

'No but that doesn't stop the guilt. And it doesn't stop

me having a vague feeling of being an outsider in my own family.'

'Those wedding photos looked as if you and your son were very close – you didn't look like an outsider then.'

'I hope so. We were close for a while when Angie died, but then ...Well, it took time for him to come to terms with me re-marrying, even though he loves Bernie to bits. He said that two years was far too soon. I suppose he thought I'd forgotten Angie; but the truth is that it was all because I *can't* forget Angie. I just couldn't face living alone after all those years together. Bernie understands. And at least I can try to be a better Dad to Lucy than I was to my own two.'

'Now I think you are being altogether too hard on yourself.' Jeanette put her hand on Peter's knee for a moment or two and looked him in the eyes. 'I bet you were a great Dad to both of them. Now, I suggest we go back and see how young Lucy and Jonah are getting on.'

'Yes. Right. I'm sorry – you must have far better things to do than listen to me going on. I can't think why –"'

'Now you stop right there,' said Jeanette firmly. 'And remember, I'm always delighted to talk about Jamaica and my fellow Jamaicans, so any time you want to tell me more about your wife or your kids, you just go right ahead. Lucy told me what happened to your wife. That was a bad business. Six years is nowhere near long enough to get over it, so just try to stop beating yourself up about it.'

****

'Of course,' Jonah explained, 'I didn't find out why Peter and Jeanette seemed to hit it off so well until much later. I was just glad that, whenever it was Peter who brought Lucy to see me, he left us together and went off somewhere else. At that stage, I still felt embarrassed at the idea of a colleague seeing the full extent of my dependency.'

****

The summer passed, with almost daily visits from Lucy,

first for mealtimes and then later to accompany Jonah for 'walks' in the garden, where he gradually became adept at controlling the electric wheelchair into which he was strapped each afternoon. He was delighted to discover that, particularly downhill, the machine had quite a good turn of speed, and he enjoyed chasing Lucy around the maze of paths between the flowerbeds. The two of them would race on ahead while Bernie, sometimes accompanied by Margaret, would follow at a more sedate pace, consciously resisting the temptation to call out to him to take more care as he narrowly avoided collisions or when the chair rocked precariously when taking a sharp bend.

One day their worst fears were realised when, racing downhill in pursuit of Lucy, Jonah was unable to slow sufficiently and the chair swayed over and landed on its side in a bed of delphiniums. Lucy turned when she heard the crash and stood, momentarily aghast, before racing back. Unable to move the heavy chair and its helpless passenger, she knelt beside Jonah with her arms around his shoulders.

Soon she was joined by Margaret and Bernie, who righted the chair and re-settled Jonah into it. He grinned up at them.

'No harm done.' He declared. 'Just a bit of driving without due care and attention, I'm afraid!'

'Hmmph!' Margaret snorted, as she started to unbutton Jonah's shirt. 'Someone who lacks sensation anywhere below the shoulders is in no position to decide whether or not any harm has been done.' She examined his torso carefully. 'I think you're going to have one or two magnificent bruises by the morning,' she concluded, 'but I can't find any broken ribs or even broken skin. You've been lucky – you could have done yourself some serious damage.'

'Sorry Miss! I'll be more careful in future.' Jonah looked up at Margaret with the air of a naughty schoolboy hoping to avoid punishment. 'And you won't need to tell the nurses about my little accident, will you? I don't want to be confined to barracks!'

'I certainly *ought* to tell them,' Margaret said sternly, "but I suppose there's no point worrying them just for the sake of it. But you must promise that you'll own up if they ask you about those bruises.'

'It wasn't Jonah's fault.' Lucy felt vaguely that Margaret was angry with her husband. 'I ran too fast. He was only trying to keep up with me.'

Margaret and Bernie exchanged glances.

'Lucy, love,' Bernie began, 'nobody's blaming anyone. We just – '

'Now you just listen here my lass!' Margaret interrupted. 'If Jonah here takes it into his head to throw himself into a flower bed then that's his problem; and he's old enough and ugly enough to take responsibility for it himself. So don't you go making excuses for him.'

Lucy looked puzzled for a moment, then broke into a smile, realising that the grownups were trying to make light of the incident in order to cover up their anxieties. 'Well, I don't think he's old or ugly at all!' she declared.

****

Bernie returned carrying a tray loaded with the teapot and fresh cups. Lucy followed her holding a large yellow envelope. She handed it to Bethan. 'I want you to see this. It's my very, very best birthday present – ever!'

Bethan opened the envelope and took out a slightly battered card, portraying a small girl standing looking up at a tall sunflower and bearing the words 'Happy birthday! 10 today.'

'Go on – open it!' urged Lucy.

Bethan did as she was told and peered down at a rather untidy scrawl in black ink. 'To Lucy,' she read aloud, 'with all my love, Jonah.' She looked up at Lucy whose face bore a radiant smile, but whose eyes were moist.

'It was the first thing he wrote himself,' she explained.

'I talked to the nurses about it afterwards and they told me how he practised for hours to get it right.'

****

'I've made up my mind.' Jonah addressed the case conference with an air of authority. 'It'll be Lucy's birthday in a couple of months and I intend to be there.' Nobody spoke, so he continued. 'Every week we have this multidisciplinary team meeting and we talk about my progress and how in a few weeks I'll be ready to go home, but after a few weeks I never seem to be any nearer getting out of here. I've never missed Lucy's birthday before and I'm determined to go to see her in *her* house, just like every other year.' He paused and looked round the room expectantly.

'I think that's an excellent idea.' Sharon the Occupational Therapist, was the first to speak. 'You're quite right, what we need is a deadline. Otherwise, you'll always be thinking, "Maybe I'm not ready yet – let's put it off for another few weeks."'

'I agree,' nodded Sanjeev, the consultant in rehabilitation medicine. 'That would be an excellent goal: a day out to show that you can manage in the outside world, without committing yourself to anything permanent. Then, if all goes well, we can expect to have you ready for discharge soon afterwards.'

'You're doing pretty well at getting around independently here in the hospital,' Sharon went on, 'but everything is arranged to make it easy and there are always staff around if you need them. Going out for a few hours would give us a chance to see whether you can cope in unfamiliar surroundings and help us to identify what modifications you'll need at home when you *are* discharged.'

'And it'll also help us to decide what training we need to give to your family before you go home,' put in Jeanette. 'I think it's an excellent idea, and Lucy will absolutely love it.'

'Right, then,' Sharon turned to a new page in her notebook and prepared to write. 'What is it that we're working towards?'

'I think,' put in Margaret tentatively, 'that, before we all get too carried away with this idea, we ought to bring Bernie into the discussion. After all, it *is* her house that will need to be made ready for him and she's going to need to meet with you all in advance to work out what needs to be done. And another thing – I don't think we ought to let Lucy know about it. It will be more fun for her if it's a surprise and less of a let-down if it doesn't come off.'

So, the following week, Bernie joined the meeting and the preparations began. Sharon made a visit to Bernie's house to assess access, after which Bernie arranged for the side gate to be widened and for a removable ramp to be constructed to give wheelchair access to the French window in the living room. They agreed that Jeanette would accompany Jonah, but that Margaret would be there too and would take care of all his needs as if there were no hospital staff present, so as to practise for when he was discharged home. Everything was planned down to the smallest detail, so that nothing could go wrong.

Jonah was now adept at browsing the internet via a specially modified computer interface and, determined that he alone would be responsible for Lucy's birthday present and card, he was inordinately pleased with himself when he succeeded in ordering a copy of "The Hobbit" to be delivered and in purchasing a suitable card from the hospital shop. Although he still only had control of movement in the first two fingers and thumb of his left hand, he was convinced that this should be sufficient to enable him to hold a pen and to write – and he was not going to be satisfied unless he managed to write a personal message for Lucy in her card.

It was a long struggle.

His first attempts were foiled by the tendency for the paper to shift under his hand as he wrote. This problem was solved by attaching it to the tray-table with masking tape. But then the pen kept slipping from his grip and he had to call repeatedly for one of the nurses to replace it in his hand. Finally, he got the knack of holding it but, being unable to move his hand, he could only write in a very restricted area of the paper. This could be overcome by asking someone to move his hand after each word, but Jonah wanted to write the whole message independently. He could not move his hand, but perhaps a mechanism could be arranged so that he could move the tray-table beneath his hand. He explained this to a friend from the Engineering Faculty at the university and eventually a device was constructed that allowed him to control the movement of a drawing board by moving his head.

That was only the beginning. Now commenced the long business of re-learning how to write. At last, he was satisfied with the results and he asked for the birthday card itself to be taped to the drawing board. Then, with painstaking care, he started to write.

****

'They sneaked me in while Lucy was at school.' Jonah smiled as he pictured the scene in his mind's eye. 'I'll never forget the look on her face when she came in and saw me there, sitting in her back room, with a parcel on my knees and the birthday cake, which she'd planned to bring to share with me at the hospital, on the coffee table.'

'And I just couldn't believe it when I opened the card and saw that he'd actually managed to write all that – just for me.'

'Of course, he'd been typing one-fingered emails for ages,' commented Bernie, 'so from a purely practical point of view, all that effort just to revert back to pen and paper was rather a waste of time.'

'Oh Mam!' Lucy was indignant.

'On the contrary,' argued Jonah. 'Even in this computer age, it's extremely useful to be able to sign my name - on cheques, for example; so I'm grateful to Lucy for giving me the incentive. But to get back to business,' he turned to Bethan, 'I suppose you want me to choose another hymn?'

'Well yes – we need eight and so far you've only chosen one. Is there something that sums up this part of your life? Or something that was particularly meaningful during that period?'

'It isn't exactly a hymn, but perhaps you could stretch a point and let me have *You'll Never Walk Alone*. I'd say that's what Lucy demonstrated to me in all those months when she came to visit me in the hospital.'

'And think what it'll do for your viewing figures,' put in Bernie. 'All those Liverpool supporters tuning in!'

****

4 O LOVE THAT WILT NOT LET ME GO

'And my next hymn,' Jonah announced, 'is easy, because it's Our Bernie's signature tune: *O Love that wilt not let me go.*'

'Don't be daft, Jonah,' Bernie protested, 'This programme is about you, not me.'

'But, like it or not, our lives have become inextricably linked,' Jonah countered, 'and if Bethan here is going to understand my story, she needs to hear yours too. Besides,' he went on, 'I've been talking quite enough. Let me have a rest while you recount how you met old Richard and became a policeman's wife.'

'Go on Mam!' urged Lucy. 'It's really romantic!'

'That it is not!' exclaimed Bernie indignantly. 'I don't do romantic, as you well know.'

'Please, Dr Fazakerley,' Bethan urged. 'It sounds quite intriguing, and I need as much background as I can get. Of course, it won't all go into the programme, but if we have lots of material then we can edit is down to make something the viewers will find interesting and, we hope, inspiring.'

'Hmmph!' Bernie sounded unconvinced, but agreed to

co-operate.

'It all began back in ninety-five,' she began. 'I was thirty-six and had been a fellow at St Luke's College for a good many years by then. It looked as if things were going to carry on much the same for probably another thirty years or so – until such time as the college authorities saw fit to insist on me being pensioned off. I had a DPhil student called Ahmed Khalifa – a Jordanian. One morning he was found hanging by his neck on the staircase outside his room. Because I was his supervisor and because I was one of the first dons in that morning, the scouts called me.'

'Scouts?' asked Bethan, puzzled.

'It's the Oxford word for college cleaners,' Jonah explained. 'Carry on Bernie.'

'I called the police and then I had a look at the body.' Bernie resumed. 'Somehow Peter Johns managed to get himself put on the case – he was a Detective Inspector and Richard had just been promoted to Detective Superintendent. I knew Peter slightly through his wife, who went to the same church as I did. He denies it, but I'm convinced that he pulled some strings when he heard about a potential suicide at St Luke's and that I was the one who had reported it. I don't know why Richard came along too – they were very much a team, but this looked on the face of it like a "routine" student suicide, so it didn't warrant someone of superintendent level getting involved. Anyway, they both turned up there, together with a pathologist and a team of SOCOs. Maybe Peter had something to do with that too.'

****

'Detective Superintendent Richard Paige,' Richard introduced himself to Bernie, as he came through the door at the bottom of the staircase known as New Quad three, holding out his warrant card to establish his identity. Now in his mid-fifties, his fair hair was starting to turn white at the temples and was thinning slightly on top. 'And this is

Detective Inspector Peter Johns.'

'Yes – I know Peter, we've met before.' Bernie reached out to shake the superintendent by the hand. 'I assume you want to see the body? It's just up here.' She turned to lead the way up the staircase. As they turned the corner just beyond the first floor landing, a body came into view, hanging in the stair well from a rope attached to the second floor bannister rail. Richard followed, avoiding looking directly at the suspended figure. He was never at ease with a corpse.

'And you are?' he enquired.

'Dr Bernadette Fazakerley, Fellow in Applied Mathematics.'

'You found the body?'

'No. Lily Dawson found the body, but she did not presume to summon the police. She reported it to the Head Scout who asked me to deal with it.'

'I see. And this,' Richard inclined his head slightly in the direction of the body, 'is one of the students?'

'He's a postgraduate student – one of mine. His name's Ahmed Khalifa. He's in the final stages of a DPhil.'

'So you knew him well?'

'Probably as well as anyone in Oxford.' Bernie agreed, but did not elaborate.

'And you would know how to get in touch with his family?'

'I rang his father while I was waiting for your lot to arrive. They live in Jordan. He's going to look into flights and get back to me.'

'What did you tell him?'

'Just that his son had been found dead and there would have to be a police investigation.' Bernie's voice had a tinge of resentment in it. What right had this policeman to question her judgement as to what was appropriate to say to the bereaved parents?

'You didn't tell him that his son had taken his own life?'

'Why would I say that when I don't believe that he did?' The resentment, if not belligerence, was clearer now.

'And why do you say that? It seems to me to be the most obvious explanation.' Richard was starting to think that he did not like this seemingly hostile woman with her aggressive manner and strong Liverpool accent.

'Sir,' Peter intervened. 'Is all this necessary just now? Can't it –'

'Dr Fazakerley?' Richard pressed Bernie for an answer, ignoring Peter's attempts to deflect him. 'I'd like to know why you don't think that this is a case of suicide.'

'Superintendent,' Bernie replied coolly. 'I draw your attention to these marks on his wrists and ankles.' She pointed at the body and Richard was forced to inspect it. 'I'm no expert, but it looks to me as if he may have been tied up before he died, which would make it quite difficult for him to attach the rope to the bannisters and drop to his death, don't you think?'

The pathologist looked up from examining the neck of the victim. 'She's quite right, you know,' he agreed. 'I'd say that he was gagged and tied hand and foot before being strung up and dropped over the rail. It's not a very professional noose and I'd guess he took some time to die by asphyxiation. There are signs that he thrashed about, trying to get free – see these chips out of the paint on the bannisters? And the matching flakes of paint on his shoes? Not a pleasant way to die.'

'All right, all right,' growled Richard, 'No need for all the gruesome details. Just put the facts in your report.'

'Very well.' The pathologist shrugged. 'Presumably, after death the bonds were removed to give the impression that it was self-inflicted.'

Bernie looked at Richard with a triumphant expression, but refrained from commenting.

'Well, we'll keep an open mind,' Richard said, then to the pathologist, 'you'll get the report to me as soon as you can, won't you?'

'We need to ask some more questions about the victim,' Peter seized the opportunity to divert the investigation on to another tack. 'Maybe we could go back to your room and talk?'

'OK. It's in Old Quad. Follow me.' Bernie led the way back down the stairs and outside.

Soon Peter and Richard were both seated in her room. Bernie picked up an electric kettle and disappeared into an adjoining room to fill it. Returning, she switched it on and turned to the two detectives: 'I'm making a brew. Would you like some tea?'

Mugs of strong tea were dispensed all round. Richard gazed with distaste at the dark brown liquid before him and surreptitiously reached for a top up from the milk jug in an attempt to render it drinkable. He gestured to his colleague to start the questioning.

'Going back to Ahmed Khalifa,' Peter began, 'he lived in college, presumably?'

'Yes – on the top floor of NQ3. He was hanging just outside his own door.'

'Are there any other students living on the second floor?'

'No. NQ3 only has one set of rooms on each floor. It's in the corner, you see, with the chapel on the other side.'

'And what's underneath his room?"

'On the first floor there's a tutor's room – Professor Philip Woodhouse, Modern History, specialising in eighteenth century France.'

'That doesn't sound like *modern* history to me,' muttered Peter.

'It's all relative. When you work for a college that was founded in 1473 the eighteenth century is *very* modern, in fact positively futuristic.'

'And below Prof Woodhouse – on the ground floor?'

'The student laundry room.'

'And does Prof Woodhouse live in?'

'No – he has a house in Summertown.'

'So, after working hours, the only people who would be likely to hear any scuffle that went on up in Ahmed's room would be students doing their washing?'

'That's right – and the laundry room is closed from ten p.m. to eight a.m. to keep the noise down at night.'

'So,' Richard observed, having listened carefully to this exchange, 'any time after ten last night, it would be fairly safe for an intruder to attack Ahmed Khalifa without being noticed?'

'Yes, I suppose so. They'd need to know the code for the door at the bottom of the staircase, but that would include every undergraduate at the college and they are notoriously hopeless at keeping codes secure. Or someone might have wedged the door open – they often do.'

'And what about Ahmed Khalifa?' Peter asked, 'What sort of person was he?'

'I'm not sure what you want to know.' Bernie shrugged. 'He was a hardworking student and a capable mathematician. He didn't mix much with the other students, as far as I know. He was very much concerned with completing his doctorate and getting back home. He didn't have time for a big social life.'

'So you don't know about anyone who might have borne him a grudge?'

'No.'

'No girlfriends or ex-girlfriends?'

'He had a fiancé back in Jordan – which is one reason why he wanted to finish his DPhil and get back there.'

'And you say he'd nearly finished his degree?'

'He emailed me a final draft of his thesis only yesterday. He was planning to submit next month.'

'And he wasn't worried about it at all?'

'Not that I'm aware of. He certainly had no reason to be. His work wasn't world-shattering but–'

'Wait a moment,' Richard interrupted. 'This "email" you say he sent. That's like an electronic letter, right?'

Bernie nodded, an amused smile on her face.

'That's right. He emailed me and attached a file with the thesis in it.'

'And the email? What did it say, exactly? Was there anything unusual about it?'

'It seemed perfectly normal to me,' Bernie answered, puzzled at this sudden interest. 'Have a look at it if you like.'

She got up and went over to a computer desk in the corner of the room. A minute or so later, she beckoned him over.

'Here it is. Nothing at all to suggest that he was contemplating suicide – if that's what you were hoping for.'

'Dear Bernie,' Richard read aloud, 'Here is my final draft for you to read. Can I come to see you tomorrow? I need your advice on something. Ahmed.'

'Do you have any idea what it was that he needed your advice on?' he asked.

Bernie shook her head.

'No – I assume it was something to do with his thesis, but it could have been more personal. Anyway – surely you will agree that someone who was planning to commit suicide within a few hours would hardly be attempting to make an appointment for the following day.'

The telephone rang and Bernie answered it.

'Professor Khalifa! Thank you for ringing back. … Ten thirty-two? … Yes, I've got that. … I'll pick you up from Heathrow. .. No, it's no trouble, I'd like to. … And how are the girls? … Good … See you this evening.'

During the brief conversation, she wrote notes on a pad. At the end, she tore off the top sheet, folded it and put in her pocket.

'That was Ahmed's father. They've booked a flight for this evening. It gets into Heathrow about ten thirty. I've said that I'll be there to pick them up.'

'*We*'ll do that.' Richard said tersely.

'No,' Bernie insisted. 'I said I'd be there and I will. It's the least I can do. At least I've met them before – better than some anonymous policeman to escort them.'

'Very well,' Richard conceded. 'You can come, but *I* drive and it *is* an official police escort, as you put it.'

Bernie looked dissatisfied, but did not attempt to argue further.

'I've got choir practice at eight, so you could pick me up from the chapel after that – about nine o'clock.'

'Right. I'll do that.'

For a moment, they looked at each other with animosity. Then Richard brought his mind back to the investigation.

'I should think the scenes of crime officers will have finished with his room by now. Would you mind coming back there with us to have a look?'

They headed back to New Quad, Bernie noting as she went that the inspector's tea remained untouched. When they got to staircase 3, they saw that the body had been taken down and transferred to a trolley, which was being wheeled towards the Porters' Lodge. The pathologist was closing his bag and making ready to follow. They made their way upstairs to the second floor, where the unfortunate postgraduate student had occupied a set of rooms comprising a small living room with an even smaller bedroom leading off it.

'Have you been in here before?' Richard asked Bernie.

'Once or twice.'

'And does it look as usual?'

Bernie looked round carefully. Then she went over to the desk. 'Is it OK for me to open the drawers?'

Richard nodded. 'Go ahead.'

Bernie opened and closed each draw rapidly, then turned to face the two policemen.

'He had his work backed up on floppies, but they've gone. He usually kept them up on that shelf.' She pointed to an empty shelf on the wall above the desk. 'I thought he might have put them away in a drawer, but it looks as if they've been taken away. And there aren't any handwritten notes anywhere either, as far as I can see.'

'Could his work have been valuable to someone?' asked Peter. 'Or could anyone have a motive for destroying it?'

'Very unlikely,' Bernie answered. 'But it's all stored on the hard drive anyway.'

As she spoke, she turned on the PC, which occupied a central position on the desk. It whirred into action, but Bernie stared at the screen in surprise.

'That's strange,' she muttered, 'it won't boot up. It looks as if someone's re-formatted the disk.'

'You mean all his work has been deleted?' asked Peter.

'It looks like it – apart from the stuff he emailed to me, of course.'

There was the sound of voices below and a uniformed police officer put his head round the door.

'Excuse me, sir,' he said, addressing Richard. 'There's a Professor Woodhouse downstairs wanting to get to his room. Can I let him in?'

'Yes – so long as he doesn't go beyond the first floor. Ask him to wait a minute though – I'd like a word with him first.' He turned back to Bernie. 'I think that's all for the moment. We'll need a copy of the file that Khalifa sent you yesterday – and anything else that you have, which could have been deleted from his computer.'

All three started to make the descent to the ground floor.

'No problem,' Bernie replied. 'I've got all of Ahmed's work in a folder on my hard drive, so I can easily copy it on to floppies for you. I'll do it this afternoon and you can have it this evening.'

They reached the bottom of the stairs and a tall man in glasses stepped forward and grasped Bernie's two hands in his.

'Bernie!' he said earnestly. 'I heard about Ahmed. It's a dreadful business – very upsetting for you. If there's anything I can–'

'Yes it is. No, there's nothing you can do.' Bernie said brusquely, cutting him off in mid-flow and snatching her hands out of his grip. 'This is Detective Superintendent Paige, who would like to ask you some questions. Superintendent, may I introduce Professor Philip Woodhouse?'

She walked off across the quad, turning briefly to call out, 'I've got to give a lecture in the Maths Institute at ten, but after that I'll be in my room if you need me again. Otherwise, I'll see you at nine.'

****

'But in fact,' Bernie said wryly, 'he was back in my room much earlier than that because, before I could copy the files he wanted, my computer was stolen. On my way back from the Maths Institute, I was intercepted by Malcolm Cameron, who was tutor in English and also the Dean of the college. He insisted on engaging me in a pointless conversation about some minor issue relating to student discipline, so it was gone twelve by the time I got back to my room. The first thing I saw when I got there was that the door, which I was certain I had locked, was swinging open and my computer was gone.'

'So, someone *was* trying to stop anyone reading your student's thesis?' gasped Bethan, gripped by this real-life drama.

'So it seemed.' Bernie agreed. 'But whoever it was evidently didn't realise that there was still a copy of Ahmed's email, including the attachment, stored on the university email server; so I was able to download another copy to my home computer and give it to Richard when he called at the chapel that evening.'

****

Richard could hear the singing as he approached the chapel. He crept in and stood waiting at the back.

'O Joy that seekest me through pain,' they sang, 'I cannot close my heart to thee.' Bernie looked up and caught sight of Richard. 'I trace the rainbow through the rain.' Their eyes met and for a moment she hesitated, then resumed as the choir continued, 'and feel the promise is not vain, that morn shall tearless be.'

Bernie slipped out of the choir stalls and walked quickly down the aisle, while the choir started singing the last verse: 'O cross that liftest up my head ...'

Bernie took Richard by the arm and guided him out.

'Sorry,' she whispered, 'I'm afraid it ran on a bit tonight. Thank you for waiting.'

Richard led the way to his car. 'I like that tune,' he commented, trying to make conversation. Getting no reply, he went on, 'Joy through pain – do you really believe in that?'

'That *has* been my experience,' Bernie answered shortly. Silence.

They got into the car and started off.

More silence. Richard racked his brain for a way to break the ice with this prickly woman. He remembered the conversation he had had over lunch with Peter.

****

'Can you tell me, Peter,' Richard asked, 'where I'm going wrong with that Fazakerley woman? She's behaving as if she doesn't trust me.'

'It's because you assumed that it was suicide. She's got a bit of a "thing" about suicide.'

'What do you mean "a thing about suicide"?' demanded Richard. 'And how to you know?'

Peter sighed, unsure how much he ought to say to his boss about his friend's past.

'Our Bernie's a good mate of Angie's. They go to the same church – the Methodist on Cowley Road – and she often babysits for us. She lives just round the corner from our house.'

'Out Cowley way? Not the most popular area for the academics.'

'I think she's trying to retain her working class roots,' Peter opined, taking care to pronounce 'class' with a short 'a', in imitation of Bernie's accent.

'And this "thing" about suicide?'

'It's like this.' Peter paused to think, then went on. 'When she was an undergraduate, our Bernie was engaged to marry another maths student in her year. They were both expected to get firsts and they were both lined up to stay on to do doctorates, so the plan was to get married shortly after their finals. Stephen – that's her fiancé – killed himself a week after finals and two weeks before the wedding.

'Bernie cut herself off from all their old friends after that. About the only person she ever talks to about Stephen is my wife. Oh! And his parents, of course: she's very close to them. They come to stay every so often and she visits them in Newcastle. Stephen was an only child, so I suppose Bernie is a sort of surrogate for them. Anyway, Bernie's view is that suicide is the worst sort of death you can have.'

****

Richard pulled himself together and decided to tackle Bernie head on. After all, the atmosphere between them could hardly get any worse.

'Peter Johns told me about your fiancé,' he began, glancing at Bernie to gauge her reaction. 'So I understand why you find it distressing to think about suicide.'

'I do *not* find it distressing to think about suicide,' Bernie retorted.

'But I can't work out,' Richard continued, pleased to have elicited a response albeit a negative one, 'why you seem to prefer to imagine that someone has been murdered rather than that they might have taken their own life.'

'I would have thought that it was blindingly obvious.'

'I suppose emotionally–,' Richard hazarded.

'Emotion doesn't come into it,' interrupted Bernie vehemently. 'My "preference" as you call it, for murder over suicide is completely rational.'

'You'll have to explain.'

'OK.' Bernie thought for a moment then began.

'With a murder there's one guilty person – or I suppose in the worst case a conspiracy of guilty people. With suicide, *everyone* is guilty: the victim's parents, siblings, partner, friends, the vicar who didn't get round to visiting, the doctor who failed to diagnose depression, the person who sat next to them on the bus and noticed they looked "a bit down" but didn't say anything ..."

'The victim's supervisor?' suggested Richard.

'Yes – you're getting the idea. Take Ahmed, for example. If he *had* committed suicide, his parents would now be wondering what they could have done to prevent it. Why hadn't he felt able to tell them there was something wrong? Did they push him too hard to succeed? Or didn't they show enough interest in his achievements?'

'And you?'

'Would be asking myself why I hadn't noticed the signs; why he hadn't felt able to confide in me if there was something wrong; was it something I said that pushed him over the edge?'

'So you're glad that it looks as if he was killed by someone else?'

'I'm not glad that he was killed, but I do think that it's easier for the survivors than if he killed himself'

'So you'll be encouraging his parents to think of it as murder?'

'I'll be encouraging his parents,' Bernie said coldly, 'to listen to the facts and wait for the outcome of the police investigation before jumping to conclusions.'

'Good.' Richard thought for a moment. 'And when it comes to the facts, you *will* refrain from going into details about *how* he died? They don't need to know, for example, that it may have been a long process.'

'I won't tell lies. I won't tell them that he died instantly and can't have felt a thing. But I won't be thrusting all the gruesome details down their throats tonight, if that's what you're worried about. If they ask direct questions then I'll tell them what I know, which isn't much.'

'Don't you think it would be kinder to–?'

'To what?' Bernie demanded scornfully. 'To tell a few white lies, so that they feel better? Or rather, so that *we* feel less awkward about telling them? And then, what? They'll probably read the pathologist's report – or else it'll all come out at the inquest – and then they'll feel betrayed, on top of everything else. You're just like the old-fashioned doctors who were afraid to tell their patients when they were dying, which must have meant that a whole lot of patients who *weren't* dying probably thought they were because they knew they couldn't trust the doctors to tell them if they really were.'

'Well, at least we've got *that* straight,' Richard murmured when Bernie paused for breath.

'Sorry,' she apologised, rather shamefaced. 'I didn't mean to rant. I just think honesty is very important.'

When, an hour or so later, they met Ahmed's parents off the plane, Richard was struck by the difference in Bernie's treatment of them, compared with her hostile attitude towards himself. She could not have been gentler in her words or more considerate in in her actions. Nothing was too much trouble.

'Professor Khalifa,' she said to Ahmed's father, 'and Dr Khalifa: let me introduce Detective Superintendent Paige. He's in charge of the investigation into Ahmed's death and will be able to answer some of your questions.' ... 'I've booked you into the college guest room, but if you'd rather stay in a hotel we can sort that out in the morning.' ... 'The Muslim chaplain will call on you tomorrow morning.' ... 'Breakfast is at eight. If you can't face the scrum of Hall, I can get something sent to your room.'

After they had said their farewells to the Khalifas and left them to settle into their room, Bernie and Richard walked back towards the porters' lodge.

'Where do you live?' asked Richard. 'I'll drop you off.'

'No thank you; I've got my bike here.'

'It's after midnight. I'll run you home.'

'But then I won't have my bike at home to come in on in the morning,' Bernie pointed out. 'I've cycled all over Oxford at all times of the day and night for the last nineteen years and I don't see why I should start worrying about it now.'

'Well I do,' said Richard firmly. 'Quite apart from the normal dangers for a woman out alone at this time of night, we have reason to believe that there's someone out there who is willing to kill in order to get hold of some information that Ahmed Khalifa may or may not have passed on to you. You may not be concerned about your own safety, but it will be highly inconvenient to the investigation if you get yourself killed before we've found out who that is.'

Bernie stared at him in disbelief. 'Do you really think–?'

Richard held up his hand to silence her and continued, pleased that he now had her full attention. 'You owe it to Ahmed Khalifa's parents not to do anything that might prevent us tracking down his killer and bringing him to justice.'

'OK. You win.' Bernie conceded. 'I'll go quietly.'

****

'It's all very dramatic,' Bethan said, writing furiously in her notebook.

'Oh, it gets better,' Lucy assured her. 'Go on Mam – tell her about the fire.'

****

Two days later, very little progress appeared to have been made in the investigation. The police had a copy of Ahmed's thesis and some of his other work, which Bernie had handed over to them, and officers were going through the files, painstakingly looking for anything that might be of interest to the killer. Bernie too was studying the files on her home computer. All of a sudden, she jumped up and went to the telephone in the hall.

'Superintendent Paige? I'm glad I've found you. I think I've discovered something in Ahmed's thesis, but I'll need to show—'

Bernie was momentarily aware of pain as a hard object struck her head from behind. She slumped to the floor, dropping the telephone receiver. For the next few minutes – or it could have been hours – she was vaguely aware of sounds around her as she drifted in and out of consciousness. A door banged, then silence. Bernie tried to get up, but her head swam and there seemed to be no power in her limbs. Then there was a crackling sound – and then a smell of smoke. The house was on fire!

Bernie managed to crawl to the front door, but was unable to pull herself upright in order to reach the catch. The hall was filling with smoke now, which set her coughing. She slid back down to the floor and lay there, remembering that she had once been told that, in a smoke filled room, the freshest air was near the floor.

There was a loud hammering at the front door and someone was shouting her name. Bernie made another effort to rise and open the door, but was unable to do so. Then there was a crashing sound and the glass pane in the door shattered over her. Bernie instinctively rolled away and, a few moments later, the door opened. She felt herself being dragged out and heard Richard's voice speaking to her anxiously.

****

'So he saved your life!' Bethan exclaimed wide-eyed and scribbling frantically.

'Yes,' Bernie admitted. 'It was extremely annoying.'
****

Bernie awoke to find herself in a hospital bed. Trying to piece together in her mind how she had got there, she recalled a jumble of people shouting, blue flashing lights and ambulance sirens, the clatter of hospital trolleys and various people peering and poking at her. She looked cautiously round and saw Richard sitting patiently in a chair next to the bed.

'Welcome back,' he said. 'I need a word with you.'

'What happened?' Bernie asked, making a deliberate decision to avoid the cliché 'where am I?'

'Someone hit you over the head and then set the house on fire. Fortunately their main concern was to destroy your computer, so the flames hadn't reached you when we arrived and got you out.'

Richard gave Bernie a few moments to digest this information before continuing.

'You'll be pleased to hear that, apart from a nasty bruise on the back of your skull and some transient damage to your lungs as a result of smoke inhalation, you are in perfect health and likely to live to a ripe old age. Although,' he continued in a deadpan voice, 'I'm probably lying about that to protect you from the hideous truth about your real condition.'

Bernie smiled broadly. 'You know, superintendent,' she said, 'given a very, very long time, I think I *might* just possibly almost get to quite like you.'

'Praise indeed!' Richard said, returning the smile. 'I will try not to allow your flattery to go to my head.'

'But back to business,' he resumed after a short silence. 'I need you to tell me what it is you found in those computer files.'

Bernie sat up, suddenly alert. 'Ahmed had hidden a list of names and dates in his bib file.'

'His *what* file?'

'The bib file for his thesis. It contains all the bibliographical references in a coded form so that it's easy for him to add them in the correct format wherever he wants them in the thesis. Normally nobody would look in the bib file, but I did because he'd got a mistake in one of the references – and one that he ought to have got right.'

'Why?'

'Because it was one of my own papers and I'd given him the BibTeX entry. The only way it could have come out wrong in his thesis was if he had altered it.'

'Bib Tec?' Richard queried. 'You've lost me again.'

'B-I-B-T-E-X,' Bernie spelled out. 'The "X" is a really a Greek chi – like in the chi-squared distribution. It's all part of a mathematical typesetting system called "laytec" – that's L-A-T-E-X. The tex file refers to entries in the bib file and, when you compile it, the references are automatically created in whatever format you specify. Oh, it's no good!' She threw back the covers and started getting out of bed. 'I'll have to show you. Get me my clothes and let's get out of here.'

It took some time to extricate Bernie from the clutches of the NHS. Eventually, however, Richard managed to convince the sceptical staff that her immediate presence at the police station was necessary to the cause of justice and that he could be trusted to ensure that, at the first signs that the blow to her head was producing further symptoms, he would get urgent medical help.

'I smell like a bonfire,' Bernie observed as they got into Richard's car. 'Do you think we could call in at my house for a change of clothes?'

'I'm afraid not. Firstly, the house is a crime scene, and secondly, the fire damage is pretty extensive. It'll be a few days before you can go in. We've got officers on duty keeping everything safe, but no civilians are allowed.'

Bernie digested this information in silence.

'When we get to the station I'll organise for a WPC to go over and see if she can retrieve some of your things: clothes, toothbrush and so on. You can make a list of anything else you'd like her to look for. And then we'll get you settled into a hotel, with a police guard – unless you have friends or family that you could stay with.'

Bernie shook her head. 'There's nobody that I'd want to impose myself on.'

'Or maybe there would be a room in college?'

'There's only one guest room and the Khalifas have got that. I suppose,' Bernie sighed, clearly not relishing the prospect, 'It'll have to be a hotel.'

About half an hour later, Richard led the way to an office where several police officers were sitting at computers. Peter Johns looked up from his vain struggles to make sense of a jumble of symbols on the screen.

'Bernie! It's so good to see you!' He got up and offered her his seat. 'How are you?'

'I'm fine,' Bernie answered dismissively. 'Now let me show you what I've found.'

'Angie asked me to tell you,' Peter interrupted anxiously, 'that you're very welcome to stay at our house until yours is fixed.'

'Thank you,' Bernie was visibly touched. 'That's very generous of you. I really appreciate it, but I know how cramped it is for the four of you as it is without having me sleeping on the sofa. Don't worry – I'll be fine. Now, look at this.'

She took hold of the computer mouse and soon had a new file open on the screen.

'This, she said,' beckoning Peter and Richard over, 'is a typical BibTeX entry.'

They peered at the screen.

```
@book{Golub,
   author   = {Gene H. Golub and
Charles F. Van Loan },
   title    = {Matrix Computations,
second edition},
   year     = {1989},
   publisher = {Johns Hopkins},
   address  = {Baltimore and London},
NB     = {Flop defn.}
}
```

'This records information about a book that Ahmed refers to in his thesis: author, title etc. The BibTeX program takes this information and turns it into an entry in the bibliography. Now,' she went on, scrolling down through the file. 'Look at these entries.'

```
@book{brothel1,
    author    = {Philip Woodhouse and
Kirsty Stainer},
    title     = {Forty minutes of
passion},
    year      = {02/02/1995},
    address   = {23 Milton Street},
NB     = {confirmed by KS 24/05/95}
}
@book{brothel2,
    author    = {Malcolm Cameron and
Andrea Wall},
    title     = {Sunday afternoon sex
romp},
    year      = {05/02/1995},
    address   = {25 Milton Street},
NB     = {confirmed by KS 24/05/95}
}
```

'Needless to say,' Bernie added, 'none of these titles correspond in any way to books to which Ahmed refers in his thesis!'

'Philip Woodhouse,' Peter read out. 'Isn't he the guy that has the room below Ahmed Khalifa's?'

'That's right,' answered Bernie. 'And Malcolm Cameron engaged me in conversation while my computer was stolen. I think that, whatever is going on, they're in it together. There are about fifty of these entries, each with dates between February and May this year. You may also notice that there is a gap of about six weeks covering the latter half of March and the first two thirds of April, which suggests that they refer to activities that took place during full term, when the undergraduate students would have been in residence. In addition, you will observe that the 'authors' are always mixed doubles, so to speak.'

'Messrs Woodhouse and Cameron seem to feature quite frequently,' Peter observed. 'And so do Kirsty Stainer, Andrea Wall, Paula Jones and Carolyn Percival.'

'Do you recognise any of the other names?' asked Richard.

'Kirsty Stainer is second year maths student,' Bernie answered. 'That could be the link with Ahmed. He tutored her on Linear Algebra in Hilary Term. I don't recognise any of the others, but it would probably be worth getting hold of a list of St Luke's undergraduates to see if any of the other names are there. The two addresses – 23 and 25 Milton Street – are both college houses. They're up the Banbury Road. It may or may not be significant that they are our two single-sex women's houses.'

'Is there still a demand for segregated accommodation?' Peter asked. 'I thought students all wanted mixed halls these days.'

'You'd be surprised how many women, after spending their first year in college, decide that they'd quite like to get away from the alcohol and testosterone fuelled attentions of the rugby club!' Bernie laughed. 'And we also have a sizeable group of Muslim women who prefer single-sex houses – which might, of course, be another way in which Ahmed could have found out something about whatever was going on there. He was quite devout and might well have got to know some of the women through the mosque or the chaplaincy.'

'The notes "confirmed by KS" suggest that his contact was probably Kirsty Stainer.' Peter said thoughtfully. 'It looks as if he checked things with her to make sure that he'd got them correct.'

'Yes – that's a good point,' agreed Richard. 'Right! I think we've got a picture of what this is all about. Peter –

get on to St Luke's and ask them for a list of students living at 23 and 25 Milton Street. In fact, get a full list of undergraduates while you're about it. And see if you can track down any of the other male names – they may well all be university staff.'

He turned to Bernie. 'Now Dr Fazakerley, we'd better get your accommodation sorted out and then you ought to get some rest.'

Ignoring her protests, he steered Bernie out of the room and down to his car. As they reached it, a policewoman came across the car park carrying a suitcase in one hand and a plastic carrier bag in the other.

'I've packed a selection of clothes,' she said, handing the case to Richard, who put it in the boot. 'And here are some toiletries and things. I hope I've got everything you need.' She handed the bag to Bernie who looked briefly inside before nodding and saying, 'That's great. Thank you.'

They got in and Richard turned on the ignition, but did not move off.

'Where do you suggest that we go?' Bernie asked.

'That's just it – I mean, well, I was thinking,' Richard stopped, unsure how to go on. Bernie said nothing, so he started again. 'I was wondering … I was wondering if, if you might prefer to stay with me, rather than in a hotel. Just for a few days, I mean – until you can get something more permanent sorted out.' The words suddenly came out in a rush and he coloured like a teenager on a first date.

'With you?'

'Yes. I've got plenty of space – a big house with just me rattling around in it. You'd sleep in the spare room, of course, and …' He trailed off, not knowing how to finish the sentence.

'Of course.' Bernie repeated. 'I would never have expected anything else.'

For several seconds neither spoke. Then Richard

opened his mouth to apologise for making such an inappropriate suggestion, but Bernie cut in before he could speak.

'Thank you, Superintendent.' She said. 'That's very kind of you – just for a few days.'

****

'And was it just for a few days?' Bethan asked.

'It was four months and six days.' Bernie replied. 'Until my house was repaired. And, before you start getting the wrong idea, I did sleep in the spare room for all of those nights.'

'But afterwards?' Bethan persisted, hopefully.

'Tell her about how he used to follow you home,' urged Lucy.

'Now *that*,' Bernie said deprecatingly, 'was just a bit of nonsense, which only serves to demonstrate how pig-headed we both were. But I suppose now that you've mentioned it I'll have to explain,' she went on, seeing Bethan's expectant expression.

'Hang on a minute,' Jonah intervened. 'You haven't finished telling us about "murder on staircase 3". You can't go on without revealing "who dunnit" and why.'

'I'm not sure that I want to go into the sordid details,' Bernie grinned. 'It doesn't reflect well on the college or the university or on academics in general!'

'Nevertheless,' insisted Jonah.

'It's all depressingly simple,' Bernie explained. 'Philip Woodhouse and Malcolm Cameron had made an arrangement with some of the women from 23 and 25 Milton Street to provide sexual favours in exchange for money. And not just for themselves – they "recommended" the service to their friends and colleagues in return for a cut of the takings. In effect, they were running a brothel.

'One of the Muslim women, who was living there, discovered what was happening and told Ahmed about it. He checked the information that she'd given him with

Kirsty, who told him everything, not realising how seriously he would take it. As far as she was concerned it was just a bit of fun and a nice little earner, she had no idea that he would be shocked.

'When she found out that he was thinking of telling the authorities, she tipped off Phil and Malcolm and they decided that the only way for them to keep their jobs was to get rid of him. Kirsty claimed that she knew nothing about the murder and the police believed her, so she got away without a criminal record. She went on to get a 2:1 and is earning big bucks somewhere in the City now.'

'So, you don't think Ahmed was blackmailing them?' queried Bethan.

'Absolutely not!' Bernie retorted. 'For him it was simply a matter of morality. He was genuinely shocked at the idea of two men in positions of authority and trust exploiting the students in that way; and he couldn't believe that the girls were really going into it of their own volition. Presumably that was what he was wanting to talk to me about the day he was killed – to ask me what I thought he ought to do about it.'

'And now,' persisted Lucy, 'Tell her about how my father used to follow you home at nights.'

'Very well!' Bernie sighed with an exaggerated air of resignation, before continuing.

'After I moved back to my own house, we got into the habit of eating together – just for convenience, to halve the amount of cooking we each needed to do. On Mondays and Thursdays, I went round to Richard's house of an evening and on Tuesdays and Fridays, he came to my place. Wednesday was choir practice for me and on Saturday, he used to visit his mother in Henley.

'He didn't think it was safe for me to be cycling back after dark; and I wasn't prepared to be taken home as if I couldn't take care of myself. So we got into a silly routine. I would cycle home and he would follow behind in his car, keeping well back so that in theory I wouldn't notice him.

When I got home, I'd go straight upstairs to the front bedroom and look out from behind the curtains to see him parked in the street opposite. I'd watch until he drove off, and then go and put my bike away. I knew that he was following me and he knew that I knew, but somehow we managed to convince ourselves that we'd neither of us given way on the matter of principle.'

'And how long did it go on like this?' Bethan asked. 'I mean – you did marry him in the end, didn't you?'

'Ah yes,' Bernie murmured. 'Well, fast-forward to 1997 and we find Richard being held at gunpoint by a group of terrorists in some sort of siege. I never did get to the bottom of exactly what it was all about; it was all very hush-hush. Peter did his best to let me know any news – not that I think there was much – but it was a very nerve-racking time. After about five days it must have been, he was released unharmed.'

****

'Richard! It's good to see you,' Peter greeted Richard as he entered the open-plan office where his team of CID officers worked. 'We were afraid you might not get out alive.'

'I have to admit I started to wonder about that myself,' growled Richard. 'Why a three-hour debrief with the Deputy Chief Constable and some idiot from Special Branch was in any way necessary, I cannot understand. By the end I was beginning to lose the will to live, I can tell you!'

He crossed the room and went into his own private office. Peter followed him in.

'Does Bernie know you've been released?' he asked anxiously.

'Bernie? What do you mean?'

'Our Bernie – Dr Bernadette Fazakerley. You were supposed to be entertaining her to dinner on Monday, remember? When you weren't at home and didn't return her calls, she got on to Angie, and I had to tell her what had happened. She's been going out of her mind with worry.'

Richard looked bemused. 'She knows I sometimes get held up by work. She wouldn't think anything of it. You must be exaggerating.'

'Believe me. I'm not.' Peter took Richard firmly by the elbow and steered him out of the office again. 'Now, don't argue,' he went on ushering him downstairs and out to the car park. 'I happen to know that she's working at home today. Take my advice, and go straight over there and show her that you're safe. Pick up some flowers on the way, or some chocolates or something.'

Seeing his friend's evident surprise at the earnestness with which he had spoken, he searched for some way of introducing a lighter note. Richard was well read; he would understand a quotation from Oscar Wilde. 'According to Angie,' he said at last, 'you've already missed three assignations with Bernie. To miss any more might expose you to comment.'

Fifteen minutes later Richard stood nervously on the doorstep of Bernie's East Oxford terraced house. Why he was nervous, he was unable to explain to himself; there was just something about Peter's behaviour that made him anxious. Peter had never shown any interest in his private life before, and Richard had never spoken to him about his relationship, such as it was, with Bernie. He pulled himself together and rang the bell.

For what seemed like a long time, nothing happened. Then he heard footsteps coming downstairs. The door opened and Bernie looked out. Richard was shocked at her appearance. Her short hair was unkempt and stuck out in all directions. Her face looked haggard and her eyes were red.

Then she recognised him and her face lit up with a smile. 'Richard!' Her voice sounded husky. 'Oh Richard! Come in.'

She stepped back to allow him into the hall. He closed

the door behind him and they stood looking at one another for a moment.

'What's wrong, Bernie?' Richard asked anxiously.

'Nothing,' Bernie said, with what Richard took to be a forced brightness. 'There's nothing wrong. I'm fine. Come and sit down, I'll make a brew.'

'No.' Richard grabbed Bernie's arm as she turned to go to the kitchen. 'I can *see* there's something wrong. You've been crying – I've never known you to cry before.'

'I *told* you,' Bernie pulled her arm out of his grip and stood facing Richard belligerently. 'There's nothing wrong – now.' She turned away and headed off in pursuit of the kettle.

The penny dropped and Richard hurried after her. 'Bernie!' he called urgently. 'Do you mean that you've been crying for me?'

'What do *you* think?' she demanded, rounding on him. 'You disappear mysteriously and I'm told that you are in the hands of some unidentified gunmen who are threatening to start killing their hostages if they don't get whatever it may be that they are demanding. No, I'm not allowed to know who they are or where they're keeping you or what the likelihood of getting you out alive might be, because it's all an official secret. Don't you think that I might, just possibly, be a tiny bit concerned as to what was happening to you?'

Neither of them would have been able to explain how it happened, but suddenly and unexpectedly Bernie was in Richard's arms with her face pressed against his chest, her arms gripping him tightly and his chin resting on her head. He held her close and kissed the top of her head.

'Peter told me to bring you flowers,' he murmured, 'but I know you think they ought to be left to grow. And then I thought of chocolates, but I know you don't approve of that sort of gesture. But if there's anything you would like, just name it.'

'Oh Richard – as if you didn't know that you've just

111

brought me the only thing I really wanted!'
****

'And presumably wedding bells followed on quite quickly after that?" Bethan suggested.

'Uh- huh!' Bernie shook her head. 'You're reckoning without our combined inferiority complex.'

'My dear Bernie,' Jonah protested, 'I would be the first to admit that you have many faults, but an inferiority complex is the last thing I would accuse you of possessing!'

'Nevertheless, in one respect it was the case then,' Bernie insisted. 'I was totally convinced that nobody in their right mind could possibly bear to live with me on a permanent basis. And Richard was equally convinced that nobody could possibly feel love or affection for him.

'His mother left when he was only eight years old and he could never get away from the idea that, if even his mother didn't love him, nobody could. He never met her again until his early forties, when she suddenly walked back into his life after his father died. He spent the rest of his life trying to be a model son to her, out of some ridiculous sense of guilt that it must have been his fault that she went away.

'She died not long after he did. She was nearly eighty. It was only when I saw the death certificate that I realised that she must have only been nineteen when Richard was born. I thought then that maybe I'd been rather hard on her. Maybe it was understandable: young mother, living with her in-laws, husband comes home from the war and a few years later, she runs away because she can't cope.

'But that's all by the by,' Bernie sighed. 'To get back to the matter in hand, it was Peter who finally got us together about three months later.'
****

'Are you doing anything at the weekend?' Peter asked Richard conversationally over lunch in the police canteen.

'I am as a matter of fact. I've got tickets for the G&S

society production of "Trial by Jury and HMS Pinafore" this evening. I thought it might cheer Bernie up after her disappointment over the Newcastle job.'

Peter stared at Richard. 'Let me get this straight,' he said, after a moment's silence. 'Did she tell you that they'd turned her down?'

'Well, I suppose those weren't her exact words, but she told me that she wouldn't be going to Newcastle after all, so presumably they must have given the chair to someone else.'

'Richard, listen to me. Read my lips. They were begging her to go. *She* turned *them* down.'

'Why on earth would she do that?' Richard sounded genuinely at a loss.

'Why do you think?'

'I don't know. I suppose she decided she didn't want to move up there after all.'

'Not move to Newcastle!' Heads turned from across the canteen. Peter lowered his voice again. 'When she's been hankering after moving closer to Stephen's parents for the last fifteen years? When she's been offered a chair at a leading university? Not to mention a professorial salary! Are you really telling me you don't *know* why she turned it down?'

'No. I don't. It doesn't make sense to me.'

'Do I have to spell it out to you?' Peter went on. 'She turned it down because she didn't want to leave *you*.'

'Do you really think so?'

'That's what Angie says, and she knows Our Bernie better than anyone else.'

They finished their lunch in silence. Then Richard stood up.

'I'd better be going,' he said. 'I've got a report to write.'

He went back to his office and settled at his desk. Half an hour later the report still comprised four section headings and a few random sentences. He got up, picked up his jacket from the back of his chair and strode out. A few minutes later, he was climbing the stairs to Bernie's college room. Sitting on the top step, were two young men clutching A4 pads.

'Is Dr Fazakerley in?' Richard asked them.

They nodded. 'We're her two o-clock tutorial,' one of them volunteered. 'The one o-clock will be out any minute.'

'Good. Would it be OK if I nip in and have a word with her before you start?'

'Be our guest!'

Richard climbed past them and stood nervously outside the door for what felt to him like an age, but which was in fact only two or three minutes. It opened and two more students emerged, a man and a woman. Richard slipped in and closed the door firmly behind him. Bernie looked up and raised her eyebrows in interrogative mode.

'Bernie!' he gasped. 'There's something I need to ask you.'

'Go ahead. You've got two minutes.'

'Bernie?' He stopped, made all the more nervous by having been given a deadline.

'Go on. Spit it out. I'm running late already.'

Richard took the plunge. 'Will you marry me?'

Bernie's expression changed instantly. 'You're being serious aren't you?' she said anxiously.

'Of course.'

'Oh Richard!' Bernie got up and put her arms round him. 'I'm not the right sort of person to be your wife. You want a nice feminine little woman, who will appreciate you taking care of her, not me complaining at you all the time for being paternalistic. You want someone who likes being given flowers and presents, and doesn't moan about the expense, someone who'll be there when you get back from a hard day, with tea on the table and the house all clean and tidy. You deserve someone who will think of all those little things that wives think of to make you feel appreciated. You deserve–"

'Bernie!' Richard interrupted. 'Just stop there. If you don't want to marry me, then that's fine, just say so; but cut out all this nonsense about you not being the right person for me. I'm fifty-seven. How long do you think I've got left to wait for Miss Right to come along? Now, if you can't face marrying someone old enough to be your father; or if you don't want to marry a policeman because they always put the job first, then that's fine: just say so. But don't give me any of this "I'm not the right person for you" stuff. You're the one who's always on about honesty and calling a spade a spade and letting people make their own mistakes. If I want to spend the rest of my life with you then that's my decision and I don't need you telling me that it won't make me happy. You're always saying how patronising it is when people do things "for your own good". It's about time you started practising what you preach.'

Bernie stared in stunned silence as Richard continued. 'Oh! I get it now. This is all to do with Stephen, isn't it? You still can't get it out of your head that he might have killed himself because he couldn't face marrying you.'

'Well,' Bernie said in a small voice, 'you have to admit it's a possibility'

'No, I won't. It's a load of nonsense. And in any case, I'm not Stephen. And you're not the same person you were back then. So now, tell me – will you marry me?'

'Yes – on one condition.'

'What condition?' Richard asked, suspiciously.

'Only that you promise that if you have second thoughts and want to break off the engagement, you'll tell me. You won't just press on regardless, out of some sort of "code of the Woosters" sense of obligation.'

'Of course. What do you take me for?'

'A kind man, who might be afraid of hurting me. Now, will you please go and tell my two o'clock tutorial partners that they can come in?'

****

'So we got married that summer, and two years later Richard died.' Bernie concluded.

'And I entered your life,' Jonah declared with an air of satisfaction. 'You see why this is all so important,' he said to Bethan. 'If our Bernie hadn't married Richard, or if he hadn't died in service, I wouldn't have gone to his funeral and my life would have been very different.

'Take my return to the police service, for example. Bernie played a pivotal role. Quite apart from the way she got all sorts of people from the university to design gadgets to help me to function as a police officer, she was always ready to argue my case. I remember one day in particular. It was summer 2010, about a fortnight after I was discharged from hospital. We were all sitting out in the garden together: me, Margaret, our younger son Nathan, down from university, Bernie, Lucy and Peter. I made some remark about wanting to get back to work and needing to fight the plan to pension me off, and Nathan rounded on me.'

****

'You can't be serious, Dad! You've got to be realistic – how could you do the job?'

'Why on earth shouldn't I? My job is ninety-nine percent brainwork and my brain is as good as ever. I've got twenty-four years' experience. It would be criminal to throw it away.'

'I'm going to get the tea things,' Margaret said, not wanting to get involved in the argument. 'Will you give me a hand, Lucy?'

Lucy obediently followed Margaret into the house, while Nathan continued to urge his father to change his mind.

'Think about it Dad! It's not as if you sit at your desk all day. What about getting out to crime scenes? You can't expect murderers and thieves to confine their activity to places with disabled access!'

'This chair is pretty good for getting around,' Jonah

argued, 'and we're working on an improved version that will be more flexible. Besides, I'm a senior officer – I have staff to do the leg work.'

'I still think you ought to take it easy. You know how tired you get now. By seven in the evening you're always done in.'

Seeing that his father was failing to be convinced, Nathan turned to Bernie.

'Bernie, won't you back me up? You're a policeman's wife. If it was Peter in Dad's place, wouldn't you be wanting him to retire: to spend more time safe at home with you?'

'I'm sorry Nathan,' Bernie said gently. 'You've chosen the wrong person to support your argument. As you say,' she went on with a wry smile, 'I'm a policeman's wife. In fact, I've made rather a habit of marrying policemen. And I can't agree with you that retirement is a good idea for your father, because I'm convinced that my first husband's death was probably partly caused by the fact that he couldn't face his own imminent retirement.'

'I don't understand,' Nathan said, puzzled.

'Richard was being forced into retirement at the age of sixty,' Bernie explained. 'The closer it got, the clearer it became that he was going to find it difficult to cope without the job that he loved, and that he'd been living for, for more than forty years. The thought of years of idleness stretching ahead of him made him take risks that he normally wouldn't have taken. And I think that's how he came to have a fatal accident just two weeks before his retirement date.'

'But this is different,' Nathan argued. 'Being told you're past it is one thing; Dad's situation is quite different.'

'Nevertheless,' Bernie said. 'If he wants to get back in the saddle, I'll back him all the way.'

Margaret and Lucy re-appeared carrying trays laden with a tea service and plates of food.

'Since we are having afternoon tea in the garden in

traditional English fashion,' Margaret said, 'I thought we ought to do it right, so we've got cucumber sandwiches, bread and butter, scones, strawberry jam and honey.'

They put the trays down on the wooden table around which they were sitting. Margaret poured milk and tea into Jonah's plastic cup, fixed the lid firmly and placed it on the shelf attached to his wheelchair, taking care to position the straw so that he could reach it. Lucy sat down next to Jonah and began feeding him as she had done in the hospital. For a few minutes, everyone was busy helping themselves to tea and sandwiches.

'I'm glad you're behind my campaign to get back to work,' Jonah said to Bernie. 'Later I'd like you to have a look at the letter I've drafted to the Chief Constable.'

'I'll be happy to.'

'Why don't you get Bernie to go to see him in person and sort him out?' suggested Peter with a grin. 'There aren't many people can say "no" to Our Bernie when she's on the warpath!'

'Are youse giving him his job back or what?' Bernie growled, putting on an even stronger and more aggressive Liverpool accent than normal and brandishing a clenched fist.

There was general laughter, but Nathan still looked anxious. All at once, he exploded with frustration.

'Oh Dad!' he shouted, jumping to his feet. Everyone else fell silent in surprise. 'Get real! Look at you – you can't even feed yourself! How do you think you're going to be able to investigate crimes? How are you even going to be able to do a desk job in the police? You've got to start accepting your limitations. What's the point of kidding yourself? And why are you all going along with it?' He added, looking round at the others. 'It's just allowing him to set himself up to fail.'

Jonah broke the shocked silence that followed. 'Lucy,' he said calmly. 'Will you come with me? I'd like to show you the rockery.'

They moved away. Nathan was the first to speak.

'I'm sorry,' he said contritely. 'I didn't mean to upset him, but ... but can't you see?' He looked round, willing them to support his view. 'It's all cloud cuckoo land. The police force isn't going to take Dad back. It's all just ...' He shrugged his shoulders despondently.

'Nathan,' Bernie broke in gently. 'Sit down and let me tell you a story.'

Nathan fell silent and dropped into his seat.

'My mam,' Bernie began, 'had motor neurone disease. I can't remember a time before she was "confined to a wheelchair" as they say. As time went on, she became more and more disabled, until she was completely dependent on other people for everything – even more than your Dad is now. You wouldn't think there was much chance of her contributing much to society or the general good, but when it came to her funeral you'd never believe the number of people who came up and told us how much she'd done for them. My Dad and I started to think that she was leading some sort of double life. It felt as if, when we went off to work and school she was somehow transformed into this other being who inhabited a different universe from us altogether. It was as if we'd been living with Clark Kent for years and now discovered that everyone else knew that he was really Superman!'

'That's all very well,' Nathan grumbled. 'I'm not saying that Dad hasn't still got a lot to offer. It's just that going back to his old job in the police isn't practical. He needs to find other outlets. And he needs to start taking care of himself. The hours he used to work: keeping at it into the night when there was an interesting case on. His health won't stand it.'

'Don't you think,' his mother put in, 'that he ought to be allowed to make that discovery for himself?'

Nathan sighed. 'I just ... I'm just worried that you're all building up his expectation of getting back to work and that will only make it all the more of a disappointment for him when he realises that it isn't possible.'

'Oh Nathan!' Bernie sighed. 'The young can be so terribly over-protective of their parents sometimes!'

Nathan stared at her, puzzled, so she went on. 'When my mam died I was convinced that my Dad would never be able to cope. I was all set to chuck in my place at Oxford, so as to stay at home and look after him. Fortunately, he managed to convince me that I owed it to Mam to go. Otherwise, I would probably have driven him insane, clucking round worrying about him all the time. Your dad's an intelligent adult. I'm sure he's well aware of the difficulties. Maybe he *is* wrong about being able to get back into his old job, but he's old enough to be allowed to make his own mistakes and all we can do is to be around to pick up the pieces if things do go wrong.'

'Hear, hear!' Jonah said fervently, emerging from behind a dense rhododendron bush where he had been eavesdropping on the conversation. 'I'm glad to hear that someone believes that there's life in the old dog yet!'

Later that afternoon Jonah managed to get Bernie on her own for a few minutes. They walked round the garden admiring the borders, which had been planted out by a working party from Bernie's church to welcome Jonah home when he came out of hospital.

'Thank you for trying to sort Nathan out,' he said. 'I know he means well, but sometimes it feels as if he's treating me like a small child!'

'It's been a big shock for him, and at his age physical disability is more horrific than for us oldies who are already starting to creak at the joints. He can't imagine being in your position and not just wanting to give up and become an invalid. He'll come round.'

'I didn't know about your mother.'

'No, well – it's not the sort of thing that comes up in conversation.'

'It explains a lot.'

'That sounds rather ominous.'

'I just meant that it explains why you understand me better than most.'

'I don't know about that: understanding isn't a quality that anyone has ever accused me of having before!' Bernie laughed self-deprecatingly, and then became suddenly serious. 'All I know is that I enjoy your company more than practically anyone else's. And I want you to remember that you must *never* start thinking that you are any less of a person now than ever you were. And you must *never, never* imagine for one moment that you are a burden to anyone.'

****

'Well,' laughed Jonah, 'with our Bernie for me, who could be against me? It took a lot more than one letter, but eventually I won my case and got my old job back. It takes a lot of organising, of course. I had to have a rota of carers to deal with my bodily functions, and my team had to get used to working in a different way. They couldn't rely on me racing round to be first at every crime scene anymore, and they had to learn to report back to me what they'd seen in places that I couldn't get to see for myself. It was all good discipline for them, actually, and they're probably all better detectives for it.'

'And your son, Nathan?' Bethan asked. 'How does he feel about it now?'

'He's still inclined to worry whenever I take on something new and I think he'd like me to slow down a bit now I'm getting older; but he's as pleased as anyone to see me back doing what I'm best at – solving crimes.'

****

O Love that wilt not let me go,
I rest my weary soul in thee;
I give thee back the life I owe,
That in thine ocean depths its flow
May richer, fuller be.

O light that followest all my way,
I yield my flickering torch to thee;
My heart restores its borrowed ray,
That in thy sunshine's blaze its day
May brighter, fairer be.

O Joy that seekest me through pain,
I cannot close my heart to thee;
I trace the rainbow through the rain,
And feel the promise is not vain,
That morn shall tearless be.

O Cross that liftest up my head,
I dare not ask to fly from thee;
I lay in dust life's glory dead,
And from the ground there blossoms red
Life that shall endless be.

George Matheson (1842 – 1906)

5 THERE'S A WIDENESS IN GOD'S MERCY

'Now, tell me about this wonderful chair,' Bethan said, indicating Jonah's electric wheelchair. 'It isn't standard issue is it?'

'No – very much custom-built,' Jonah replied. 'Yes, there's quite a story behind this chair and all the other gadgets that I rely on – and it's mainly down to these guys.'

A slight movement of his index figure made the screen in front of him swivel round so that Bethan could see that it was displaying a photograph of two young men. They were facing the camera and smiling broadly, with their arms around one another's shoulders.

'That's Dean on the left.'

Bethan looked at the shorter of the two men. A long fringe of dark brown hair covered his forehead and threatened to obscure his deep brown eyes, which were surrounded by long thick lashes – so luxuriant that, had he been a woman you might have suspected that they were artificially enhanced. A very attractive young man, Bethan thought.

'And the other is Wayne,' Jonah went on.

Bethan switched her gaze to the other face. This man

was taller and more heavily built. His fair hair was cut short. His eyes were a nondescript blue-grey colour.

'It all started while I was still in hospital,' Jonah continued. 'Bernie realised how tedious it was for me lying there, unable to read or use the telephone or email or any of the things that need manual dexterity, and she harnessed the might of the Oxford University Engineering Department to sort me out.'

'That's putting it a bit strongly,' Bernie laughed. 'The thing to remember about a collegiate university is that academics naturally get to know people outside of their own departments, because each college has tutors across lots of disciplines. So all I really did was to buttonhole our Engineering Fellow in the Senior Common Room. Ken Thomas is an electronic engineer so I thought he would be just the person to tell us how to fix something up so that Jonah could control a computer with his three fingers without being able to move his hand.'

'I never cease to be amazed,' Jonah commented, 'at how ready everyone is to help. A couple of days later he came out to see me with an assortment of laptops and notepads and keyboards and mice and joysticks and stuff, so's he could get an idea of exactly what I could and couldn't do. And it was only a week or so before he managed to produce a mini keyboard and roller-ball mouse combination that was small enough for me to reach all the keys without needing to have my hand moved, but big enough that I didn't keep hitting several keys at once. That, together with a bit of Heath Robinson stuff to get a computer screen suspended where I could see it from my bed, got me online.'

'Which Ken must really have regretted,' put in Bernie, 'because that meant that Jonah could email him with questions and ideas for new modifications at any time of the day or night!'

Jonah gave Bernie a withering look and continued. 'Anyhow, the best thing that Ken did was to suggest that designing more bits of kit for me would make a good final year project for a couple of students. And that's where Wayne and Dean came in.'

****

'I think I've found the right students for the Jonah Porter project,' Ken told Bernie over coffee in the Senior Common Room. 'There's one of mine – Dean: Dean Rutter –'

'I know Dean,' Bernie interrupted. 'He's a nice lad. I hadn't twigged he was an engineer. I know him through the choir. He's the Organ Scholar.'

'Is he now? I never knew that!' Ken paused for a moment. 'I suppose those long artistic fingers would be right for playing an instrument. Anyway, I put the idea to my third year tutorial group and he jumped at it immediately. He's very quiet and doesn't usually put himself forward, so he must be keen.'

'Then the other one is at Teddy Hall. His name's Wayne Major. He looks a bit of a bruiser, but he's really a gentle giant. Moreover, he's a very talented engineer. Again, he was very keen to take on the project, which I think is important.'

'Yes,' agreed Bernie, 'I'd hate to feel that we might let Jonah down.'

'I certainly hope that we can do something for him. And it's a perfect opportunity for the students to do a project that has real-life applications.'

'Even if nothing much comes out of it,' Bernie added, 'it will give Jonah something positive to do. It must be soul-destroying just being stuck there like that. I mean, he does have regular physiotherapy and the OTs are working on ways of making him a bit more independent with various things, but he was such an active person before, that it must be mind-numbingly boring for him in between therapy sessions.'

****

'I have to admit that I was a bit disappointed when

Wayne and Dean turned up,' Jonah said mischievously, 'I was hoping for an attractive pair of female students who would pet me and spoil me and tell me how terrifically brave I was.'

'Whereas Wayne is built like a tank and used to play rugger for his school,' Bernie said with a smile. 'But you have to admit they knew their stuff.'

'Indeed they did,' agreed Jonah. 'And they weren't afraid of hard work. The hours they put in, to get everything just right to make it as easy as it could be for me to use their gadgets, were phenomenal. The actual project was quite restricted in scope, because it had to fit into the timescale for a student project, but they did all sorts of other things as well. Basically, every time they spotted something I couldn't do they tried to find a way of enabling me to do it. I began to worry that they might be spending so much time working on my problems that they'd fail their exams. Of course, that was just in that first year after my injury. Amazingly they carried on after they graduated, which is when they developed this chair.'

'Yes,' urged Bethan, 'Tell me about the chair.'

'Well it's developed a lot over the years,' Jonah explained. 'In fact, I now have several different models. This is the all-purpose version, which I use for my work and basically, whenever I go out of the house. It's manoeuvrable enough to be used inside as well, but I've also got a more lightweight one that takes up less space. However, that doesn't have all the features of this one. Then there's an all-terrain version that allows me to go off-road.'

'Under strict supervision,' Bernie interjected, 'because he can't be trusted not to go too fast and turn it over!'

'I can control it using the joystick or by voice commands, which is handy for occasions when my hand slips off the controls, but can be rather tricky, particularly in a noisy environment. Here, Bethan – have a go!'

Bernie gently moved Jonah's left hand into his lap and

motioned to Bethan to place her own on the arm of the chair. Bethan tentatively put out her hand and grasped the joystick. Bernie stepped forward and adjusted her hand on the controls so that she could move the joystick with her index finger while resting her second finger on what turned out to be a control that determined the speed in a forward or backward direction. Bethan gasped as the chair lurched around in response to her inexpert attempts at manoeuvring it.

"It's harder than it looks," she declared. "You make it look so easy!"

Bernie replaced Jonah's hand on the controls and he gave an impromptu demonstration of the chair's capabilities.

'The height is adjustable,' he explained. 'So that I can look people in the eye whether they're standing up or sitting down, and whatever height chair they're sitting on.'

Bethan watched as Jonah rose so that his head was about six feet from the floor. Then he sank back down to bring him level to where she was sitting.

'There's a tilt mechanism.' The chair tilted slowly about thirty degrees, first to the left then to the right. 'That shifts my weight, so that I can spend long periods of time in the chair without developing pressure sores.' Jonah explained. 'And the grandchildren love it – they call this Grandad's boat!

'And it reclines,' he went on, 'like a dentist's chair, so that I can rest in a lying position; but more importantly, that helps my carers to transfer me into bed. Here at home I've got hoists and other equipment to get me into and out of bed and so on, but this means that I can stay away from home with just one carer. I'm quite a weight so it wouldn't be safe for Bernie, for example, to try to lift me from a sitting position into bed. This way, it's just a matter of positioning the chair and then rolling me on to the bed.'

He demonstrated the reclining feature, so that Bethan found herself gazing down at Jonah stretched out full length. Then he returned the chair to its upright position and looked her in the eye. 'Neat isn't it?'

'I'm impressed,' she confirmed. 'And all this is down to Wayne and Dean?'

'Loosely. Of course, there's lots of equipment on the market for disabled people these days, so they didn't have to design everything from scratch. But it's always easier when something is exactly tuned to my size and shape and abilities. And the OTs – that's Occupational Therapists, if you're not familiar with the term – had a lot of input too. But by and large, yes, this is all down to Wayne and Dean.'

'Maybe we could include them in the programme?' Bethan suggested.

'I'm sure they'd be delighted. It would be free advertising for them. They've set up their own company now, designing and manufacturing equipment for disabled people.'

'So that's another very positive element to your story,' Bethan commented. 'Your disability providing the springboard for two young people to make a future for themselves. We definitely ought to try to include that.'

'Talking about Wayne and Dean's future together,' Lucy chipped in, smiling and exchanging glances with Bernie, 'brings in a whole new dimension to the story.'

'Indeed it does,' agreed Bernie. 'It must have been round about the beginning of Hilary Term when we first started having our suspicions.'

****

Wayne and Dean were just leaving, as Bernie entered Jonah's room at the hospital on a cold January afternoon.

'How goes the work?' she enquired.

'Pretty good,' Wayne answered. 'We've satisfied the original spec, but now we can see all sorts of things that we didn't think of that could do with being incorporated.'

'Don't get carried away,' Bernie advised. 'If you've done what you set out to do, write it up and hand in your dissertation before spending lots of time on more advanced modifications.'

'That's what Ken says,' Dean admitted, 'But there's so much more we could do, it seems a pity to stop.'

'Whatever you do,' Jonah called out from where he was propped up in a chair next to the window, 'don't jeopardise your degrees. We need more qualified engineers with an interest in this sort of thing.'

'We won't.' Wayne promised. 'Come on Dean; let's go back to my room. There's some new stuff come through from my Dad that I'd like you to see.'

He put his hand lightly on Dean's shoulder and steered him out of the door. Bernie watched them go and closed the door behind them, before sitting down facing Jonah.

'Do you think there's something more going on between those two,' she asked seriously, 'than just a tutorial partnership?'

'I don't think that's any of our business is it?' Jonah asked mildly.

'No, it isn't,' Bernie agreed, 'but ... well, it's just that ... Dean's quite a leading light in the college CU, and they tend to be a bit ... well ... dogmatic about gay relationships. I can't help being afraid that someone may get hurt.'

'I thought young people were all quite relaxed about that sort of thing,' Jonah observed, 'and it was just us oldies who still had hang-ups.'

'Not in conservative evangelical circles.'

'Or Catholic ones, I suppose.'

'Why do you say that?' Bernie asked sharply.

'Aren't *you* a catholic? I mean Lucy talked about going to mass, and your name, Bernadette, that's definitely not one you come across in the Baptist circles that I was brought up in.'

Bernie laughed. 'I reckon I'm about twenty percent catholic.'

'How d'you work that out?' Jonah asked, intrigued.

'My father was a Catholic and my mother was Salvation

Army,' Bernie explained. 'I compromised and became a Methodist, but I'm also in the choir at the college chapel, which is C of E, so I reckon that, by now, I'm fifty percent Methodist, ten percent C of E and twenty percent each Catholic and Sally Army. I take Lucy to mass occasionally, so that she appreciates her heritage. She had her first communion at Whitsun, so she was full of it when we started visiting you back in the summer.'

'So you came from a mixed marriage,' joked Jonah. 'How did the families get on? Was it open warfare?'

'Not over religion,' Bernie laughed. 'But I have to admit my Mam's folk did find it quite hard to come to terms with idea of having an Everton supporter in the family!'

Jonah joined in the laughter, which came more from the sheer joy of being together than because her witticism was particularly funny.

'For me,' Bernie went on, 'the main consequence was that weekends were very busy. What with band practice, confession, mass and two services at the citadel, Friday night to Sunday evening was pretty packed. And of course, during the football season, there was almost always a match on as well.'

'You played in the Salvation Army band!' Jonah said in a tone of some surprise. 'What instrument?'

'The cornet.'

'I played the cornet in the Boys Brigade. We weren't much good – as far as I remember, we only ever learned one tune. I wouldn't even be able to get a note out of it now. How about you? D'you still play?'

'Not up to band standard – I don't get round to practising often enough – but I can still manage to get a tune out of it, just about.'

'Well, well, well,' Jonah shook his head in wonder and lapsed into silence. Since his injury some seven months previously, he had got to know Bernie very well, as he thought, but still there were occasions when he realised that it takes a long time to know someone who has fifty years of unshared history behind them.

'But getting back to Wayne and Dean,' Bernie persisted. 'I'm not saying that we ought to be prying into their relationship, but I'd like to think that we'd notice if they were having problems.'

'What sort of problems?' Jonah asked, sounding a bit suspicious. 'Sometimes', he thought to himself, 'Bernie is altogether too keen to get involved in other people's affairs.'

'I don't know.' Bernie shrugged. 'Some sort of identity crisis, maybe – or one of them misinterpreting something the other does or says. And there's a frighteningly high rate of suicide and self-harm among young gay men.'

'You're jumping the gun a bit aren't you?' Jonah still sounded sceptical. 'You don't even know if they are–'

'I know,' Bernie interrupted. 'Could you just keep an eye on them though? I mean, keep an eye out for any signs of anxiety or depression – not a probe into their sexual preferences.'

As the weeks passed, Bernie was convinced that she could detect signs of growing affection between the two young men. They certainly spent a large amount of time in on another's company; but then they had a lot to talk about. As well as finishing and writing up their final year project, they were starting to make plans for a joint enterprise after they graduated. Wayne's father was a successful businessman, with his own engineering firm, and he was prepared to fund the setting up of a subsidiary company to support Wayne and Dean in developing their ideas for equipment to assist people with disabilities. The planning for that entailed several trips to Wayne's home in the West Midlands and many hours of discussion over spreadsheets and business plans.

Their enthusiasm was infectious and soon Jonah was demanding to see the proposals. The therapy team on his ward heard about their ambitions and provided contact details of professional organisations and disability charities who might be willing to offer advice and, ultimately, to endorse their products.

As the six-week Easter Vacation approached, everything seemed to be going extraordinarily well. Their dissertations were nearly complete. Jonah was delighted with the mechanism that they had designed and built to enable him independently to move his computer screen around so that he could view it from his bed or the chair in which he now spent the majority of his day. Dean was to spend a week at Wayne's family home mapping out with Wayne's father exactly how the new enterprise would operate. Revision for their exams was well in-hand and Ken was optimistic that they would both get good marks.

However, when Dean returned to Oxford after the vacation, he was strangely subdued. Jenny, the college chaplain, noticed it when he arrived to play the organ for the first Sunday Evensong of term. Bernie felt there was something wrong the following Wednesday evening at choir practice. Then that Sunday evening he simply did not turn up to chapel.

Jenny was worried. It wasn't like Dean to let them down. She looked at her watch – already five minutes late. They would have to start without him. Bernie manfully led the choir in singing the hymns and responses unaccompanied. As the congregation left at the end of the service, Jenny quizzed everyone as to whether they knew where Dean could be. Nobody had seen him since lunchtime.

Jenny and Bernie left the rest of the chapel-goers to their after-chapel drinks and nibbles and headed off to Dean's room. The door was locked. They knocked and called, but there was no reply. Jenny put her ear to the door and heard the sound of music playing. She beckoned Bernie to listen too.

'It sounds like the radio,' she said. 'That's odd, if he's gone out.'

Their eyes met and suddenly they were both hit by a conviction that Dean was in there and that all was not well.

'You stay here,' Bernie ordered. 'I'll go to the porter's lodge and get a key.'

Jenny resumed banging on the door and imploring Dean to answer her. After what seemed like an age, Bernie returned with the master key. They opened the door, fumbling with agitation. They entered and immediately saw Dean slumped in a chair, his head drooping forward and slightly to one side. His eyes were hidden beneath his fringe. His hands rested in his lap. Then they saw the dark stain on his trousers, beneath his hands.

Bernie leapt forward and grasped his arms. The wrists were bleeding. She raised both hands above his head and gripped the wrists firmly, pressing down on the cuts to stop the blood.

'Is he breathing?' She demanded urgently.

Jenny put her face close to Dean's mouth and, with a great feeling of relief, felt the warmth of his breath on her cheek. 'Yes,' she answered, at the same time pulling her mobile phone from her pocket. She called for an ambulance and then looked at Dean again, trying to work out if there was anything else they could do.

'Let's get him on the floor,' she suggested. If he's lost a lot of blood it would be better if his head is on a level with his heart, I should think.'

'OK,' Bernie agreed. 'Can you move him, while I keep the pressure on his wrists?'

Dean's eyes flickered open and he moaned slightly as his body slithered to the floor. Jenny tried to make him comfortable, while Bernie continued to grip his wrists, conscious that his life depended on it. Jenny sat on the floor cradling his head in her arms and trying to think of something reassuring to say to him.

'The ambulance will be here soon,' she told him. 'Just lie still and hang on until then. Everything's going to be alright.'

He blinked his eyes and looked as if he was trying to speak, but no sound came.

'Don't try to talk,' Jenny instructed. 'Just relax and wait for the ambulance. It won't be long now.'

Eventually – in fact, it was only twelve minutes – the ambulance did come. Jenny went in it with Dean while Bernie telephoned his parents to break the news to them. They were dairy farmers in a remote part of Cornwall and would not be able to make the journey to Oxford until the morning.

Then Bernie rang Ken, to let him know that one of his students had been taken to hospital, and Peter, to tell him that she might not be home for some time. Then she rang Wayne's mobile.

'Wayne? It's Bernie Fazakerley, I need to see you: can you tell me where you are?'

About half an hour later, a taxi dropped Bernie and a rather white-faced Wayne at the Accident and Emergency Department. Jenny was waiting for them.

'They think we found him in time,' she reported. 'Fortunately he didn't make a very good job of slitting his wrists so they're very hopeful that he'll be OK.'

'Can I see him?' Wayne demanded, trying to hide his distress beneath an aggressive façade. 'Where is he?'

'We'll have to wait,' Jenny said, leading the way through some double doors to a lobby area with seating round the wall. 'They'll call us when he's ready.'

Bernie looked at her watch. Not yet nine o'clock. This was turning into one of the longest evenings of her life.

Wayne sat restlessly for a few minutes then got up and paced round the room, with his hands in his pockets, looking moodily at the notices on the wall, which reminded visitors of the need to wash their hands when entering clinical areas and forbade entry to anyone suffering from coughs, colds or vomiting. Jenny meanwhile was frantically trying to find out, without asking the question out loud, why Bernie had felt it necessary to bring Wayne. Eventually Bernie realised what Jenny's pantomime of looks and nods was intended to convey.

'Dean's parents can't get up until tomorrow,' Bernie said, her eyes continuing to watch Wayne as he moved round the room. 'So I thought it would be a good idea if his best friend could be there when the medics have finished with him.'

A health care assistant arrived.

'Reverend King?' she enquired, looking around. Jenny got up.

'You came with Dean Rutter?' the health care assistant went on. 'He's out of danger now, but he needs to stay in overnight. He'll be assessed by the doctor again in the morning. I thought you'd like to have a word with him before we take him up to the ward.'

She led them through more double doors into a wide corridor. They saw a patient trolley standing against the wall and, as they got closer, they saw that Dean was lying on it. His arms were hidden under a light blanket. Wayne, who had never been in a hospital before, turned very white at the sight of a bag of blood hanging from a drip trolley with the line disappearing under the blanket. Bernie took his arm and whispered, 'Take a few deep breaths. Better not to pass out if you can avoid it!'

Jenny went over and spoke quietly to Dean, but he did not respond.

Wayne closed his eyes and breathed in. Then he forced himself to walk up to the trolley and look down at Dean, who was staring vacantly into space.

'Dean?' Wayne said, tentatively, his throat suddenly very dry.

At the sound of Wayne's voice Dean moved his eyes to look at him with an expression of deep sadness. He struggled to speak. 'Wayne? Why – What are you doing here?'

'I've come to see you, of course!' Wayne spoke with a heartiness that he did not feel.

'But … why?'

'Because I love you, you great twat!' Wayne mumbled, flushing red briefly before going very white again.

'No!' Dean became agitated. 'No – don't *say* that.'

Jenny intervened. 'Dean,' she said calmly, pushing Wayne aside. 'Listen to me! Whatever you are and whatever you've done, God loves you just as you are. Dean! Do you hear me?'

He turned his face towards her and gave her a small nod.

'Now, we've got to go,' Jenny continued, seeing a porter approaching to take Dean to the ward. 'Try and get a good sleep and we can talk again in the morning.'

Peter was waiting for them at reception when they left.

'I've brought the car,' he explained, 'I'll give you all a lift back to college – no point paying taxi fares. How's Dean doing?'

'He's going to be alright,' Bernie answered, giving Peter a reassuring smile. She knew that his real motivation for being there was concern for her having to face the prospect of the suicide of a young man of whom she had become fond. 'They're keeping him in, but he's going to be alright.'

'We were supposed to be seeing Jonah tomorrow morning,' Wayne said, as they drove back to the city centre. 'Do you think I ought to tell him what's happened?'

'Of course.' Bernie's tone indicated that she thought the question not worth asking.

'I mean – you don't think it might be upsetting for him?'

Peter broke in before Bernie could reply. 'Of course it'll be upsetting,' he said gently, but firmly. 'It is for all of us. But he's a police officer; he's seen it all before. He won't thank you for hiding things from him as if his physical injuries have made him some sort of emotional cripple too.'

They started walking to the car park.

'Bernie – do you think *you* could ring Jonah and tell him?' Wayne asked. 'I wouldn't know what to say.'

'OK. I'll ring when we get home, and make sure he knows before you get there tomorrow.'

They got in the car. For several minutes nobody spoke. Then Wayne could no longer hold back his anguish.

'Why?' he demanded. 'Why did he do it?'

Bernie broke the stunned silence that followed, speaking very softly and tentatively. 'I have a horrible suspicion that he thought that he had to choose between you and God.'

She gave a short, rather embarrassed laugh and, in an effort to lighten the mood, went on, 'I suppose you should be flattered that he found the choice so hard to make!' Immediately the words were out of her mouth, she felt angry with herself for making such a crass remark.

'I don't understand.' Wayne looked round, bewildered. 'I knew he was religious, but I don't see what that has to do with – well, with him and me.'

'Traditional Christian doctrine forbids homosexual relations,' Jenny explained. 'These days there's a wide variation in attitudes towards gay relationships, but Dean may well have been worried that … that ….' She stopped, unsure how to go on.

'I think,' Bernie continued for her, 'that he was afraid that the feelings that he had for you were wrong, but he couldn't bear to give you up – and so he couldn't see any way out except …'

'So his religion says it's wrong to be gay?' Wayne sounded incredulous. 'What's he supposed to do – become a monk, pretend to be straight …?'

'The Church of England,' Jenny resumed, 'requires gay clergy to remain celibate, but doesn't lay down any specific rules for lay people.'

'And what about you?' Wayne asked. 'What do *you* think?'

'I think,' Jenny said slowly, trying rapidly to formulate an opinion on a subject that she had not previously found it necessary to think through, 'that the church ought to be inclusive and accept people as they are.'

'And you?' Wayne turned to Bernie. 'You're religious, aren't you? What do *you* think?'

'I think that there's got to be something wrong with any doctrine that drives a young man with such a bright future ahead of him to attempt to take his own life.'

'I'll go and see him tomorrow morning,' Jenny promised. 'They'll let me in outside of visiting times. And I'll try to show him that things aren't quite as black and white as he thinks.'

They dropped Wayne off at St Edmund Hall before going on to St Luke's, from where Bernie and Jenny both had bikes to retrieve. As Wayne got out of the car, Bernie leaned out and said earnestly, 'Wayne, whatever else you think, *please* believe that it's not your fault.'

****

'Of course,' Bernie said to Bethan, 'He did blame himself – anyone would in his position.'

'But at least in this case he got another chance,' Jonah observed, 'unlike with a successful suicide.'

'Yes,' agreed Bernie. 'We all felt that we'd been given a second chance to help Dean – and now we felt a big responsibility for looking after Wayne too. So, as soon as I got home that night, I rang Margaret and put her in the picture. She understood at once and arranged to take the morning off work to visit Jonah to break the news.'

****

Margaret was still there when Wayne arrived. He stopped in his tracks when he saw her. Her close-cropped hair was dyed a deep magenta and her nails and lips were painted to match. The same colour featured again in the floral pattern of her cream-coloured dress.

'Wayne!' Jonah called to him. 'I don't think you've met my wife. Margaret – this is Wayne.'

'Pleased to meet you,' Wayne mumbled.

'And *I'm* pleased to meet *you*,' Margaret replied. 'I've heard such a lot about you – and about Dean, of course. Bernie told us what happened. We're both very shocked – and sorry.'

'It's lucky for those CU-types I don't have the use of my arms anymore,' Jonah said grimly. 'Putting stupid ideas into his head like that. I'd like to wring their necks with my bare hands!'

'Jonah!' Margaret reproached him. 'Don't forget – they're only young. We said the same sorts of things ourselves at that age.'

'But society has moved on a lot since then. We were just reflecting what most people thought then.'

'I'm not so sure about that. Your idea that sexual orientation was purely a matter of choice was outdated even then. Don't you remember arguing about it? I can't think how we got on to the subject. It wasn't that long after we met – you must have been all of twenty, I suppose. You had some very odd ideas in those days!'

'While you, at the grand old age of twenty-three and with a medical qualification, were much more well-informed and could speak with complete authority!'

'Of course.' Margaret smiled. 'When you're twenty-three you know everything! It's when you get to fifty-three that things start getting blurred about the edges. Those CU-types, as you put it, just haven't learnt yet that the world isn't black and white.'

'Which is a pity,' Jonah said drily, 'because if they only stopped to think about it they'd realise that it's actually glorious Technicolor!"

Suddenly they both remembered that Wayne was there. 'I'm sorry,' Jonah apologised. 'Ignore us – we got carried away. You didn't come here to listen to us reminiscing about our youth or pontificating about the narrow-mindedness of the CU.'

'No, please – I'm interested. I want to know why Dean

… why he thought … well, what he thought, I suppose. Anyway,' he went on, trying to concentrate on the original reason for his visit, 'we'd better get on. We wanted to show you an idea we'd had for an improvement to your writing board – to make it easier to move it with your head.'

The conversation was interrupted by Wayne's mobile phone. It was Bernie with an update on Dean.

'The doctors are quite happy with his physical condition,' she reported, 'so they're hoping to discharge him later today. They're trying to arrange a psychological assessment first. His mother's on her way to visit. Jenny will pick her up at the station. His dad couldn't get away – nobody else to milk the cows apparently. Visiting is at two this afternoon. I assume you'd like to be there?'

'Yes, of course.'

'I'll drive you, if you like. Tell you what – why not come to St Luke's when you get back from seeing Jonah and I'll take you to lunch.'

'OK. Thanks – if you're sure?'

'I'm sure.' Bernie said firmly. 'See you later. My room's at the top of Old Quad two. Come as soon as you like.'

Jonah and Margaret were eager to hear what Bernie had said, and delighted that Dean was making a full recovery. When it was time to go, Margaret offered to drive Wayne back to Oxford.

'There's no point you taking the bus,' she declared, getting up and giving Jonah a kiss on the cheek by way of farewell. 'I don't need to get into work until the afternoon – my registrar can cope with my morning clinic – and I've arranged to have lunch with Dean's consultant. So I'll drop you off at St Luke's and then go to the hospital and catch up with him.'

'Thanks,' Wayne said, hurrying after her, feeling rather bemused.

'You know the doctor who's looking after Dean?' he asked as they walked briskly to the car.

'The trauma surgeon mafia,' she explained with a grin. 'I rang the hospital this morning and it turns out that Dean's under an old friend of mine – well, actually he was my first registrar, just after I became a consultant – I taught him all he knows!'

'And will he tell you more about how Dean is?'

'Strictly speaking, he's bound by patient confidentiality not to. I was thinking more that I might tell him why we'd all be extremely grateful if he could see his way to giving Dean extra specially good treatment! But I think if he was worried about anything he'd probably tip me off – in my role as a friend of the family, rather than as a nosey doctor.'

'So you're a doctor? You look after people like Dean?'

'Yes.' Margaret unlocked the car and they both got in.

'And what do you think makes them do it? I mean, it can't always be down to religion.'

'You know, Wayne?' Margaret looked at him seriously. 'I think the underlying reason is almost always lack of self-esteem. The reasons why are different, but I think that's what it usually comes down to. People try to kill themselves when deep down they don't think they *deserve* to live.'

'But that's nonsense!' protested Wayne. 'Dean's the nicest, kindest most …' his voice trailed away engulfed in a deep wave of misery.

'Of course,' Margaret agreed. 'So, Wayne, what we all need to do is to show him how much we all value him, in the hope that then he'll value himself too.'

They sat in silence. Wayne fought back tears, trying desperately to understand what was happening. How had the joy that he had felt – that he thought that he and Dean had shared – during the Easter holiday, turned into this? Eventually he was able to speak again.

'One thing I'd like to know,' he said, then stopped unsure how to go on.

'Yes?' Margaret encouraged gently.

'Why is everyone being so nice to me?'

'Well, in my case,' Margaret said in a matter of fact voice, trying not to show her amusement at the naïve question, 'I'm deeply grateful for what you've both been doing for my husband. And,' she went on with a smile, 'I have a vested interest in seeing that your partnership continues so that all those plans you have for him come to fruition.'

Wayne smiled weakly.

'But as for everyone else,' Margaret continued. 'You know, I think you just have to accept that we like you – I mean, like you both.'

****

'Over lunch I tried to reassure Wayne that he wasn't to blame,' Bernie told Bethan. 'But of course we couldn't get away from the fact that if he and Dean hadn't fallen in love, Dean probably wouldn't have tried to kill himself. And he asked all sorts of questions about "religion" as he called it and why Dean's beliefs could have provoked such self-loathing.'

'Those must have been difficult questions to answer,' suggested Bethan.

'Very,' agreed Bernie. 'Especially difficult to answer them without slagging off the conservative evangelicals.'

'I wouldn't have worried about that,' Jonah growled. 'They ought to learn to engage their brains before opening their mouths!'

'And then Wayne was very nervous about meeting Dean's mother,' Bernie said, trying to steer the conversation on to safer ground. 'He didn't know what Dean had told his parents about them, but we both thought that it was likely that they thought that he and Dean were just university chums. We agreed not to say anything to disabuse her of that when we met at the hospital. She'd already had enough of a shock.'

'And did that meeting go off OK?'

'Yes. Dean's Mam took to Wayne right away. He's a

very likeable lad; they both are. By the time we got there, Dean had already told her enough about their relationship to explain why it had driven him to despair. Her main worry then was that it might have been anxiety about how his parents would react to his "coming out" that had driven him to try to take his own life. So, she was doing everything she could to reassure him that it didn't bother them, including being quite determined to like Dean's lover, pretty much whatever he'd been like.

'I think it was probably a good thing his father wasn't there. When I met him, much later, he still seemed to be having difficulty handling it. I think he was glad that Dean didn't come back to live locally. It meant that most of the time he could just ignore it. Not that he was ever actually hostile: it just isn't the sort of thing that they talk about when the farmers meet up at the livestock market or the county show.'

'So, in the end things didn't work out too badly,' Jonah concluded. 'And now, I've got a hymn to illustrate this part of the story: *There's a wideness in God's mercy.*'

'Yes, I see,' Bethan said, 'Showing that God welcomes everyone, even-'

'Even the CU,' Jonah finished for her, with a wicked grin on his face.

'Jonah!' Bernie said reproachfully. 'That's not a very charitable attitude. They're very sincere.'

'I know – that's half the problem with them.'

'They just have a completely understandable desire for certainty,' Bernie argued.

'Hmmph!' Jonah snorted, 'That's just ignoring reality. Life just *is* uncertain. In my opinion, certainty negates freewill. If we could always be certain about what was the right thing to do *and* be certain that doing right demonstrated that we were "saved", as they would put it, then doing right would be just as self-serving as doing as we please, because we would be expecting a pay-off in the next life, if not in this.'

Bethan looked from Jonah to Bernie and back again. She wasn't sure that she was following this.

'I think that's one for a completely different programme,' Bernie said. 'You could call it "Inspector Porter does Philosophy".'

'Definitely one for BBC2,' Lucy suggested.

'Or Radio 4,' Jonah agreed.

'But actually,' Bernie said, backtracking in the interests of fairness, 'the CU did have a pretty torrid time of it themselves, according to Jenny the chaplain.'

****

The Reverend Jennifer King had just returned to her room after the brief morning service, which she led in chapel each weekday, when there was a knock at the door. She opened it and saw, waiting nervously in the corridor, Victoria Cunningham, the president of the college Christian Union.

'Vicky! Come in.' Jenny stood back and Vicky entered.

'Are you busy?' she asked anxiously. 'I can come back later, if you like.'

'No, no,' Jenny assured her. 'Sit down. Would you like a coffee … or tea … or something cold?'

'No. I'm OK. I've only just had breakfast. I wanted to talk to you, to ask you something I mean.'

'Go on,' Jenny said encouragingly, sitting down in one of the easy chairs in front of the empty fireplace. Vicky sat down in the other chair and gazed at Jenny for a few moments before having another attempt at explaining her predicament.

I heard that Dean Rutter tried to kill himself. Is that true?

Jenny nodded. 'Yes, I'm afraid it is, but he's out of hospital now and going to be fine.'

'Oh! Good. Only, I haven't seen him around.'

'He's not living in college at the moment. He's staying with one of the tutors; just for a while, while he gets his head back together.'

'You don't think he'll try again, do you?' Vicky's eyes were wide with anxiety.

'No, no, no. It's just to give him a chance to sort himself out in peace.'

'Oh. I see.' Vicky paused, preparing herself to ask the big question. 'Do you know why he did it?'

'I'm not sure that I ought to discuss it with you. It's rather private – confidential.'

'Oh.' Vicky thought for a while. 'Well, can you tell me if it was … was it anything to do with him thinking he was gay?'

'And was there a particular reason why you ask that?' Jenny leaned forward slightly and looked Vicky in the eye. 'Was that something that he talked to you about?'

Vicky nodded. Then she got up and strode around the room, trying to think how to put into words what she wanted to say. Jenny watched her silently, waiting for her to be ready. After a few minutes, Vicky returned to her seat and spoke earnestly to Jenny.

'I'm so afraid that it may be because of what I said to him,' she groaned. 'I told him that what he'd done was a sin, but that everything would be alright if he repented and put it all behind him. I thought I was saying the right things. I never thought he would …,' she tailed off in tears.

Jenny offered her a box of tissues. After a minute or two the tears subsided.

'Why don't you tell me all about it?' Jenny suggested.

Vicky nodded then took a gulp of air and began.

'It all started in seventh week last term. Our Bible study group was reading one Corinthians chapter six. There's this verse that says that homosexuals won't inherit the kingdom. Dean said it didn't seem very fair because gay people didn't choose to be that way, and we had a discussion about whether people were born gay or if it was caused by their environment and whether gay people could become straight. In the end, we all agreed that it didn't

145

really matter because the Bible didn't say that it was wrong to *be* gay, only that gay sex was wrong.

'Afterwards Dean came to see me and asked if I thought there could be some other way of interpreting that verse, because it still didn't seem fair to him that gay people weren't allowed to have the same sort of relationships as straight people; and, if two people loved each other, did it really matter about their gender? I told him that Christian teaching was very clear and that it was only the same as me not being permitted to have it off with someone else's husband. I nearly asked him whether he thought he was gay, but …

'Anyway that was all, until we came back from the Easter vac. Dean came to the Bible study meeting in first week, but he didn't say a word – which is very unusual for him. He seemed very down altogether, so I went to see him the day after. He told me that he'd been to stay with this guy from Teddy Hall over the holiday and they'd had sex. He knew it was wrong, but he couldn't tell the guy in case …well, because he didn't think he could bear to lose him.

'I told him that, if he really cared for this guy, he ought to be trying to bring *him* into the kingdom not encouraging him in sinful sexual acts. I said that God would give them both the strength to fight their urges. And I promised to pray for them: and I did too, every night!' Vicky collapsed into tears again.

'Vicky – listen to me.' Jenny leaned forward and took Vicky's hands in hers. 'You mustn't blame yourself. You only said what you thought was right.'

Vicky looked up, blinking to see through her tears. 'What would you have said, Jenny, if he'd come to you?'

'When I was your age, probably exactly the same as you.'

'And now?'

Jenny thought for a few moments before replying.

'Vicky,' she began at last. 'You say you were reading the

first letter to the Corinthians? Tell me, has your Bible study group got to chapter fourteen yet?'

Vicky shook her head, so Jenny reached out to take a Bible from her bookshelf and thumbed through it while she continued.

'Well, in that chapter it says that women ought to keep quiet in church meetings and mustn't be allowed to be in charge. See – here.' She handed the Bible to Vicky and pointed to the place on the page. 'Naturally I can't take that as applying literally to the church today or I couldn't be in this job!'

Vicky read the passage then said slowly, 'yes – I suppose I always thought that, well, times have changed.'

'In fact,' Jenny went on, 'St Paul isn't even consistent about this. If you read Chapter eleven, he says, "Any woman who prays or proclaims God's message in public worship with nothing on her head disgraces her husband." That doesn't make sense if women are forbidden to speak at all, does it?'

Vicky looked at Jenny with a puzzled expression on her face. 'So, what are you saying?'

'That if times have changed as far as women's role in the church is concerned, and if St Paul isn't providing a consistent list of rules about that in any case, maybe we shouldn't be too quick to apply other things that he says to twenty-first century life. Look, Vicky, I've been reading up a bit on this, since Dean … Well, anyway, I came across a lecture that the Archbishop of Canterbury gave a couple of years ago. He's my boss, so I have to take notice of what he says.'

She went across to her desk and came back with a piece of paper. 'I'd like to read you a bit of it.'

'OK.'

'He's talking about ways of interpreting the Bible. He says:

Thus Spirit through the events of God's initiative stirs up the words and makes sense of them for the reader/hearer in the Spirit-

sustained community. As Karl Barth insisted, this leaves no ground for breaking up Scripture into the parts we can "approve" as God-inspired and the parts that are merely human-'

'Of course!' Vicky interrupted. 'The Bible is the Word of God. That's why I don't understand-'

'No, but hear how it goes on,' Jenny urged gently.

'The whole is human and the whole is offered by God in and through the life of the body; always shaping and determining the form of that life.

'What he's saying is that, while the Bible is *inspired* by God, it was written by fallible human beings, for fallible human beings who were living thousands of years ago in circumstances very different from the ones we're in now.'

'Then how do we know what to do?' Vicky said disconsolately. 'I thought we just had to read the Bible and think about what Jesus would have done.'

'I think we just have to do our best and when we realise we've got it wrong, pick ourselves up and have another go. Even Jesus didn't always get it right first time, you know.'

'What do you mean? That's impossible!'

'I was thinking about the story of the Syrophoenician woman who came to Jesus asking him to cure her daughter of demon-possession and he said that he had come only to the lost sheep of Israel, but when she argued with him he changed his mind and healed the girl. It's in Matthew's gospel – I can give you the reference if you like.'

'So you're saying that it's OK for Dean to have sexual relations with that guy?' Vicky brought the conversation back to her main problem.

'I'm saying that I'm not confident enough that it isn't OK to criticise them for it, especially after seeing them together. They really do love each other, and I'm finding it difficult to work out an argument why that's a sin.'

Vicky continued to look unconvinced. So Jenny continued.

'But Christians are really divided on this. There are plenty of people who agree with you that it *is* sinful, and

I'm not here to make you change your mind; but, as you've seen, you have to be very careful what you say about it because for someone like Dean it's a lot more than just a theoretical question.'

Later that day Jenny accosted Bernie on the terrace outside the Senior Common Room. They sat down together over a pot of tea and scones. Jenny enquired after Dean's welfare and Bernie assured her that all was well.

'Wayne's parents are being tremendously supportive,' she confided, 'which is a big help to them both. I think everything's going to work out OK.'

'Good, good.' Jenny stirred her tea and prepared for her next question. 'Bernie?'

'Yes?'

'Vicky Cunningham came to see me this morning – you know, the CU president.'

'Oh, aye?'

'She thinks she may have pushed Dean over the edge by telling him that homosexuality is a sin.'

Bernie raised her eyes to heaven and gave a sigh. 'She said that, did she? Well, I'm afraid she may not be wrong – about pushing him over the edge, I mean.'

'She wanted to know what I would have said to Dean, if he'd asked me. I gave her some flannel about how I'd have said much the same as her when I was her age – which is perfectly true, by the way – and tried to make her feel less responsible. Then I tried to explain biblical criticism to her in five minutes, which I don't think was a particular success. I was wanting to ask you, what you would you have said.'

'To make her feel less guilty, or to convince her that she needs to adopt a more liberal attitude?'

'Either – both. I just mean, well, I got the impression that you knew all about Dean and his friend and so I thought perhaps you'd thought this stuff through rather better than I had."

'Well, if the only thing I was concerned about was

making Vicky feel better I might tell her that she was only confirming an orthodox Christian belief and was presumably motivated by a desire to save Dean's soul from eternal damnation – glossing over the fact that driving him to consider suicide, which is also a mortal sin, was unlikely to have the desired effect.'

'And if you wanted to encourage her to change her thinking?'

Bernie thought for a few moments. 'I suppose perhaps I'd start from St Peter's dream in Acts. You know – what God has made clean, do not call unclean. With conservative evangelicals the only way to argue is by a sort of battle of biblical texts.'

'They'd probably argue that Peter's vision is about circumcision, not homosexuality.'

'But then, logically, if circumcision isn't necessary for Christians neither is the rest of the stuff in the Jewish law, which knocks out the quotations from Leviticus that they usually rely on – and probably Sodom and Gomorrah as well – which as far as I can remember, leaves us with just a couple of dubious references in St Paul's letters.'

'Yes – that's where it all started apparently. I tried to convince Vicky that you need to approach Paul's letters with caution, but I'm afraid all I did was to worry her. She's looking for certainty, and I wasn't able to give it to her.'

****

'But to get back to Wayne and Dean?' Prompted Bethan.

Bernie took up the tale. 'Dean came out of hospital the day after he went in. There was a move to send him home, so that there would be someone to keep an eye on him, but then there was the problem of making sure he kept terms.'

'Kept terms?' Bethan queried.

'University regulations say that students have to reside within six miles of Carfax for six weeks each term.' Bernie explained. 'So if he'd gone home for more than a couple of weeks he wouldn't have been eligible to get his degree.'

'So he came to stay with us,' Lucy put in, 'which was all to the good really, because he got to stay in the magic Spare Room!'

Bethan looked from face to face, wondering what this was all about. Eventually Bernie took pity on her.

'My daughter,' she explained, 'is referring to the way that people who stay for more than a few days in our spare bedroom have a habit of getting married within a couple of years as a result.'

'My Mam stayed there when her house burned down,' Lucy chipped in, 'and that led to her marrying my father. And Peter stayed there after his wife died, and then married my Mam. And, while Dean was staying here, it gave Wayne lots of opportunity to visit and get things sorted out between them.'

'That's once Dean managed to get himself sorted out,' Bernie added.

****

Dean looked blearily round the kitchen, wondering where everyone else was. He had woken from a fitful night's sleep to discover the house strangely silent, in stark contrast to the lively bustle of the evening before. He had dragged himself reluctantly out of bed and made his way downstairs, struggling to remember which day of the week it was and whether or not he had a lecture or tutorial to attend.

He looked at his watch, which revealed that it was shortly after ten on the Wednesday following his suicide attempt. Could it really be Wednesday already? The intervening two days were shrouded in a fog of misery and half-memories. Eventually he managed to focus his eyes on a note lying on the table at the place where he had sat for his supper the previous night.

'Gone to college. Back by lunch time,' he read. 'Help yourself to breakfast, Bernie.'

Dean filled the electric kettle and switched it on. Then he found a loaf in the breadbin and put two slices in the toaster. He tried several cupboards before locating a plate and mug. A few minutes later, he was sitting down with toast and marmalade and a mug of strong coffee. He started to eat, but didn't feel hungry, so he pushed the toast aside and sat with his elbows on the table sipping the coffee slowly.

The door from the garden opened and a stranger entered. Dean looked up to see a man who looked to be in his seventies with steely grey hair and brown eyes. His gnarled hands were clutching three plastic containers, rather like the poultry drinkers that Dean was familiar with on his parents' farm, but smaller. Their eyes met and the old man smiled and nodded in greeting.

'You must be Dean,' he said, closing the door behind him. When Dean did not answer, he continued, speaking softly in a broad Geordie accent. 'Stan Corbridge. I'm an old friend of Bernie's. She's kind enough to allow me to keep my birds in her garden.'

'Birds?' Dean echoed, not quite knowing what to make of this.

'Yes – I keep racing pigeons. Our house doesn't have enough space, so Bernie let me put up a loft at the bottom of the garden here. Would you like to see?'

'Er – yes, yes I would.'

'Right you are!' Stan, always delighted to share his hobby, sounded enthusiastic. 'You finish your breakfast while I clean these out and then I'll take you down to meet the flock.'

So saying, he deposited the drinkers in the sink and proceeded to scrub them vigorously under the tap. Dean forced himself to eat up the toast and then finished his coffee. Soon they were on their way down the garden.

When they reached the pigeon loft, Stan put his burdens down on the ground and took both hands to the bolt that held fast the outer door. The bolt was stiff and he struggled to open it.

'Here – let me do it.' Dean stepped forward and took hold of the bolt. It grated as it slid across allowing the door to open.

'Thanks, son. This arthritis has got to be a real nuisance these last couple of years. Still – mustn't grumble! My old dad was dead before he got to my age.'

'The door's dropped a bit on its hinges,' Dean said, experimentally opening and closing it and checking the alignment of the bolt. I could fix it for you, if you like, so it slides easier. I do a lot of this sort of stuff back home on the farm.'

'Thanks. I'd appreciate it. I used to be pretty handy with that sort of thing myself, but these days I don't have the strength in my hands. That's old age for you.'

'Just show me where you keep your tools. I'll do it right away.'

'No – there's no rush. You wait until those stitches in your wrists are out. Our Bernie'll be on the warpath if I let you do anything that might open them up again. Now come inside and I'll show you my beauties.'

They went inside the pigeon loft and Stan spent a happy half hour showing off his prized birds. Dean was a good audience, asking intelligent questions and showing a proper appreciation of the finer points of pigeon-keeping. After they had checked the welfare of each of the birds and topped up their feeders, they returned to the kitchen for 'elevenses'.

'Now, son,' Stan said, looking at Dean over his mug of steaming tea into which he was dunking a digestive biscuit. 'Tell me why you did it.'

'Did what?'

'You know.' Stan looked meaningfully at the dressings on Dean's wrists, which were clearly visible as he held both hands round his own mug on the table.

'I don't really know,' Dean said slowly. 'It just seemed the best way.'

'But why?' Stan persisted. 'Was it your college work? Were you afraid you were going to fail your exams?'

'No – it wasn't that. I just couldn't bear to ... I just thought ... how much better off everyone would be if I just wasn't there.'

'I'm sure your parents wouldn't have thought so,' Stand said vehemently. 'Or that friend of yours – Wayne isn't it?'

Dean looked Stan in the eyes.

'Did Bernie tell you about me and Wayne?'

'Our Bernie told me nothing. But I can tell by the way she's been clucking round your Wayne ever since your little escapade that there must be something very special going on between the two of you.'

'Would it shock you if I told you that I'd had a,' Dean hesitated, 'a *physical* relationship with Wayne?'

Stan shook his head. 'Look son, I'm too old to get shocked by anything you're likely to have got up to. What you and Wayne do in the privacy of your own bedroom is no business of mine or anyone else's. All I know is that the way your Wayne's been on the phone all the time to Bernie wanting to talk about how you're doing, there must be something a lot more than just "carnal desire" involved.'

'And do you think that makes it alright? The CU say it's a sin.'

'Well,' Stan spoke slowly. 'That's certainly a point of view. But when *I* think about Sin, I think of it as something that harms someone else – or that *might* harm someone else, I suppose. So promiscuity is wrong because people get hurt – quite apart from spreading disease; but I don't see what harm there can be in a long-term gay relationship, any more than in a straight one.'

'But what about the Bible? And the CU say that gay relationships *are* harmful, because that's not the way God intended us to be. They say it's Satan leading us astray.'

'Well now,' Stan put his mug down and clasped his hands together on the table. 'I left school when I was fourteen and went straight into the shipyards, so I'm not

154

educated like your university friends, but I did do some studying for my Local Preacher's exams. And one thing I learned was that the Bible was written by lots of different people for people living very different lives from us, and rules that worked for nomadic tribesmen in the Middle East don't automatically work in twenty-first century England.'

'But don't you believe that the Bible is inspired by God?'

'Inspired maybe, but not dictated. So you've got to make allowances for the other influences that the writers had on them.'

Dean looked puzzled, so Stan went on, warming to his subject.

'Look, son, let me tell you what I mean. I worked as a welder for fifty years. It was a man's world in the shipyards. Probably the worst thing you could say to anyone was to suggest he was a poof. Nobody ever talked about it – it was just assumed that it was shameful and at the same time a bit of a joke. And nobody would have wanted to admit that any of us big strong working men could possibly be "one of them".

'Now think about me going in as a lad of fourteen. I just accepted it all – even though I got my own fair share of ribbing for going to chapel and for *not* going to the pub! It never occurred to me that I'd ever actually meet a homosexual and I never thought about what it really meant to be one.'

'So what made you change your mind?'

'Hang on a minute, son, we'll come to that later. Let me finish what I was saying.' Stan paused to collect his thoughts.

'The point I was trying to make,' he resumed, 'is that the people who wrote the Bible were probably like me and my mates at Swan Hunter. We never even thought about whether homosexuality was right or wrong. We certainly didn't ever talk about it. We didn't need to talk about it –

we all *knew*.

'Let's take another example. A lot of the Bible assumes that women are just chattels of their fathers and husbands. That's because that was how people thought then. Or again, the Bible assumes that slavery is normal – because that's how people thought then. I never had a problem with reinterpreting it to fit in with how we think now about those things, but to be honest I never thought about gay rights until the discussion about civil partnerships and gay clergy and all that started.

'You asked me what made me change my mind. Well, I'm ashamed to say that it wasn't as much *changing* my mind as *making up* my mind, because I never bothered to think about it properly before.'

'So now,' Dean said cautiously, 'you think it's OK for me and Wayne to ... you know?'

'Son,' Stan sighed. 'That's up to you and your conscience. All I know is that your Wayne deserves better from you than to be cast off like an old glove just because of your religious notions. One thing Christianity definitely *doesn't* hold with is human sacrifice!'

He got up and carried the two mugs to the sink.

'And now I'd better be getting on. My wife'll be wondering what's taking me so long.'

He walked to the door and opened it to go out. Then he turned and looked at Dean.

'Tell me straight, son,' he said seriously. 'Did you not consider at all how devastated your Mum and Dad would be when they found you'd killed yourself?'

Dean shook his head slowly. 'I never thought. I just thought about how they'd feel if they found out that I was ... I mean, I thought then they wouldn't ever know that I was gay. I thought it would kill them to know. I never meant ...'

Stan nodded abruptly and went out closing the door behind him.

****

'Anyway,' Jonah said, with a rather grim smile, 'What with Stan's words of wisdom and one or two heart-to-hearts with our Bernie-'

'Not to mention your efforts to undermine completely his faith in the CU,' Bernie put in.

'Dean got himself sorted out,' Jonah continued, ignoring the interruption, 'and eventually managed to believe that he *wasn't* condemned to the fires of hell for all eternity after all.'

****

Wayne pushed his bicycle through the side gate and stood it up against the back wall of Bernie's house. He stood for several minutes, going over in his mind the speech that he had prepared to deliver to Dean when they met. It was important that he got it right.

He looked up and saw a group of people seated around a wooden table on the patio. He started walking towards them. Dean and Bernie were sitting opposite him, but who were the other two? What a nuisance! If Bernie had visitors, he would have to put off his heart-to-heart with Dean. The unknown couple had their backs to him, but turned to look at him when Bernie called out.

'Wayne! Come and sit down. We're just having a brew.'

Wayne stopped in his tracks as he recognised his parents.

'Hello Wayne,' his mother called to him. 'We just popped down to visit Dean.'

'To tell him how much we're looking forward to working with him,' his father added, 'and to check he isn't having any second thoughts. I'm looking to get a good return on my investment you know!'

'And to say that we hope that he'll soon feel that he's part of the family as well as the business,' his wife added.

Wayne continued to stare in silence.

'Come along – sit down!' his mother urged, indicating a chair next to Dean's. 'What's got into you?'

'I – I just wasn't expecting to see you here, that's all.'

157

Wayne sat down and Bernie poured him a cup of tea.

'Graham and Barbara have been telling me about a flat they've seen in Bromsgrove,' Dean told Wayne. 'They think it would suit us.'

'Not that we're trying to run your lives.' Barbara Major was keen not to appear overbearing. 'It's just that we saw it and it seemed perfect: handy for the office and close enough to us for you to come over sometimes, but not so close that we'd be living in each other's pockets.'

'Thanks.' Wayne was still trying to adjust to the unexpected parental apparition.

'I said that maybe we could go over and have a look this weekend,' Dean said tentatively. 'If you think it's a good idea.'

'Yes – yes, of course.' Wayne answered absently.

'Well, we must be getting off,' Graham Major declared, getting to his feet. 'Time and tide and all that.'

His wife got up and they both made their excuses to Dean and Bernie and then headed off. Bernie accompanied them to their car.

'Thank you for coming,' she said, once they were out of earshot of Wayne and Dean. 'I know it means a lot to Dean to know you accept him – them – you know.'

Meanwhile, Wayne was still lost for words.

'If you'd rather not see the flat ...' Dean started, tentatively.

'No – it's not that, Of course we'll go. I just got a shock seeing my Mum and Dad here – and saying such weird things!'

Bernie returned and started packing the tea things on to a tray – all except Wayne's untouched cup of tea.

'I'll leave you two lads to chat,' she said. 'I'll be in the study if you need me.'

'No, wait!' Wayne said abruptly. 'I've got something to say – and I'd rather like you to be here, Bernie. I want you to know, so that you can stop people jumping to conclusions.'

Bernie raised her eyebrows in surprise and bewilderment. Wayne launched into his speech, speaking rather quickly and going rather red in the face.

'Dean, I've been thinking a lot about – well, about us and about your religion – and I wanted to say that I don't really understand much about it, but I do know that it's very important to you and so,' he took a deep breath and carried on, 'and so I wanted you to know that, if your religion says that you and I can't – well, you know – then it's alright by me. Well, not exactly, but I mean I don't mind – at least if it's going to make you miserable then I'd rather … Look, what I'm trying to say is, I'm sorry if I pushed you into doing things you didn't really want to do and … and I just hope that we can go on being friends and setting up the business together. Oh – that all came out wrong!'

He tailed off and sat staring morosely at his feet.

'No it didn't.' Dean reassured him, putting his arm round Wayne's shoulders and blinking back tears. 'I understand perfectly. And I can't tell you how much it means to me to hear you say it. But …'

'But?' Wayne asked nervously.

'But, it's OK. I've been thinking it through too and I don't think God would want to stop us expressing our love however we want to.'

Bernie picked up the tray and carried it silently into the kitchen, smiling to herself. Whatever might be going to happen next, she was confident that she was no longer needed there.

****

'And they got married?' Bethan asked.

'Well, it was a Civil Partnership, to be precise,' Jonah answered, 'because marriage wasn't available back then. They moved in together that summer and then a couple of years later they tied the knot.'

'They spent their honeymoon helping at the London Olympics,' Lucy said excitedly. 'Show her the pictures,

Jonah.'

Jonah frowned in concentration as he searched for photographs on his computer. A few minutes later, he swivelled the screen so that Bethan could see.

'This is their wedding album. Here they are coming out of the registry office.'

'They look very happy,' Bethan observed.

'Of course,' said Lucy. 'Isn't everyone supposed to be happy on their wedding day?'

Bethan watched as Jonah scrolled through pictures of the reception. Then the quality of the photographs changed as they moved on to record highlights of the couple's time at the Olympics. These were clearly snaps taken on a mobile phone.

'They were stationed at the Royal Artillery Barracks, where the shooting competitions took place.' Lucy provided a commentary as Jonah flicked through the pictures. 'There they are with the British shooting team. And now this is one of the other volunteers, Lisa something-or-other.'

'Lisa Price-Williams, wasn't it?' Bernie suggested helpfully.

'Price-Davies,' Lucy corrected her. 'It was a bit sad, really – she had been hoping to be in the team herself, but she came off her bike and broke her elbow, which meant that she wasn't able to qualify.'

'Now here we have the flat in Bromsgrove,' Jonah continued, 'and there they both are, with Wayne's Dad, signing the agreement setting up their company. It's been a huge success, although I'm sure they'd make more money if they didn't spend so much time with their disabled clients customising their equipment to suit their individual needs.'

'I don't know about that,' Bernie disagreed. 'I think that's their unique selling point: recognising that everyone is different.'

****

There's a wideness in God's mercy,
Like the wideness of the sea;
There's a kindness in His justice,
Which is more than liberty.

There is plentiful redemption
In the blood that has been shed;
There is joy for all the members
In the sorrows of the Head.

There is no place where earth's sorrows
Are more felt than up in Heaven;
There is no place where earth's failings
Have such kindly judgment given.

There is welcome for the sinner,
And more graces for the good;
There is mercy with the Saviour;
There is healing in His blood.

There is grace enough for thousands
Of new worlds as great as this;
There is room for fresh creations
In that upper home of bliss.

For the love of God is broader
Than the measure of our mind;
And the heart of the Eternal
Is most wonderfully kind.

But we make His love too narrow
By false limits of our own;
And we magnify His strictness
With a zeal He will not own.

If our love were but more simple,
We should take Him at His word;
And our lives would be all sunshine
In the sweetness of our Lord.

Frederick Faber (1814 – 1863)

6 DEAR LORD AND FATHER OF MANKIND

'Now, to get back to my choice of hymns,' Jonah said, taking a draft of tea through his straw. 'We *must* include *Dear Lord and Father of Mankind*.'

"And why have you chosen that?" Bethan asked.

'It was Angie's favourite hymn and we must include something to commemorate her. I know I said that Bernie was the main instrument in getting me back into the police force, but actually Angie's role was vital too.'

'Angie?' Bethan looked puzzled. 'You'll have to remind me who she is.'

'Angie was Peter's wife,' Lucy explained.

'Peter's *first* wife,' Bernie added emphatically.

'I remember now,' Bethan said, still looking puzzled. 'But I don't understand – didn't she die *before* your accident?'

'Yes,' Jonah chuckled. 'But even from beyond the grave she managed to convince the powers that be that I could still hack it as a detective! It's quite remarkable what an influence she's had on my life, considering that I don't think I ever met her.'

'If you don't *think* you met her then you definitely

didn't,' Bernie said decisively. 'Nobody could meet Angie and *not* remember!'

Bethan looked from one face to another, wondering whether they were teasing her. Soon Jonah took pity on her confusion.

'Look, this is how it happened …'

****

'*While it is greatly to your credit that you wish to return to your post as Detective Chief Inspector,*' Jonah read out from the screen in front of him, '*your recent medical report shows that your continuing disability makes you incapable of carrying out the duties of the role.* What do they know? And look, here!' He scrolled further down the page. 'See – here! *We have considered alternative positions for you and have concluded that there is no suitable employment available for someone with your current level of disability.* And here – look! *I therefore strongly recommend that you accept the generous early-retirement package offered to you.*'

Bernie looked seriously at the hardcopy of the letter, which she held in her hand. It was July 2010 and she was at Jonah's house, plotting with him the next stage in the campaign to get him back into his job.

'And to cap it all,' Jonah went on indignantly, 'He has the nerve to *take this opportunity to thank you for the years of loyal service that you have given and to wish you a long and happy retirement.* How would he like being thrown on the scrap heap at fifty-one?'

'Fifty-one, eleven months and thirteen days,' Bernie pointed out.

'Fifty-two then,' Jonah conceded. 'But the point it still the same. I'm not ready to be put out to grass.'

'We really need to do something to demonstrate that you can still do the job,' Bernie said. 'They're just looking at you and seeing all the things you *can't* do. And you've been telling them how you can get around them, but maybe we ought to be focussing on what you *can* do and showing them that those are the things that you need in order to solve crimes.'

'If they'd let me back into the job then I'd soon show them,' Jonah growled.

'Yes,' mused Bernie. 'That's what you need – a case that you could solve to demonstrate that you can still do it. I wonder … I wonder if Peter could be persuaded to let you in on one of his.'

'Well, it certainly wouldn't be hard for me to show that I can solve a case quicker than old Peter!'

'Jonah!' Bernie reproached him, 'Why are you always so dismissive of Peter's abilities? Is it just because he's never managed to get as far up the greasy pole as you?'

'No – it's just that he's a plodder.' Jonah answered, 'He always has been. He's a good police officer – very careful, very thorough – but he lacks imagination. He's – well, boring, I suppose. I wouldn't have thought he was your cup of tea at all. Why did you marry him?'

For a moment, Bernie was taken aback by this sudden and unexpected question. The she recovered herself and said lightly, 'Because he was there!'

'Seriously though?' Jonah persisted.

'I *am* serious. He was there, occupying my spare bedroom, and we decided that it would be more efficient if we were to get married so that we could legitimately share my room – halving the number of sheets to be washed, for example.'

'Come off it Bernie!' Jonah laughed. 'Nobody gets married out of consideration of the laundry bill! What really happened to bring you two together? What was he doing in your spare bedroom anyhow?'

'You really want to know?'

'I really want to know.'

'OK, but it's a long story. We really have to go right back thirty years to summer 1979.'

'The year Margaret and I met. I was a humble police constable and she helped to get me into CID. Now that,' he went on, 'is an example of what I meant when I said I couldn't imagine you marrying someone as boring as old

Peter. From the moment I first rode pillion on the back of her motorbike I knew that I would never be bored if I hitched up with Margaret!'

'Do you *want* to hear about me and Peter or not?'

'Sorry! Yes – go on.'

'I was in my final undergraduate year and I was engaged to be married to another third year mathematician called Stephen Corbridge. He was from Newcastle. His dad was a welder with Swan Hunter – the shipbuilders. My dad was a docker, so I suppose we were brought together by the contrast with all the Public School types that we were surrounded by. You know: the ones who belonged to the Oxford Union and went to the opera and the ballet and thought our accents were absolutely hilarious.

'We'd both got the promise of a grant to stay on to do a DPhil, so we planned to get married shortly after finals, only …' Bernie broke off, apparently suddenly very interested in the state of her fingernails.

'Only …?' Jonah prompted.

'Only, two weeks before the wedding he decided to jump off the top floor of the Engineering Tower.' Bernie said quickly, as if trying to get something unpleasant over and done with.

'And why would he want to do that?'

Bernie shrugged. 'Since he didn't have the courtesy to leave a note, we could only speculate. The general consensus was that he probably thought he'd done badly in the exams and couldn't face the prospect of failure. It's not uncommon, apparently, to get suicides just after Schools. But if that *is* the reason, he must have been incredibly bad at judging how well he'd done, because they marked his papers and it would have been a first.'

'And do *you* have a hunch at all?' Jonah asked. Then light suddenly dawned and he went on without waiting for an answer, 'You don't think – you couldn't possibly believe – that he killed himself to get out of marrying you?'

'My head says, "No, of course not. Don't be

ridiculous!" But my heart says, "It has to be a possibility." Consider the timing: what else could have been bothering him?'

Jonah shook his head in exasperation, but realised that argument would be futile. What could he say that Bernie had not thought about during the thirty-odd years since her fiancé had so inexplicably, and, Jonah thought, selfishly, killed himself? Instead, he tried to think of something to lighten the mood.

'At least now I understand,' he said, 'how come you were still available when Richard was finally ready to plunge into matrimony. I'd always wondered how it could be that you hadn't been snatched up years before!'

Bernie laughed. 'Now you're just acting daft! I'm under no illusion that I'm highly desirable matrimonial material. The wonder is that not only one, but two, people have actually gone through with it!'

Jonah opened his mouth to protest at this continued self-deprecation, but changed his mind and instead urged Bernie to get back to the point of her story.

'Which brings us back to my original question: you still haven't explained how you came to marry Peter.'

'Or how he came to marry me – which is at least as baffling, I would have thought.' Bernie sat for a moment in thought and then resumed her tale.

'You remember that I said that I became a Methodist as a compromise between Roman Catholicism and Salvationism?'

'Yes.'

'Well, that wasn't exactly the whole story. The real reason was that Stephen and his whole family were lifelong Methodists. When we were going out together, we started going to the John Wesley Society – that's the student Methodist society – and going to the big Methodist church in the centre of Oxford, where most of the students go. We decided that, when we were married, we wanted to belong to the same church and go along as a family. So, I became a member of the Methodist Church.

'Anyway, after Stephen died, I couldn't face going to Wesley Mem, where everyone knew about it – and knew Stephen – and would be trying to help. I wanted a chance to be, well, anonymous: to tell people in my own time – or not to tell them at all. I was living down Cowley Road way, so I started going to the Cowley Road church, which is where I met Angie. Did you know her? She and Peter must have been married when you worked with him.'

'No, I never met her, as far as I remember. I just remember that Peter always seemed very devoted to her and was always very keen to get home at the end of his shift. She was a nurse, wasn't she?'

'That's right. When I met her, she was still working at the old Radcliffe Infirmary. She came from Jamaica. In 1979, she'd been in the UK for four years and she'd been married to Peter for just over a year. Hannah was born the following year.

'We hit it off right away. Angie was a tremendously easy person to talk to and she was the only person who really seemed to understand how I felt about Stephen. No, that's not fair,' she corrected herself. 'Stan and Sylvia – that's Stephen's parents – understood, but that was different. They understood because they were going through the same thing, whereas Angie understood, because she understood *me*, if that makes sense.'

'Perfectly.' Jonah nodded.

'Anyway, we became what you might call best friends. When the kids were born, I was their main baby-sitter. With Angie and Peter both working shifts, they needed someone quite often.'

'I know the feeling,' Jonah nodded. 'We were in the same predicament when the boys were young. We envied people who had grandparents living near who could provide free childcare.'

'Of course, Angie's family were all in Jamaica and Peter was a product of the National Children's home. Come to think of it, I believe that's how they met: at a fund-raising event for NCH.'

'Really? I never knew Peter had been in care. It's strange how you can know people for years without really knowing much about them at all. But go on with your story.'

'I was lucky. I finished my DPhil and managed to get a couple of postdoc posts following on from that, and in the end I landed a fellowship at St Luke's, which had just started taking women and wanted some female dons to make them feel more at home.

'I bought myself a house just round the corner from Peter and Angie's. I didn't see much of Peter, because of his work, but Angie and I were in and out of each other's houses most days. When the kids got older, I was sometimes drafted in to help with their homework. There was a time when Eddie looked as if he might be going off the rails, and I think I helped by encouraging him to turn his interest in computers into a career instead of a distraction from his schoolwork.

'I think maybe Peter underestimated the impact on the kids of being mixed race. I don't mean that there was overt racism shown towards them exactly, but I think they probably did feel that they didn't really belong in either community. Hannah seemed to handle it better, but I think Eddie found it quite hard sometimes.

'After Richard and I were married, Angie and I became if anything even closer, because we now shared the joys, or otherwise, of being police wives. And Peter and Richard worked together a lot, so often if one of us was wondering what had become of their husband the other would know that they'd been called away to investigate a suspicious death in Summertown or Kennington or wherever.

'And then when Richard died Angie was a tower of strength. I really don't know how I'd have coped without her. And when Lucy was born – well, she knew so much more about childrearing than I did. Peter and Angie were

Lucy's godparents – and that's when I really started to get to know Peter properly. He loved Lucy to bits and spent a lot of time with her. According to Angie, he did all sorts of things with Lucy that he'd never had time to do with his own kids. I suppose, when they were growing up, he felt he had to devote his time to his career, whereas by the time Lucy came along he was established as a Detective Inspector and didn't particularly care about progressing any further.

'Anyway, everything went along very nicely until just after Lucy's third birthday. Then one morning, after Peter had gone to work, Angie was found stabbed to death in her own kitchen, with the word "SCUM" written in blood on the wall above her.'

Jonah shook his head in astonishment. 'I was seconded to the Met that year, so I was a bit out of touch. I vaguely heard that Peter's wife had been killed, but I had no idea …'

'Understandably Peter was very shaken up, but he did his best to put on a brave face for the sake of the children. Well, they weren't really children by then: Hannah had a job and a boyfriend in Leeds and Eddie was in his final year at Manchester University. Once he'd finished his degree, Eddie went off to the West Indies to find his roots and Peter was left alone in Oxford. I told him that our spare bed was always made up, ready for unexpected guests, and if ever he wanted to get out of the empty house, he could just turn up any time, day or night.

'He stayed a couple of times while Eddie was still up at Manchester then, a month or two after he left for Jamaica, Peter came for a weekend and never quite got round to going back – apart from moving back into the family home whenever Hannah paid a flying visit to check that Dad was OK.

'I imagine that lots of people made wild, unfounded assumptions about the actual sleeping arrangements, but he really did occupy the spare room for over two years. As anyone with an ounce of common sense would understand, he was far too devoted to Angie's memory to be in the least tempted to do anything else.'

'So what changed?'

'Nothing really. I suppose it was just a matter of time. One evening Peter came downstairs after putting Lucy to bed and I made some remark about how much she liked having him reading her bedtime story. We were sitting together on the settee in the living room. He said something along the lines of, he supposed the sensible thing, under the present circumstances, would be for us to get married. And I asked him if that was a proposal. And he said that he supposed it probably was.'

'How incredibly romantic!' Jonah observed.

'Yes, wasn't it?' Bernie agreed, with a grin. 'Anyway, one thing led to another and we got talking and in the end we fell asleep in each other's arms and the next thing we knew was Lucy, age five and a half, demanding to know what we were doing downstairs at that hour in the morning! And I'll never forget what she said after that. She said, "If you want to sleep together you'd be more comfy upstairs. Mam's bed is big enough for two people."'

They both laughed.

'And then,' Bernie resumed, 'Peter asked her how she'd feel about him coming to stay with us permanently and sharing my bedroom. And she was absolutely over the moon at the idea of having him for her Daddy. It was as much as we could do to stop her broadcasting the news to everyone she met before we'd had a chance to let important people, such as Hannah and Eddie, know.'

'So, did you marry Peter in order to give Lucy a father?'

'That was part of it,' Bernie admitted. 'But Peter would probably say that I mainly married him because I felt that I owed it to Angie to see that he continued to eat properly and didn't turn to drink after her death.'

'Well,' Jonah said slowly. 'I can see the benefits for Lucy, who gets a new father, and for Peter, who gets a housekeeper-cum-nursemaid-cum-social worker to keep him on the straight and narrow, but what do *you* get out of the arrangement?'

'A father for my daughter, and the opportunity to repay my debt to Angie for arriving just too late to prevent her murder, and –'

'Stop right there!' Jonah interrupted. 'My dear Bernie, please tell me – is there any human disaster that you do *not* believe yourself to have been personally responsible for?'

'I'm sorry. It's the twenty percent catholic coming out,' Bernie giggled. 'We're very good at doing guilt, I'm afraid. But, to finish answering your question, I also get a companion for the long winter evenings, a confidant, and someone who can change the battery on the smoke alarm without having to get a ladder.'

'And,' she went on, more earnestly, 'I *do* love him, you know. And he loves me – although there'll never be any question of me being anything approaching a replacement for Angie. I know that he's still in love with her and won't ever care for me in the same way. And he knows that I know. He'd never forgive himself if he ever felt the same about anyone else as he does about Angie.'

'And that doesn't bother you?'

'It makes things a lot easier. There's no competition. I'm not trying to be as good as Angie and he isn't competing with Richard. He's one of the few people who knew Richard well and I'm the one person that he can really talk to about Angie – the one person who really knew her. I mean, the kids obviously knew her too, but only as their mum, not as a friend.'

'What did you mean, you arrived just too late to prevent Angie's murder?' Jonah asked sharply, having just digested the implications of Bernie's earlier remark. 'Are you telling me that you were there? You found the body?'

Bernie nodded. 'I'd arranged to go over to Abingdon with Angie to help her look for something to give to Peter for their silver wedding anniversary, which was coming up in a few weeks' time. I was about half an hour late, so I was expecting Angie to be waiting for us, but-'

'Us?' interrupted Jonah, moving into detective-interrogating-a-witness mode.

'Me and Lucy. Fortunately, I'd left Lucy in the car, because I was expecting us to be going off straight away, so she was spared the worst of it. When I rang the doorbell, there was no answer. Then I heard a noise from inside the house. It sounded like a door banging and then there was a crash and some shouting, but I couldn't hear what – men's voices I think, but I can't be sure. Definitely not Angie.

'I had a key to their house, so I let myself in and called out for Angie. She didn't answer so I took a look around. When I went in the kitchen – there she was.'

'And the intruders? The voices that you heard?'

'Scarpered. It was one of those old two-up and two-down terraced houses with a back lane running along behind the gardens. They must have bolted through the kitchen door and over the back wall when they heard me.'

'And Angie was already dead?'

'Yes. The pathology report at the inquest said, "multiple stab wounds to the chest and abdomen, including one puncturing the abdominal aorta." There was blood everywhere. The thing that convinced me that she was dead was when I tried to feel for her pulse and found that her carotid artery had been severed.'

'So the murderer, or murderers, must have had blood on them when they left.'

'You'd think so – but nobody ever came forward to say they'd seen anyone fleeing the scene covered with blood that morning, or any family members with unexplained blood stains on their clothing.'

'So was the murderer never found?'

'No. Not for want of trying. Of course, the police were extra motivated, with it being the wife of one of their own. And what with it being a racially motivated killing and with the ink hardly dry on the Macpherson report –'

'Three or four years,' Jonah observed drily. 'It must have been rather slow drying ink!'

'It was still very much in everyone's minds. Nobody wanted to be the next police force to be accused of institutional racism. So they pulled out all the stops, but every lead seemed to just point up a blind alley.'

'It must be difficult for old Peter,' Jonah said, breaking the silence that ensued. 'Not knowing. And feeling that justice hasn't been done.'

'Is that how *you* feel? I mean, about the person who shot you?'

Jonah thought for a moment. 'I don't think so – not yet. I suppose I'm still assuming that some new evidence will turn up.'

'After more than a year?'

'It wouldn't be unheard of. Sometimes it takes a long time for witnesses to come forward – especially if they're giving evidence against someone they know. But, I suppose what I was thinking about was more how I'd feel if someone had murdered Margaret. I think I'd find it hard to accept that they couldn't be found.'

'I know Peter finds it hard when he has to go back to that area of Oxford,' Bernie admitted. 'He can't help thinking that everyone he passes might be the murderer. It could be someone he knew – perhaps one of the neighbours. I think that's one reason he was glad to move out of that house and come here.'

'Funny they didn't move sooner. I would have thought that, with two kids, they'd have wanted a bit more than a two bedroom terraced.'

'Something more like your five bedroom detached in its own grounds with open aspect across the golf course to the rear?' Bernie asked with a touch of sarcasm in her voice. 'You're forgetting that Peter's wife wasn't bringing in a top surgeon's salary – and *you* don't have a family back in Jamaica to support.'

'How d'you mean?'

'One of Angie's brothers has severe cerebral palsy. She used to send a good chunk of her salary home each month to help pay for his care – especially after her father had an accident and couldn't work anymore.'

'It must have been a blow to them when she died.'

'Of course – but not financially: Peter kept up the payments out of his own salary.'

'Even after he married you?'

'Of course. We don't need the money and it makes a big difference to them. And that,' Bernie added, 'is another benefit of our marriage: only one house to maintain between us. Richard's ancestral home is quite big enough for the three of us.'

'Especially now that you aren't obliged to sleep in separate bedrooms,' Jonah added, smiling.

'Yes – especially now that we share the same bedroom, which means that we even have plenty of space for guests. So, Peter sold his house and split the proceeds between Hannah and Eddie. We can all live perfectly well on my salary and Angie's family don't lose out. Of course, we did both have to give up our widow's pensions, so, on a strictly financial basis, we're probably worse off really, but I know it's a big relief to Peter not having the Cowley Road house to worry about.'

'I'm beginning to see that there's more to old Peter than meets the eye.' Jonah spoke more seriously than before.

'Certainly there is – especially when the eye is a jaundiced as yours.'

'And he really doesn't have any idea who killed his wife?'

Bernie shook her head. 'None at all.'

'It must be hell for him.'

For a few minutes there seemed to be nothing more to be said.

'I wonder,' Jonah mused aloud. 'I wonder if this is the

case we're looking for. Why don't I look into it again? A fresh pair of eyes might just spot something that was missed first time around. Or maybe someone will remember something they didn't mention before. It must be worth a try.'

'If the idea is that this is the case that you're going to solve to prove that you're still up to the job,' Bernie remarked, 'then you certainly can't be accused of lacking in confidence. Is it really sensible to choose a case that has baffled the force's finest for seven years?'

'If I solve it then it'll prove my point conclusively.'

'And if you don't?'

'If I don't, I can at least produce a report of what I did, which will demonstrate that I can still conduct an investigation. Now, let's get down to business. Who was the investigating officer?'

'He was a Glaswegian.' Bernie tried to remember. 'Tall … and heavily built. We called him "Big Mac". I can't think what his name was, though.'

'Gordon MacBride?' suggested Jonah.

'Yup,' Bernie nodded. 'That's the one. And he had two sidekicks: DI Alison Brown and DS Arshad Khan. I assume someone decided that the team ought to include a woman and someone from an ethnic minority.'

'Or maybe they were just the best people for the job.'

'Pardon my cynicism.'

'Right! I'll get on to MacBride and see if I can twist his arm to let me have access to the files. Can I count on you to fill me in on the background and what you actually saw?'

****

'And did you manage to solve the case?' Bethan asked eagerly.

'I did indeed!' Jonah declared.

'He said modestly,' Lucy added.

'It was a hard nut to crack,' Jonah continued, ignoring the interruption. 'But-,'

'With the finest mind on the force …,' Bernie continued for him, with a grin.

'I wasn't going to mention that,' said Jonah, 'not being one to blow my own trumpet. But I have to admit I did make a pretty good job of that investigation.'

'Tell me how you did it,' Bethan prompted.

'To my surprise, MacBride was very co-operative,' Jonah said. 'Actually, I suspect that he told his superiors that I'd been on to him and they told him to give me plenty of rope, in the hope that I'd find out for myself that I wasn't up to the job and give up pestering to be allowed back.

'Anyway, he let me see all the old files – and they were pretty extensive: lots of interviews with local people, none of whom admitted to having seen anything. I mean – you'd have thought that the murderer would have found it pretty difficult to get away without being noticed, given that he must have got blood all over himself.

'They'd also interviewed all the likely suspects – known neo-Nazis, gang members, that sort of thing – but they all seemed to have been living exceptionally blameless lives on that particular morning, and had alibis to prove it.

'It seemed that the murderer, or murderers, must have got away over the back wall into the lane that runs down the backs of the houses, and it was likely that they got in the same way, but there were no footprints to show that. But then, it was the middle of a heat wave and the ground was hard and dry, so it wouldn't have shown up footprints anyhow.

'I discovered that both Bernie and Peter had been considered as potential suspects, but they'd been ruled out quite quickly. Peter could have killed Angie before leaving for work, but he wouldn't have had time to clean himself up, dispose of the knife and his blood-stained clothes and get to police HQ in Kidlington between the earliest possible time of death and the time he was known to have arrived.'

'And anyway,' put in Bernie, 'what about the sounds that I heard? It was quite clear to me that Angie was killed well *after* Peter would already have got to Kidlington.'

'But you could have made that up in order to protect Peter. It could even have been a conspiracy between the two of you. Fortunately for you, you didn't leave Headington until after the postman had called with a recorded delivery package that you signed for. That meant that you couldn't have arrived at the Johns's early enough to have done the deed yourself and then changed your clothes and disposed of the knife before reporting that you'd found the body.'

'Well, I'm glad we were both in the clear. It had never occurred to me-,'

'I bet you wouldn't have invited Peter to stay with us if you'd known,' Lucy chortled. 'It must have looked very suspicious – the bereaved husband shacking up with the Other Woman!'

'To continue,' Jonah said, giving them both a hard stare. 'I soon saw that I would have to look for some new evidence. So I started on a round of house to house visits.'

'Fortunately it was the long vacation,' Bernie put in. 'So I was able to fit my work in around ferrying Jonah to and from East Oxford.'

'Peter would say, "Work, what work?",' commented Lucy.

'He doesn't think dons do much,' Bernie explained, 'especially outside term time. He has a very low opinion of academics all round.'

'Don't we all?' said Jonah. 'But, to get back to how we solved "Murder in an East Oxford Kitchen": we'd anticipated that Bernie would drop me off and then I'd be able to go round in my chair knocking on doors and interviewing people, but we soon realised that she'd need to come with me to every house. It wasn't just the number of houses that had steps to negotiate before you could even get to the front door – and you have to remember that the chair I was in then wasn't as manoeuvrable as this one – but there was also the question of how to knock on the door or ring the bell to alert the inhabitants that I was there.'

'But, of course, in a real house-to-house the police would normally go in pairs anyway, so it was a perfectly fair test of whether Jonah would be able to cope,' Bernie said. 'All I did was to get him to the front door and ring the bell. Jonah took over completely from there. It was great fun. I'd never taken part in an investigation before.'

'For a long time we didn't make any headway at all,' Jonah resumed. 'Some of the houses had changed hands, so the people living there hadn't been around when the murder took place. Those that were still there either couldn't remember or just said the same things they'd said to MacBride and his team. Nobody seemed to have seen or heard anything.

'Then we had a wander down the lane at the back of the house, where we thought the murderer had got away, and we realised that anyone running off down there would be invisible from any of the houses. Moreover, we didn't meet anyone all the time we were there, so the chances were that the murderer didn't either. Then, when we looked at an aerial view of the area, we realised that you could get all the way to Iffley Road along back alleys, where you'd probably not be seen. And from Iffley Road it was but a small step to the river, where a bloody murderer could wash away all signs of his guilt and dispose of the murder weapon.

'So now we had an idea of how the murderer got away with it, but we weren't any closer to knowing who they were. The real breakthrough came one day in September. We'd picked Lucy up from school and gone over to Cowley Road, in the hope of catching people on the way back from work or from the school run. Outside one of the houses opposite where Angie and Peter lived, an elderly Afro-Caribbean lady was sitting in a deck chair. A boy in his early teens was sitting on the doorstep, playing with some sort of electronic game device, and on the patch of grass in front of the house there was a baby girl, sitting propped up with cushions, and a girl about Lucy's age was building towers of plastic bricks for her to knock down.

'We went over and struck up a conversation with the woman, whose name was Celeste Gilbert. The children were her grandchildren and great granddaughter: Daniel, Stella and baby Serena. Lucy soon made friends with Stella and they sat on the grass playing with Serena while we chatted with Celeste.'

****

'Oh, I remember it well – a dreadful business, dreadful business,' Celeste said, shaking her head. 'They were a lovely family. He was a policeman and she was a nurse. They kept themselves to themselves but if anyone was in trouble, Angela would get to know about it and do whatever she could to help. And Peter was very helpful when my Grace – that's their mother,' she explained, pointing at Daniel and Stella, 'got into trouble with the police. The children were always very polite. I could never understand why anyone would do something like that.'

'Tell me what you remember about the day it happened,' Jonah prompted gently.

'It was one of those very hot days and I was just opening the window in the front room to let in some air when this lady's car drew up and she got out.' Celeste waved her hand towards Bernie. 'I went back into my kitchen to clear up the breakfast things and the next thing I knew there were police cars and an ambulance and all sorts outside with blue lights flashing and everything!

'I went outside to see what was going on. This lady-,'

'Dr Fazakerley,' Jonah said.

'Dr Fazakerley,' Celeste continued, 'was there in the front garden, with a little girl holding her hand. They were talking to one of the policemen. Then there was a lot of rushing about and they taped off the house with that blue and white tape that they use. Then another police car came and Peter Johns got out of the passenger side. I saw his face – it was white as a sheet. He went in and then a few minutes later he came out again and got into the car with Dr Fazakerley and the little girl and they drove off.'

'Peter couldn't investigate his own wife's death,' Bernie explained, 'so I took him home with me while the police went over the house looking for clues.'

'I went over there a few days later and took them a cake I'd baked. He was there with the two kids. He looked like – well, I don't know! He looked like he was lost, I suppose. Like the world had come to an end but he was still there.'

'Now Mrs Gilbert,' Jonah said gently, 'I'd like you to think back to the days and weeks *before* it happened. Do you remember seeing anything that could have a bearing on what happened? Anyone hanging around outside the house, for example?'

'No – not that I recall.'

'And what was it like living here? Did the neighbours get on?'

'Pretty much. There wasn't much of what you might call community spirit. Everyone kept themselves to themselves, but generally we got on OK.'

'So you weren't subject to any racial abuse at all?'

'No, I wouldn't say so.'

'Only police harassment – like always.'

Everyone looked at Daniel, who made this contribution without looking up from his game console.

'Now Danny,' Celeste rebuked him. 'Mind your manners. Inspector Porter here is a police officer himself.'

Daniel shrugged his shoulders and carried on with his game. 'Suit yourself,' he muttered. 'But it don't make any difference. Leroy said that Angela had it coming to her – marrying white police scum.'

'I really must apologise,' Celeste said, embarrassed. 'Danny – you tell the officer that you're sorry, d'you hear me? Fancy saying something like that about poor Angela!'

'I was only telling you what Leroy said,' Daniel retorted sulkily. 'He said she was betraying her own kind and she thought she was too good for the likes of us.'

'And can you tell me who Leroy is?' asked Jonah, trying not to sound too eager at the thought of a possible new lead.

'He's my other grandson,' Celeste explained. 'Danny's half-brother. My Grace never had much luck with men. She had three kids all with different fathers, none of them any good.'

'She's lucky to have you to help with bringing them up,' Jonah said. 'Did they all live with you back then?'

'No. I just had the boys. Stella and Grace lived with Stella's Dad until a year or so after that.'

'And then?'

'He came back drunk one night and accused Grace of going with another man. They argued at the top of the stairs, in the house they was renting, and he hit her and she fell down and cracked her head on the stone floor in the hall.'

'Was she badly hurt?'

'She died.' Celeste said baldly. 'So I took Stella to live with me.'

'I'm sorry.' Jonah paused for a few moments then pursued his questioning. 'Going back to 2003, if you don't mind, did Leroy say anything to you about Mrs Johns' death? Do you know what he thought about it?'

'Oh! He wouldn't talk to me about anything in those days.' Celeste declared. 'He had no time for us old folks. He was rather wild back then. He got in with the wrong crowd and they led him astray – into drink and drugs and that.'

'But he's turned himself around now,' she went on, some pride creeping into her voice. 'Or rather his girlfriend, Olivia, has turned him around. He's doing an apprenticeship at the motor works now and they've got a flat in the Windrush Tower. That's their little girl,' she indicated the baby, who was gurgling with delight as Lucy and Stella played with her.

'And he was, how old, when Mrs Johns was killed?'

'Fourteen.' Celeste frowned in thought for a moment. 'I remember now! It was that same day. He played truant from school and went off with some of his friends and came back filthy, with his clothes all covered in mud.'

Jonah smiled encouragement to her to continue, so she went on. 'It was very hot that day and they decided to bunk off school and go swimming in the river. They went down Jackdaw Lane and went in the stream there, but it was all very muddy and they got bogged down and never made it to the real river – which was probably just as well or they might all have ended up drowning themselves.'

'You know,' Jonah said, 'I'd really like to speak to Leroy. If he and his mates were out and about that morning, they may have seen something that would help us to find out who killed Angela. Where can I find him?'

'He'll be coming here when his shift finishes,' Celeste answered, 'in about half an hour – to pick up Serena'

'D'you mind if I wait for him?'

'Not at all. I'll be glad of the company.'

'And now Danny,' Jonah turned to the teenager. 'Can you tell me – you called the police "scum"; is that how Leroy and his mates used to refer to them?'

'Yeah – sometimes.' Daniel answered sulkily without looking up from his game.

****

'And it turned out that was the key to the whole case,' Jonah said with satisfaction. 'The original investigation had all been based on the assumption that the word scrawled in blood on the kitchen wall was intended as a racial insult to black people. The victim was black, so they all thought that the crime must have been committed by white racists. As soon as we realised that the word was aimed at the police, everything looked different.

'Leroy was reluctant to talk at first, but Celeste gently persuaded him that he could trust me. In the end, I think he was relieved to tell someone what had gone on.'

'And what *had* happened?' asked Bethan.

'Leroy had somehow got roped into a gang of boys – young men really – all quite a bit older than he was. Being the youngest he was keen to be accepted and was easily persuaded to go along with anything they decided to do. That day he set off for school as usual, but he didn't go. He went round to one of his mates' houses and changed out of his school uniform. Then they all went out, basically looking for trouble.

'There were three of them plus Leroy. The others had all been drinking already, although it was only nine in the morning. In fact, I gather they were just topping up the excesses of the night before, which hadn't ended until the early hours. They'd had a run in with the police and there was a lot of talk about police harassment of black youth. Leroy just happened to mention that there was a black woman in his street who was married to a police officer.

'The leader of the gang, one Sebastian Tyler, expressed the opinion that for a black woman to marry a white man was a betrayal of her race, and that to marry a white policeman was unforgiveable.'

'Only he used rather more colourful language,' Bernie put in, smiling as she remembered Leroy's account of the conversation.

'Anyway,' Jonah continued. 'The upshot of it all was that they decided to teach the "police scum" and his traitorous wife a lesson. They went down the back lane and got over the wall into the garden. Leroy was left in the lane to be the lookout. He was adamant that he never went in the house and had nothing to do with what happened, and I believe him. He also said that the plan was simply to trash the place. They weren't expecting anyone to be at home.

'Leroy waited in the lane for perhaps half an hour,

maybe less, and then all of a sudden the others came bursting out of the back door like bats out of hell. They climbed over the wall and hared off down the lane, leaving Leroy to follow as best he could. It wasn't until they got well away and all stopped for a breather that he noticed that Tyler was holding a flick knife and had blood all down his arm and the front of his tee shirt.

'They decided to go down to the river to wash off the blood and dispose of the knife. Only Tyler had any noticeable amount of blood on him, so they walked as a group, with him in the middle to make it less likely that he'd be noticed.'

'Of course,' Bernie interjected, 'the blood wouldn't show up so easily on dark skin. And he was wearing a black tee shirt, so that would only have looked wet rather than bloody.'

'And they didn't meet anyone in the back passages behind the houses,' Jonah continued. 'The only dangerous part from their point of view was getting across Iffley Road and down Jackdaw Lane. But then again, I don't suppose anyone who did see them would have wanted to stare too hard at a group of young black men walking close together in a pack like that. Anyway, nobody *did* notice them – or at any rate, they didn't remember or didn't think it was relevant to the enquiry, which they'd been told was a white on black hate crime.

'They all cleaned themselves off in a backwater of the Thames called Shire Lake Ditch. The weather was warm, so they hung about there until they dried off and then wandered the streets until Leroy reckoned he'd better get home. He went back to his mate's house and got changed back into this school uniform and tried unsuccessfully to make out to Celeste that he'd been at school all day.

'He claims that he didn't realise that Angie had been killed, until he got home and his grandmother told him. The other boys had just said that she'd found them trashing her kitchen and Tyler had used his knife to keep her off them while they got away.'

'So then what happened?' Bethan asked. 'Were they prosecuted?'

'Yes. Leroy gave us the names and we managed to match Seb Tyler to DNA collected from under Angie's fingernails where she'd tried to fight him off. He was already serving a sentence for GBH, so it wasn't hard to track him down and charge him. One of the others had cut his hand on a glass that they'd smashed, so we had his DNA too.

'Once they both realised that they were likely to be convicted, they confirmed that the third lad was there as well and told us where we could find him. In the end, he admitted to being involved. Both of the others claimed that Seb was the one who killed Angie and that they never intended to do more than smash things up. They both described him as going into a sort of frenzy, once he saw the first blood, and that he didn't seem to be able to stop himself stabbing her over and over again.

'In the end, Leroy pleaded guilty to being an accessory, and he got a community sentence in view of his having given evidence against the others and because of his family responsibilities and his recent exemplary behaviour.'

'Peter gave evidence in his favour as a character witness,' Bernie put in.

'Seb got life for murder and the others were given custodial sentences of varying lengths for their part in the business,' Jonah concluded.

'Leroy finished his apprenticeship,' Bernie added, 'and now he's got a good job at BMW. He and Ollie have two little girls now and Ollie is the head stylist at the hairdresser's where she works. Stella is in the sixth form working for her A' levels. She'd like to become a police officer, but she's going to do a degree first and then apply for graduate entry.'

'You seem to know a lot about Leroy and his family,' Bethan observed. 'It sounds like you've been keeping in touch with them.'

'Well, Peter has,' Bernie explained. 'It's been very liberating for him to know who was responsible for Angie's death, because now he can speak to his old neighbours without having at the back of his mind the idea that maybe they were the ones who did it. So he's been able to pick up with the likes of Celeste where he left off back in 2003.'

'And he really doesn't blame Leroy?' Bethan asked in wonder.

'Our Peter has hidden depths,' Jonah said seriously. 'If you really want someone to inspire your viewers, he'd make a much better subject for your programme than me.'

'Except that he doesn't really believe in God,' Bernie said, 'which could be a bit of a problem for your afternoon religious slot.'

'Well, we'd certainly like to include him,' Bethan said, diplomatically, 'if you think he'd be willing – or would he not want to be involved in anything religious?'

'Oh, he's not *against* God,' Bernie assured her. 'In fact, he doesn't exactly *disbelieve*. I think he'd *like* to believe, if only out of solidarity with Angie for whom faith was very important. It's just that he finds it hard to be sure, and he's too honest to pretend.'

'Would you ask him then?'

'You can ask him yourself, unless you're in a tearing hurry to get off. He's been visiting his daughter in Leeds, but we're expecting him back any minute. He promised he'd be back by tea time.'

'Which is in forty-three minutes,' Jonah added, glancing down at the time on his computer screen. 'Why don't you stay? I'm sure there'll be plenty.'

'Yes,' Bernie agreed, 'you'll be very welcome. It's scouse, which I suspect will be a new experience for you.'

'Well, if you're sure …' Bethan thought for a moment. 'Forty-three minutes! You're very precise about mealtimes.'

'I do try to keep to a regular routine,' Jonah admitted.

'It helps avoid problems with my digestive system.'

Bethan looked puzzled, so he went on.

'You see – and stop me if this is too much information – the bowel is controlled by reflexes which cause the sphincter muscle at the exit to relax and allow the bowel to empty in response to the rectum becoming full. Now in your case you get a message to your brain to let you know that the bowel is ready to be emptied. But the messages can't get through to my brain, so I need to try to make sure that this only happens at appropriate times. Keeping to a fairly strict eating pattern helps to do that.'

'I see. I hadn't thought about that sort of thing – I just thought that you couldn't move your arms and legs.'

'And to avoid accidents, we make a point of forcing a bowel motion every morning,' Jonah went on. 'That's Bernie's job – or Peter's or Lucy's depending on who's on bowel care duty that day.'

'And … what does that involve exactly,' Bethan asked cautiously.

'What does a constipated mathematician do?' Bernie asked, with apparent irrelevance. 'Work it out with a pencil!'

'Oh! Ah! Yes,' Bethan said, reddening. 'I think I get the picture.'

'It's called "digital stimulation",' Lucy explained. 'We have gloves to wear and, once you get used to it, it's not nearly as bad as it sounds.'

'The main problem,' Bernie agreed, 'is that it adds to the time it takes to get going in the morning. We start the process of getting Jonah up at six, in order to be sure of being in the office by nine.'

There was the sound of a key being turned and the front door opening.

'Excuse me,' Bernie got up. 'That'll be Peter.'

She left the room. Lucy collected the crockery together on a tray and followed her. Bethan and Jonah sat looking at one another.

'And presumably, after you'd been so successful with solving that murder, the police force gave way and let you back in?' Bethan asked.

'I still had a bit more persuading to do, but essentially – yes. It took time, but gradually I became accepted as just another member of the team. I started out part time but, after a few months, I was properly back in the saddle. But, as Bernie said, everything takes a lot longer than it did, so I spend a disproportionate amount of my non-working time on basic things like getting up, getting washed and getting dressed and undressed.'

'And Bernie? She's your full-time carer? She goes with you everywhere?'

'Well, she does now, but that was later. At first, I relied on professional carers from an agency. They were very good generally, but it wasn't as flexible as I'd have liked. Police work isn't nine to five. Sometimes you need to carry on beyond the end of a shift and it was frustrating when I had to hand over to someone else just because my carer needed to go home. Bernie works the same hours as I do, even when that means extra hours at short notice. Essentially the two of us together make one full-time police officer.'

****

Dear Lord and Father of mankind,
Forgive our foolish ways;
Reclothe us in our rightful mind,
In purer lives Thy service find,
In deeper reverence, praise.

In simple trust like theirs who heard,
Beside the Syrian sea,
The gracious calling of the Lord,
Let us, like them, without a word,
Rise up and follow Thee.

O Sabbath rest by Galilee,
O calm of hills above,
Where Jesus knelt to share with Thee
The silence of eternity,
Interpreted by love!

With that deep hush subduing all
Our words and works that drown
The tender whisper of Thy call,
As noiseless let Thy blessing fall
As fell Thy manna down.

Drop Thy still dews of quietness,
Till all our strivings cease;
Take from our souls the strain and stress,
And let our ordered lives confess
The beauty of Thy peace.

Breathe through the heats of our desire
Thy coolness and Thy balm;
Let sense be dumb, let flesh retire;
Speak through the earthquake, wind, and fire,
O still, small voice of calm.

John Greenleaf Whittier (1807-1892)

7 ALL PRAISE TO OUR REDEEMING LORD

'And now,' Bethan said firmly, 'I really do need to press you to choose some more hymns. You're up to number five so far. We need three more.'

'Well there's one that I'd really like to have: "All Praise to our redeeming Lord, who joins us by his grace; and bids us each to each restored together seek his face."'

'Why's that?' Bethan asked

'It's what we've just been talking about – how so many people all pulled together to get me through after I was injured. There are lots of good bits in it: "'build each other up", "hand in hand go on", "We all partake the joy of one". I particularly like the last verse, because it reminds me that we haven't lost Margaret and Angie and Richard and my Dad and everyone else that has died: "And if our fellowship below in Jesus be so sweet, what heights of rapture shall we know When round His throne we meet!"'

There was a knock on the door and a man's face appeared. His hair, although largely grey, showed signs of having once been a fiery carrot shade, and his complexion was the blotchy red and white associated with that colouring.

'I was told I had to come and introduce myself,' he said, coming in and addressing Bethan. 'Peter Johns.'

Bethan stood up and shook his hand. 'Bethan Abbott. I'm very pleased to meet you. I've been hearing a lot about you.'

'All good, I hope.' Peter sounded slightly nervous

'All very much to your credit, I can assure you,' Jonah answered. 'But, since we focussed rather a lot on the death of your wife, I'm not sure that we could say that what we talked about was all good. Now sit down. Miss Abbott here is hoping that you might agree to appear on TV.'

'We'd like to show people how Jonah's friends help him to lead a full and active life despite his injuries,' Bethan explained. 'And you seem to have played a big part in enabling him to get back into police work – as well as welcoming him into your home, which is quite a remarkable thing to do in itself.'

'Oh, it's more Lucy and Bernie who make the running.' Peter was dismissive. 'I just go with the flow.'

'That's not strictly true,' Jonah admonished. 'The plan for me to come to live here on a permanent basis when Margaret died was definitely your idea.'

'It's quite a long story,' he went on, turning to Bethan. 'I suppose it all started one Friday afternoon in – February, I think it was – 2013. I got a call from an ex-colleague who had moved to West Mercia. He'd been investigating a murder in Worcester and had just been called over to Oswestry to look into another suspicious death, which they thought might be linked. They were both remarkably similar to three recent unsolved murders in the Didcot area, which I was investigating, so he wanted us to compare notes. He was hoping that I could come up right away and check out whether it was likely that it was the same killer. I said "yes" and then it dawned on me that my agency carer had to get off home to his kids at five. Margaret was on-call that weekend, so she couldn't come with me. So, in the end, I rang Peter.'

'Peter had retired a couple of years earlier and I thought he might enjoy doing a bit of detective work on the side, but he had his young granddaughter staying with him.'

'My daughter, Hannah, was expecting her second and I was trying to give her a bit of a rest,' Peter explained.

'Bernie, however,' Jonah resumed, 'was delighted to come – and that was how our detective double-act started.'

****

'This must be the place.' Bernie drew into the car park of a budget hotel on the outskirts of Oswestry. She went round to the back of the modified people carrier, let down the ramp and climbed in to release the straps that held Jonah secure in his chair. Then she stood back to allow him to descend, before stowing the ramp, taking out a large trolley case and a rucksack and then locking the car.

'Now, we're already getting on for half an hour after your usual tea time, so number one priority, after we've checked in, is food. I don't want you and your old friend starting talking about the case and forgetting the time. And I absolutely forbid you to allow him to take you off to visit the crime scene or interrogate witnesses or view the body. That can all wait until tomorrow.'

'Yes Miss,' Jonah said, putting on the voice of a nervous schoolboy, up before the headmistress. He headed off towards the double doors marked Reception, which opened automatically at his approach. Bernie followed with the luggage.

'Paul!' Jonah called out as they entered. A man of about forty, with curly light brown hair and brown eyes, jumped up from one of the armchairs in the reception area. He stared at Jonah for a moment before recovering himself sufficiently to respond.

'Jonah! It's been so long – I didn't recognise you.'

'You mean you didn't recognise me in this.' Jonah immediately perceived his ex-colleague's dismay at the sight of his wheelchair. 'I'm sorry. I hadn't realised that you didn't know.'

'What happened?' Detective Inspector Paul Godwin continued to stare in disbelief. 'When?'

'A bullet in the back of my neck, nearly four years ago.' Jonah replied laconically.

'Who? Why?'

'No idea, and haven't a clue.'

Bernie deposited the bags on the floor behind Jonah's chair and walked unobtrusively to the reception desk to check in.

'I'm sorry.' Paul continued to feel embarrassed. 'I wouldn't have dragged you all this way if I'd known. I suppose that's why you insisted on booking the room yourself?'

'Well, it does make things easier to speak direct to the staff about what I need,' Jonah admitted. 'Not that it's all that much – this chair enables me to get pretty well anywhere and it's got all sorts of gadgets built in to help.'

Bernie came over and addressed Paul.

'Well now, Paul!' she said stridently in the exaggerated Liverpool accent, which she occasionally adopted for effect. 'How're you doing? You ignoring me, or what?'

'Bernie!' Paul noticed Bernie for the first time. 'What are you doing here? Oh! I suppose you're with Jonah?'

'That's right!' Bernie confirmed with a grin. 'I'm his temporary nursemaid – just for the weekend.'

'I gather you two know one another,' Jonah remarked.

'You could say that.' Bernie slapped Paul on the back. 'This lad here was Peter's sidekick for years. He danced at our wedding.'

'Really? I'm impressed,' Jonah said smiling. 'I didn't realise you had talents in that direction,' he added looking at Paul.

'I didn't really dance,' Paul protested. 'It was just that Lucy-,'

'We let Lucy choose one of the hymns,' Bernie cut in. '"She wanted *If I were a Butterfly* – she was only just turned six, remember – and Paul led the way in getting the congregation to join with the actions.'

'It sounds delightful. Why wasn't I invited?'

'You were, but you were otherwise engaged. You sent your apologies and a climbing rose – despite our having given strict instructions to all the guests not to give presents. After all, we already had two of everything!'

'Well, in my defence, (a) You didn't have even one of those roses, and (b) it wasn't for you, it was for Lucy. I thought she might feel neglected, what with it being your Big Day and all.'

'But to get back to business,' Bernie said, shouldering the rucksack again. 'Our room is on the ground floor. I'll drop the bags off there, and then we must eat – I'm simply starving!'

Jonah felt a small surge of affection for Bernie, realising that she was making efforts to ensure that he kept to his regular feeding regime without the embarrassment of having to explain it to his colleague.

'The restaurant is just over there.' Paul pointed. 'Or they do sandwiches and soup and pies and things in the bar.'

'Why don't you two get something from the bar?' Bernie suggested, 'and bring it to the room. Then, if you want to talk police business while you eat, you won't need to worry about being overheard.'

'OK,' Paul agreed, 'but let me help you with the luggage – you seem to have a lot to carry.'

'My fault, I'm afraid,' Jonah said apologetically, 'so many bits and pieces that I need. No chance of travelling light these days.'

'I'm fine,' Bernie insisted. 'We've got this down to a fine art. You go with Jonah and pick up some soup and sandwiches and I'll start unpacking. The room number is easy to remember – it's double O seven. Just down that corridor there.'

They went their separate ways. Once Bernie was out of

earshot Jonah said to Paul in a low voice, 'Of course, the real reason Bernie suggested eating in our room is to save me the embarrassment of having the whole restaurant turning to watch her feeding me.'

'Is that what happens?' Paul asked, trying to make conversation while not quite sure how to deal with the unexpected situation. Questions raced through his mind. Should he try to ignore Jonah's disability and carry on as if nothing had changed? But then, how would he avoid looking as if he was expecting Jonah to do things of which he was now incapable? Was it insensitive to ask questions? Would it look as if he didn't care if he did not?

'People try not to stare,' Jonah answered, 'but you know how it is when you're trying not to look at something? Somehow, your eyes get drawn back there all the time. And of course, it can be quite an entertaining spectacle – especially when we get the timing wrong! That's usually my fault: I keep talking too much.'

Entering the bar, they saw a slim woman in her mid-twenties chatting with the barman. She was smartly turned-out in a pinstriped trouser suit with her black hair fastened neatly at the nape of her neck in a plastic clip. She turned round as they approached and her large brown eyes opened wide when she saw Jonah, putting him in mind of Bambi.

'Karen!' Paul greeted her. 'Let me introduce-,'

'DCI Jonah Porter!' the young woman completed for him in tones of awe, her distinctive Welsh accent revealing that she originated from the Aberystwyth region. 'So *this* is your old friend from Thames Valley! Why didn't you tell me?'

She turned to Jonah, holding out her hand to shake hands with him then hastily withdrawing it in some confusion as she realised that he could not reciprocate. 'DS Karen Evans, sir.' She said a little breathlessly. 'And can I say how much I admire you, sir?'

'Certainly you can,' Jonah replied, smiling broadly and

hoping that she would take this as a sign of pleasure rather than revealing his amusement over her transparent delight at meeting him. Clearly, she considered him to be a celebrity. 'Although I fear that you may well have cause to revise your opinion after this weekend. I'm told that I'm a very difficult person to work with.'

Karen opened her mouth to protest, but Paul cut across her. 'I'm going to brief DCI Porter on the case over supper in his room. So you can consider yourself off-duty until the morning.'

He turned to Jonah. 'DS Evans is working with me on this case,' he explained. 'She spent a couple of years as a constable in this area before coming to CID, so she has local knowledge which may be useful.'

'I'm sure that her assistance will be invaluable.' Jonah agreed seriously, struggling to keep a straight face as he observed the pleasure in Karen's face at this sign of approval by her hero. 'Well now, Detective Sergeant Evans, I look forward to catching up with you again tomorrow morning.'

They made their purchases and then Jonah led the way to the room that he and Bernie were to share. Paul followed with the tray. When they got there, the door was open and Bernie was inside, with her back to them, busily unpacking the trolley case, which lay on one of the beds. Paul noticed a box of latex gloves and some mysterious plastic tubing lying on top of a pile of neatly folded clothes in the open trolley case. Hearing them enter, she flapped the lid down and turned to greet them.

'Put the tray down there,' she instructed Paul, pointing at the wooden bench, which ran along one side of the room and served as a desk and dressing table.

She inspected the soup, which was a rather thick tomato, tipping the bowl to see how it flowed. 'Do you think it'll make it up the straw?' she asked Jonah. 'Or had we better resort to a spoon?'

'Water it down a bit and I'll suck hard,' Jonah

answered, gesturing with his head towards the kettle, which stood on the bench next to the tray. 'Better than letting you loose with a soup spoon!'

Ignoring this completely unfounded slur on her ability at spoon-feeding, Bernie disappeared into the bathroom for a few minutes to wash her hands and fill the kettle. When it boiled, she poured Jonah's soup into a plastic cup and added some of the warm water. Then she stirred it, tested the temperature with her finger and added a little cold water before putting the lid on the cup, inserting a long drinking straw and placing the cup into a holder at the side of Jonah's chair, positioning the straw so that he could reach it with his mouth. 'Go carefully,' she warned. 'It's still quite hot.'

Soon they were clustered round a rather inadequate round table from which Paul had removed an assortment of leaflets advertising local tourist attractions. Before they could start eating, they were interrupted by a beeping noise. Jonah cancelled the alarm by pressing a button on the small keypad attached to the arm of his chair beneath his left hand. He exchanged a look with Bernie who nodded and then went over to the bed to rummage in the suitcase. 'Better get it sorted before starting our tea,' she murmured to Jonah.

'Excuse us,' Jonah said to Paul, who was looking a little bemused. 'It's just another little inconvenience caused by my condition. You see,' he went on, 'I have no control over my bladder, so I have a urine bag secreted down one trouser leg. That beeping noise was an alarm connected to a sensor, which tells me when it needs to be emptied. We won't be long.'

Jonah followed Bernie into the bathroom and the door closed, leaving Paul with a jumble of thoughts going through his mind. The day was turning out so differently from what he had expected when he decided to invite his old boss to join him. He felt irrational guilt at having brought Jonah such a distance when a more junior member of his team could have done just as well; or else they could have communicated remotely, without the need for a long and tiring journey. But then, why did nobody tell him that Jonah was no longer the irrepressibly active officer that he had been when they had worked together more than a decade ago? What exactly was Bernie's relationship with Jonah? What was it like to be so completely paralysed? Admiration for Jonah's pluck was mixed with scepticism that he could really still be an effective police officer.

Before Paul could finish assembling his thoughts, Jonah and Bernie emerged from the bathroom. Soon they were all eating their supper of soup and sandwiches. Try as he would to look elsewhere, Paul could not help watching with interest as Jonah ate. Bernie seemed to know instinctively when he was ready for another bite of sandwich and there was only one occasion when she offered it to him just as he turned aside to take a draft of soup. Miraculously, at the same time, Bernie managed to eat her own food and Jonah outlined what they knew so far about the three Didcot murders and questioned Paul on his own cases.

'We think it's a case of internet grooming,' Jonah said. 'All three girls seem to have spent a lot of time on social media and not to have had any real-life boyfriends. The parents of a fourth girl have come forward saying that their daughter arranged to meet a boy whom she'd made contact with on Facebook. She had the sense to tell her mother, and mother and daughter went together to the rendezvous. The boy never turned up, but they gave us the description of a middle-aged man who seemed to be coming up to them and then walked past. We think he may have been masquerading as a teenager to lure girls into meeting him and he got scared when he saw this one wasn't alone.'

'So maybe after that, he decided to move location,' suggested Paul. 'Our girls seem to have been killed in the same way: strangled with some sort of ligature.'

'Our forensics people say it was bailer twine in all three of our cases. I've brought a sample of the sort they think was used.'

'That would certainly be consistent with what we found in Worcester. We haven't got that far yet with this latest victim. I'll ask them to compare your sample with the marks on the body.'

'That could be important,' Jonah agreed. 'Unfortunately, details of how the girls died got out to the media, so there's always the possibility that this is a copycat murder and not the same man at all. Strangely, there's been no sign of sexual assault, which is odd, given the grooming factor. Presumably, our killer got his kicks out of the actual killing – something to do with the feeling of power and control, I suppose. From our point of view it means that we don't have any DNA evidence to confirm that it was the same person each time.'

'I've arranged to talk to the parents again tomorrow morning. Would you like to come?'

'Absolutely! And perhaps we could have a look at the place where the body was found. Presumably the pathologist won't be keen to talk to us over the weekend?'

'She can probably be persuaded. I'll give her a ring in the morning.'

Once they had finished eating, Bernie quietly collected the dirty crockery together on the tray and left the room to return it to the bar. Paul took the opportunity to tackle Jonah on an issue that had been bothering him all evening.

'Does Peter know that you are sharing a hotel room with his wife?' he asked, trying but failing, to keep a tone of sharp criticism out of his voice.

'Certainly he does. Why d'you ask?' Jonah was amused at the thought that Paul somehow felt that this arrangement was improper. Paul was clearly struggling to formulate an answer, so he continued. 'It's not as if I'm in any position to threaten Peter's marriage by having my wicked way with his wife in the night, is it?'

'No, no, I didn't mean … It's just, well … You could hardly help seeing …'

Paul stumbled to a halt, unsure now what it was that he wanted to say and wishing fervently that he had never started out on this tack. However, Peter had played a crucial role in both his career and his personal life and he hated the idea that his wife might be betraying him in some way.

'Look, Paul,' Jonah said, detecting Paul's embarrassment and trying to speak in a matter-of-fact tone. 'Once I've been put to bed, I can't even turn myself over without help. So Bernie only needs to put me facing the wall and she has complete privacy. There's no question of my being overcome with desire at the sight of her naked body emerging from the shower! And it's the turning business that makes it more convenient for us to share a room: I need someone to turn me over every few hours to prevent pressure sores. It's less disruptive for Bernie if that just means waking up and going to the next bed.'

Bernie's return saved Paul from having to find a suitable answer.

'Now, I don't know about anyone else,' she said brightly, 'but I'm ready to turn in. It was a long drive up and I get the impression that we have a packed programme tomorrow.'

Jonah noted to himself that Bernie had, once again, taken steps to safeguard his well-being without admitting that she was thinking of anyone but herself.

'Yes. Right. OK. I'll go then. My room's on the first floor: One, one, four.' Paul stood up to go, and then hesitated. 'Unless you could do with any help?' he added, looking from Bernie to Jonah and back again.

'No, that's fine,' she assured him. 'We can manage. Tell you what,' she went on, seeing that Paul was uneasy. 'If you go on up and get ready for bed, I'll come, in, say, about forty-five minutes, and tuck you in and tell you a bedtime story. How's that?'

'OK.' Paul smiled. 'I'll be waiting for you.'

He left and Jonah looked enquiringly at Bernie. 'Now what was that all about?'

Bernie laughed. 'It's nothing,' she declared. 'I always tell Paul a bedtime story whenever we're sleeping under the same roof. It's a sort of tradition.'

'And you always tuck him in a night too?' asked Jonah raising his eyebrows. 'And what, might I ask, does Peter think about that?'

'Peter is absolutely fine about it,' Bernie assured him emphatically, still smiling. 'It's all perfectly innocent. Peter and I are the parents he never had, that's all.'

'How come?'

'OK. I'll explain,' Bernie conceded, 'but no more procrastination – it's time you were in bed.'

While they went through the lengthy business of preparing Jonah for bed, Bernie explained.

'Paul came to work with Peter shortly after Peter was promoted to Inspector. That was a couple of years after Richard died. Shortly afterwards he had some sort of crisis with his accommodation and Peter suggested that he could lodge with me for a while – just until he found somewhere else. He knew I'd occasionally taken in students temporarily in the past.

'Lucy was two at the time and bedtime stories were an important part of her routine. I can't remember exactly what started it off, but Paul asked me something – about Richard, I think – and I said it was a long story and I couldn't answer there and then, but if he was a good boy I'd tell him at bedtime. And after that, it became a bit of a ritual. It was a vehicle for telling him things that were difficult to talk about in normal conversation.'

'I must say,' Jonah observed, 'That he has a nerve. Just now he was lecturing me on the inappropriateness of our sharing a hotel room, because of the damage it might do to Peter's feelings as your husband – and now it turns out that you regularly go into his bedroom to kiss him good night!'

'How did you know about that? The kissing, I mean.' Bernie asked, amused.

'That's what you always used to do when you tucked Lucy in at night.'

'Well, Paul never had much of a routine when he was a child. His parents were both alcoholics, so his home-life was rather chaotic. That's what I meant by us being the parents he never had. These days, he usually comes to us for Christmas and we go to stay with him for a few days in the summer. He's into model railways and models in general, which made his house very attractive to Lucy when she was a bit younger. They still manage to spend many happy hours playing at being the Fat Controller!'

'So, I gather Paul is still single?'

'Yes.' Bernie paused for a few moments, thinking. 'Yes – that's another story really. He had a bad time a few years ago: the love of his life turned out to be a murderer.'

'Are you serious?' Jonah sounded incredulous. 'That must have been dreadful for him.'

'Yes. I think that was what made him want to move away – to get away from the memories. It was also one of the things that brought us closer together – that and the way he supported Peter after Angie died. To be honest, I think he covered up a lot for Peter when his mind wasn't really on the job.'

Bernie smoothed down the covers, checked that the urine bag was clipped securely to the bed frame and headed for the door.

'I won't be long,' she promised. 'Try to get off to sleep.'
****

The door opened and Lucy appeared. She announced that the meal was ready and they were all to proceed to the kitchen. Jonah led Bethan out of his study and down the hallway into a spacious room, fitted with worktop round three walls. There was a large wooden table in the centre with empty chairs arrayed along both sides. An elderly couple sat at one end. Bernie introduced them.

'These are two great friends of mine: Stan and Sylvia Corbridge.'

'They moved down here to help look after me, after Angie died.' Lucy added.

'So you all live here together?' Bethan asked, shaking hands with Stan and Sylvia.

'Oh no,' Stan said. 'We live in Bernie's old house in Cowley. She very generously allows us to stay there rent free.'

'In return for uprooting yourselves from Newcastle and providing endless free childcare and housekeeping,' Bernie said quickly. 'So not very generous of me at all.'

'But we're up here most days, because Stan keeps his racing pigeons here and he needs to see to them,' Sylvia added, thinking that some explanation for their presence was needed and not wishing Bethan to think that they had come with a view to getting themselves included in the television programme.

'Bernie very nearly married our son, Stephen,' contributed Stan, 'but unfortunately he died. So Bernie is like a daughter to us.'

Jonah steered himself to a gap in the centre of one of the long sides of the table. Peter ushered Bethan to a seat opposite Jonah and sat down next to her. Lucy went over to the sink and washed her hands before sitting down in the chair immediately to Jonah's right.

Bernie bustled round, distributing plates of what looked to Bethan like some sort of stew. Peter helped Bethan to water from a large jug in the centre of the table and offered her bread to accompany the scouse. Bernie sat down next to Peter and looked round at them all.

'Tuck in,' she instructed. 'I suppose, Bethan, you would probably call this '"dinner"', but I still find it hard not to consider dinner in the evening as disgustingly pretentious, so we call it "tea".'

Bethan started eating, trying not to stare, as Lucy, on the other side of the table, somehow managed to combine consuming her own food with spooning small portions into Jonah's mouth.

'Jonah was just telling me,' she said, addressing Bernie, 'about the first time you accompanied him on a case.'

'Our adventure in the wild borderlands of darkest Shropshire, you mean? Poor Paul! He was completely taken aback to see Jonah – though how he can have managed not to hear about it, I'll never know. It was in all the papers and on the radio and television news.'

****

Bernie knocked on Paul's door and then went in. As promised, he was already in bed. When Bernie entered, he put aside the papers that he was studying and looked up at her. She came over and sat down on a chair next to the bed.

'Thank you for going along with the early night,' she said gratefully. 'He drives himself too hard sometimes – well, to be honest, most of the time.' She sighed, before continuing.

'He has to keep proving to himself that he can do his job just as well as before – which means refusing to admit to getting more tired or needing to allow time for taking care of himself properly. You have to admire it, but …'

'You know Bernie – I think you're a bit in love with Jonah.'

'Oh, I freely admit it.' Bernie said cheerfully. 'Me and Lucy both – head over heels, in fact. But it's alright – we've got it cleared with his wife!'

'You've what?' Paul asked, puzzled.

'I 'fessed up to his wife,' Bernie answered with a grin, 'and she said she could live with that and we agreed that we'd share him.'

Paul thought for a few moments.

'If he's got a wife,' he said, at length, 'why isn't *she* here lumping his luggage around and putting him to bed and

205

changing his urine bag?'

'Because she's a top trauma surgeon and she's on call this weekend.' Bernie replied rather shortly. 'Jonah officially went off duty at five this evening, so the plan was for them both to stay at home, with me and Peter available at the end of the phone in case she had to be out at the hospital for longer than he could safely be left alone.'

'So I messed everything up by asking him to come over. I'm sorry. I didn't know.'

'Don't be. He wouldn't have come if he didn't want to.' Bernie tried to reassure him. 'Don't worry! He's enjoying himself. He's never happier than when he's working, and this has the added attraction of being an opportunity to put one over on you!'

'And what about you? I've messed up your weekend too.'

'Nonsense! It certainly beats marking second year mechanics exercises, I can tell you! After thirty-odd years, I've already seen every possible way of failing to master the equations of motion of a vibrating membrane, and I'm not sure I want to have to carry on correcting them every year for much longer. This is a wonderful chance for me to see a police investigation at first hand instead of just getting recorded highlights afterwards. Highlights, incidentally, usually consisting of moans about the unreasonableness of senior officers, the intransigence of suspects in answering simple questions and the inability of witnesses to remember anything with any sort of accuracy!'

'Sounds about right,' Paul agreed, smiling. Then his face fell again. 'But it's just so awful!' he said bitterly. 'Seeing him like that! When he used to be so active. He was, he was …' he struggled to find the right words, 'almost *indecently* energetic. When I think of how he would go striding around a crime scene, checking on everything and everyone. Always demanding that we get things done by yesterday …'

'*Almost indecently energetic*,' Bernie echoed. 'He'd like that description.' She smiled with pleasure.

'But he's still got plenty of energy for the job,' she continued. 'And they wouldn't have allowed him to come back if he weren't up to it. I know it's a shock at first, but he really doesn't need our pity. Now, no more chatter. What would you like for your bedtime story?'

'Well, I suppose what I'd really like to hear about is how you came to know Jonah in the first place.'

'OK. Settle down now.' Bernie leaned back in her chair and began. 'Once upon a time there was a young police constable called PC Jonah Porter, who longed to become a detective. By chance, he met a Detective Inspector called Richard Paige, who thought that he had potential and managed to arrange for him to have a trial with CID. They worked together for several years, until DC Porter was promoted and moved into a different area.

'Many years later, he heard strange rumours that Detective Superintendent Paige (as he now was) had, at the age of fifty-seven, taken a wife. Porter found this difficult to believe since everyone agreed that DS Paige was firmly wedded to his job and never looked at a woman with love, or even with lust. Moreover, the wife in question was said to be an Oxford don, which seemed an impossible choice for a man who had, until that time, gone through life with the attitude that the university was responsible for most, if not all, of the ills besetting the city of Oxford and who had a particular antipathy towards all academics and to clever women in general.

'And then one day, some two years later, the venerable Detective Superintendent had cause to follow a criminal up on to the rooftop of an Oxford college, and fell to his death. (Although nobody afterwards could explain why someone of his rank should take it upon himself to chase suspects across the leads when there were numerous lower ranking officers, many of more athletic build and with better heads for heights, who could have been called upon to undertake this duty.)

'His death was the cause of much wailing and gnashing of teeth among the ranks of the police force – even by those who had previously been eagerly awaiting his departure from the force so that they could fill his place – and so word came to the ears of Detective Inspector Porter and he determined to travel to the funeral to pay his respects and to see who this woman might be, who had won the heart of the misogynist superintendent at such an advanced age.

'And lo! While he was there, DI Johns, who had become DS Paige's right-hand man in recent years, let slip that a baby was on the way. DI Porter treasured this information in his heart and made a vow that he would honour this child in memory of his good friend DS Paige. And so, each year on the anniversary of her birth, he would travel even unto Headington to see the child and to bring her gifts.

'And thus it continued, until the year of our Lord two thousand and nine, when it came to pass that some person with villainous intent did strike down DI Porter by shooting him with a .22 calibre bullet in his neck, rendering him paralysed. And thus it was that Lucy Paige and her mother came to start visiting DI Porter in his hospital bed and struck up a friendship with him and his wife. And that friendship has continued, even unto the present time.

'So now you know all,' she concluded. 'Now, snuggle down and I'll tuck you in.'

Paul obediently lay down and allowed Bernie to arrange the covers over him.

'But what about Peter?' he demanded as she kissed him on the cheek and then got up to go. 'If I was married, I wouldn't want my wife going off to spend the weekend in a hotel bedroom with another man, even if he was paralysed.'

'That's another story,' Bernie said firmly, 'and it will have to wait for another bedtime. Now I must get back to my other charge. He had strict instructions to go to sleep, but no doubt, instead of doing so, he will be anxiously awaiting my return to check that I don't linger in your boudoir for an unseemly length of time!'

****

'This is turning into some sort of Whitehall farce,' Peter commented, contributing to the conversation for the first time.

'And all because everyone is so concerned with preserving your honour and my reputation,' Bernie replied, smiling at him across the table. 'But we haven't got to the best bit yet. You should have seen Karen Evans' face when she saw me emerging from Paul's room that evening! I wasn't there when Paul introduced her to Jonah, so I couldn't understand why this complete stranger should be giving me a dirty look just for walking down the hotel corridor at night.'

'Not that it would have been any of her business *who* Paul chose to have in his room at night,' Jonah commented. 'She'd no right to pass judgement even if he'd been entertaining the Dagenham Girl Pipers!'

'Ah yes,' Bernie retorted with a twinkle in her eye. 'But she had a massive crush on our Paul. She must have thought that she'd died and gone to heaven when she saw the two of you in the bar: a weekend away from home with both her greatest hero *and* the man of her dreams! She must have felt really sick at breakfast the next day when she realised that this middle-aged scouse imposter was muscling in on the act and cramping her style.'

'At least she probably had a proper night's sleep,' Jonah commented, 'which is more than you were able to get.'

****

The alarm went off and Bernie rolled sleepily out of bed to move Jonah into a different sleeping position. As soon as she touched the bottom sheet, she realised that there was something wrong.

'Jonah?' she spoke softly, gently taking him by the

shoulder and rolling him over to face her. 'I'm afraid you seem to have a leak in your plumbing. The bed's wet. We'll have to give you a complete change.' She switched on the light and they blinked at each other as their eyes adjusted to the glare.

Bernie stood for a minute, thinking. Jonah had spare pyjamas in his suitcase, brought against just such an eventuality as this, but they did not have any fresh sheets for the bed and it would be unreasonable to seek out hotel staff at this hour to ask for supplies. The only solution was to move Jonah into her own bed. She could sleep in the armchair or lay out the abundant supply of cushions and pillows to form a makeshift mattress on the floor.

Calmly she set to work. She went to the wardrobe and got out their suitcase. She opened it and selected a plastic sheet, which she spread out on her bed, having first drawn back the covers. She covered this with a large bath towel.

Then she turned her attention to Jonah. She carefully peeled off his sodden pyjamas and inspected the length of plastic tubing that connected him to the urine bag attached to the bed. As she had suspected, the sheath had come off his penis, allowing urine to flow on to the bed. She looked closely at his skin. There were red patches, which felt hot to the touch.

'Right,' she said, speaking softly so as not to disturb guests in neighbouring rooms. 'I'm going to roll you on to my bed and sponge you down. Then we'd better put on some more moisturiser as well. Margaret will have my guts for garters if I send you home with ulcers on your backside.'

She pushed the bed up against Jonah's to enable her to roll him carefully on to the towel. He lay patiently as she washed him all over and patted his skin dry with a soft towel.

'You're very good to me, Bernie,' he remarked, as she gently massaged moisturiser over his buttocks. 'There aren't many people who'd do this for me in the middle of the night without even complaining.'

'If I didn't love you so much,' Bernie replied gruffly, moving without a pause to apply the soothing ointment to the inflamed skin on his thighs. 'That might indicate some sort of virtue on my part. As it is, I'm only doing what comes naturally.'

Jonah digested that statement in silence. Although Bernie had spoken in a matter-of-fact way, he somehow knew instinctively that she meant what she said. What she was doing was truly an act of love and not a duty. He suddenly felt a tremendous sense of loss that he could not take her in his arms and hug her, in thanks for her kindness, but also to show that he loved her too.

A few minutes later Bernie stood up and stretched. 'I think you'll do. Now let's get you back off to sleep.'

She gently lifted him off the towel and removed towel and plastic sheet from the bed, making sure that the bottom bed sheet was stretched smoothly over the bed to avoid wrinkles pressing on his skin. She re-connected the urine bag, taking care that the sheath was firmly attached this time. Then she dressed him in fresh pyjamas, settled him into a comfortable sleeping position lying on his left side and pulled the bedclothes up around him.

'What about you?' he asked. 'Where are you going to sleep?'

'I'll make up a bed on the floor. These hotels always leave loads of cushions lying around.'

'Don't be ridiculous!' Jonah said scornfully. 'We can't have you sleeping on the floor.'

'OK. I'll snuggle down in a blanket on the armchair then, if it's so important to you.'

'Look,' Jonah insisted. 'I need you to be fresh and ready for anything tomorrow, which you won't be if you don't get as much sleep as you can in the limited amount of night that we have left. The bed's plenty big enough for two. Just move me a bit closer to the edge and get in behind.' Bernie looked doubtful. 'Go on – what're you waiting for? You can't be worried that I'll ravish you in the night!'

Bernie gave in. It would do neither of them any good to prolong the argument. Jonah was quite right that what they both needed was to get back to sleep as soon as possible. She gently moved him over and got in next to him, lying on her right side so that they were back to back. She felt the warmth from his body and realised for the first time how cold she had become through being out of bed for so long in only her pyjamas.

Jonah felt the bedclothes move against his neck as Bernie drew them over her shoulders, and became aware of the soft rhythm of her breathing as she settled down to sleep. He knew that she was close to him – that probably they were actually touching, but he could not feel her back against his. All of a sudden, the awfulness of his situation felt overwhelming. It was quite unlike him to feel self-pity, but now a deep sense of loss came over him. He was completely dependent on friends like Bernie, who had to put up with broken nights and unpleasant – almost sordid – tasks. And now, here she was in his bed and he could not even feel her back against his.

He fiercely blinked back the tears, which he was unable to prevent coming to his eyes. He *must* not give in to emotion. Bernie *must* not know how he was feeling. However, it was no good. The tears would not stop and soon his body was shaking with silent sobs.

Bernie felt the movement. For a moment or two, she was sure she must be mistaken. Jonah was so strong. He never showed resentment at his situation. He never entertained bitterness or self-pity. But what else could be producing that shuddering in his upper body, those stifled gasps as he drew air into his lungs through his mouth? She turned over and put her right arm round him. She nestled her face up to his shoulder. She felt around to find his left hand and took hold of the three functioning fingers, squeezing them gently and receiving an answering squeeze in return. The sobbing paused briefly, then resumed.

Bernie frantically tried to think of something to say. But what was there to say? That she understood how he felt? But of course, she did not – nobody could. That his friends would stick by him however bad things became? But he knew that anyway – that might well be part of the problem. So she just hugged him tightly to her, kissed his neck and waited until the sobs died away and he lay still at last.

Bernie gently removed her hand from Jonah's and got out of bed. She found a box of tissues and, standing at Jonah's side of the bed, carefully dried his eyes and helped him to blow his nose. He smiled his thanks, not trusting himself to speak.

Bernie bent over him and put her face close to his. For a moment, Jonah thought that she was going to kiss him, but she just whispered softly, but fiercely, 'remember what I said before: never, ever, for one minute, think that you are a burden.'

****

Peter and Bernie cleared the plates away and Sylvia brought out from the oven a steaming jam roll, which she served to everyone. Peter passed round a large jug of custard for them to help themselves.

'For some weird masochistic reason of her own,' Jonah said to Bethan, 'Bernie failed to be put off by that experience and it even seemed to spur her on to volunteer to take me on full time.'

****

Jonah woke the following morning to the sound of Bernie 'making a brew'. He opened his eyes, but his view was restricted to the small part of the room directly in front of him. He lay there wondering whether to call out to Bernie to let her know that he was awake or to wait until she came to help him up. The kettle boiled and he heard her pouring the tea. Then she came over to him and was about to touch him on the shoulder to waken him when she realised that his eyes were already open.

'That was quite a night!' she observed brightly. 'Are you ready for a warm drink to get your bowels into gear?'

She lifted him into a sitting position and propped him up with pillows. Then she fetched the plastic cup and looked around for a suitable place to put it for him to drink. Unlike at home, or in the room at Bernie's house that Jonah used on occasions when he came to stay, there was no secure place where the cup could be placed within reach. Bernie shrugged her shoulders and climbed on to the bed next to Jonah. She held the cup on her lap and offered him the straw. He took a draft then stopped and looked at her.

'Bernie,' he said, 'It's silly really I know, but I do miss being able to drink tea from a proper china cup. The straw is great, because it makes me independent, but it would be nice, just once in a while … I wouldn't ask normally, but if you're going to be sitting there holding it anyway, d'you think you could …?'

'Of course.' Bernie got up and transferred the tea into a mug. 'Not proper bone china, but better than plastic,' she observed.

She got back on the bed and they sat together companionably as she held the cup up to his lips to allow him to take sips.

'I'm sorry about last night,' Jonah said. 'I mean about the maudlin self-pity. I don't know what got into me – over tired I suppose.'

Bernie resisted the impulse to say something kind, realising in time that sympathy might well make them both become emotional again.

'My dear Jonah,' she said, adopting a tone of admonishment. 'Have you any idea how arrogant that sounds? Or how inadequate it makes us ordinary mortals feel to hear you apologising for failing to live up to your own superhuman standards by falling infinitesimally short of total perfection.'

Jonah laughed. 'Oh Bernie! You are very good for me. Anyone else would have told me how terrifically brave I am and how completely they understand what I'm going through. I should have known better than to try to fish for compliments from you.'

'Absolutely! Surely you knew I don't do sycophancy.'

'Well you can't blame me for trying.'

'I think I probably could, but I have a very forgiving nature.'

'Of course I ought to have realised that, while you may happily massage my bum, you would never massage my ego.'

'An ego the size of yours can well do without any encouragement from me.'

They collapsed into helpless laughter, which lasted for several minutes until Bernie looked at her watch and declared that it was time to get up.

'I've been thinking,' Bernie said, as she worked methodically through the early morning routine of preparing Jonah for the day ahead.

'Sounds dangerous,' Jonah commented flippantly. 'Have you done a risk assessment?'

'I'll be fifty-five this summer,' Bernie continued, ignoring him.

'I know – me too. And several people have been keen to remind me that many police officers retire at that age.'

'What sort of people?'

'The boys, for a start. Only the other day, Nathan was saying that he understood why I wanted to go back to work after my injury, but surely I'd made my point now and it was time to take it easy.'

'I take it you're not planning to follow his advice.'

'Certainly not! There's a lot of life left in the old dog yet. But I interrupted you – what was it you'd been thinking?'

'I've been thinking that I'm not sure that I want to see any more spotty students, each cohort coming up to

Oxford knowing less than the year before. So I was thinking about retirement. It certainly seems to suit Peter, but he's very happily settled into his house-husband role and I can see he's not keen on having me under his feet at home all day, so I was wondering … I hoped that maybe you might consider taking me on as your carer: while you're at work, I mean.'

Jonah did not answer, so she went on. 'Then you wouldn't keep getting different people from the agency and having to teach them what you need. I could take the same leave as you and work the same overtime. Of course the down side is that you'd have to put up with-'

'I think that would be great,' Jonah interrupted. 'But are you sure? You really would like to do it – for yourself, I mean, not just for me?'

'Honestly – I'd love it. It's fascinating to see you at work and, surprising as it may sound, I actually enjoy looking after your bodily needs.'

'Well, let's see if you still feel the same after you've had that pleasure for the rest of this weekend. You may find that the experience palls.'

****

'That was delicious!' Bethan declared as she finished her jam roll.

Peter and Bernie gathered in the dessert bowls and piled them next to the sink.

'Come along, Bethan,' Jonah commanded, leading the way from the room. 'At least I have the perfect excuse not to help with the washing up. We'll adjourn to the living room and I'll do my best to give you the rest of the information you need for your programme. I'm afraid we've been rather wasting your time with digressions.'

'Not at all,' Bethan assured him, as she followed his lead into a large, airy room at the back of the house. There was a long settee and an assortment of easy chairs arranged so that they had a view out through French windows over an extensive garden.

'The producer will be delighted to have so much material to choose from. Just so long as you understand that he'll be quite selective with what goes in – based on what will be most interesting to the viewers.'

'And what is suitable as a topic for discussion in the Sunday afternoon religious spot.' Jonah suggested. 'Not too much of the nitty-gritty of life with a spinal injury that might not be pleasant viewing for those who are enjoying their afternoon tea while watching!'

'Yes – we will have to bear that in mind. But to get back to business: you were telling me about the first case that Bernie helped you with. Did you find the killer in the end?'

'Yes, but for those of us involved that wasn't the only important thing that came out of that weekend.'

****

'Right, let's get going,' Jonah said, as the four of them assembled in the carpark outside the hotel. 'It'll be easier if we just take my car, so I suggest that Bernie drives and Paul sits in the front to give her directions. Karen, are you alright to come in the back with me?'

'Yes, of course.' Karen answered. She was unsure whether she was more pleased with the prospect of being placed in such close proximity to this heroic figure, who was so revered among her colleagues (especially the female ones), or annoyed at not having been given the chance of going alone with Paul in his car. She decided to make the most of the situation as it had turned out and resolved to be an indispensable assistant to the Great Man.

'It's all a bit remote,' Paul was saying, as they prepared to leave. 'So we've got a portable incident room set up near where the body was found. The girl's parents have agreed to come in at about eleven to answer some more questions. If we get off there now, we can have a good look round the site before they arrive.'

'OK, just tell me where to go,' Bernie said, tucking in a thick rug around Jonah's knees before climbing out of the back of the car and into the driver's seat.

'Now Karen,' Jonah said kindly, 'It is alright for me to call you Karen?' Karen nodded eagerly. 'Now Karen, Paul tells me that you are a bit of an expert on this area and the people who live here. He's told me the basic facts of the case, but d'you think you could go through it again, in your own words, filling me in a bit on the background and who everyone is?' Karen nodded again. 'The girl's parents, for example – what do they do?'

'Her parents are Robert and Daphne Ellis,' Karen said, marshalling her thoughts quickly, determined to give a good impression. 'He works at the local auction mart, selling cattle and sheep and so on. They live on a farm out in the hills. Their land straddles the border, but the house is in England. Alice's body was found about three miles away, as the crow flies, in a wood also just on the English side of the border.'

'I can see it's a good thing we've brought a native with us,' Jonah commented. 'In case we have to cross into Wales in hot pursuit of a suspect! We may need an interpreter.'

Karen was about to explain that the Welsh language was not much spoken in this particular region, but she realised in time that this was a joke and continued to outline the case.

'Daphne – the mother – runs the farm as a horse-riding establishment, in partnership with an old school friend of hers, Sandra Parry. Alice used to help out there at weekends. Apparently, she was very popular with other girls at school, because she was able to get them free rides and the opportunity to groom and muck out the horses.

'She went missing just over a week ago – last Friday night. She goes to school in Oswestry and normally comes back on the school bus, which drops her at the end of the lane that their farm is in. She told her parents that she wouldn't be coming home that afternoon, because she was going to the cinema with some friends, and that one of their parents would drop her off at about ten p.m.

'When she wasn't back by half past ten, Mrs Ellis started ringing round all of Alice's friends, but they all denied having gone to the pictures with her. So then, they contacted the police. The following Monday, when she was still missing, one of her friends admitted that she had told her that she was meeting a boy that she'd made friends with on the internet. Apparently, he was planning to come from his school in Shrewsbury on the bus and they were to meet at the bus station.

'We've got CC TV footage of her waiting at the bus station and speaking to a woman there. At about half past four she goes off with the woman and we don't have any further sightings of either of them. We also don't know who the woman is. The pictures are very unclear and neither her parents nor her friends recognise the woman or have any idea who she might be. The best description we can come up with is that she's about the same height as Alice – so five foot six – and with curly blonde hair. She was wearing a long dark-coloured coat, but that's not surprising at this time of year. Her face was turned away from the camera for the whole time, so identifying her is going to be difficult and it also means that we don't have any idea of her age. She definitely looked like an adult, though – not a teenager. We put out an appeal for people to come forward if they saw Alice or the woman after they left the bus station, but we haven't had any response.'

'Thank you, that's all very clear. Now: what about the body?'

'That was found on Wednesday afternoon. Sandra Parry was exercising one of the horses and she took her red setter with them. The dog found the body, buried in a pile of leaves, about twenty yards from the bridle path. Sandra recognised her and immediately contacted us. She'd been strangled and also had some bruising to her face and arms.'

'The pathologist has agreed to meet us at ten,' Paul

informed them. '"So she'll be able to fill you in on the details of the post mortem.'

'Now, tell me more about the family,' Jonah said to Karen. 'Alice was an only child, I gather. How did she get on with her parents?'

'As far as we know, very well. Her friends all seemed to think that Alice had less trouble with her parents than most of them did. And her parents claim that she was no more difficult than any teenage girl. They were adamant that she'd never deceived them before and that she was usually totally reliable about coming home on time. Sandra Parry confirmed that they got on well and that there hadn't been any rows recently.'

'And did Alice have a boyfriend at all?'

'Not that anyone knew about – except this unknown one from Shrewsbury. We've got her computer and some of the internet crime experts are going through it to see if they can find out anything about the boy from that.'

'So it does fit in with the same pattern as our Didcot murders,' Jonah said. 'Except that, this time, we know that she was approached by a woman. Presumably it couldn't have been a man dressed as a woman?'

'It certainly didn't look like one.' Paul answered, 'but I suppose it wouldn't be impossible.'

They arrived at the incident room, where they were greeted by two uniformed police officers. Paul declined their offer to accompany them to the place where the body had been found. When she saw the state of the bridle path that they would have to follow, Bernie asked for Paul's help to transfer Jonah into the all-terrain wheelchair, which she brought out from a storage cabinet in the back of the car. Paul watched as she assembled it with care, noting mentally that she was clearly very familiar with this task.

'One, two, three – lift!' and the transfer was completed. They set off down the muddy track, Jonah shamelessly showing off by racing ahead, making the others break into a jog to keep up.

'I keep intending to get the engineers to put a governor in that thing,' Bernie panted. 'It's not safe to drive it at this pace.'

'Not very dignified for the likes of us bringing up the rear, either,' agreed Paul, with a grin. 'I take back everything I said last night about what a tragedy it is that Jonah isn't active anymore.'

'Of course,' Bernie said, deliberately speaking loudly enough that Jonah would hear, 'if he could be trusted to behave sensibly, there would be no *need* to restrict its speed. But he always goes off like a dog that's just been let off the lead when he gets in that buggy.'

****

Jonah and Bethan were soon joined by the rest of the party. Bernie came in carrying the inevitable tray containing teapot and mugs. Sylvia and Stan briefly made their excuses and left for their own home. The others sat down and started passing round mugs of steaming tea.

'Where are you up to?' Lucy demanded.

'Just viewing the scene of crime,' Jonah answered. 'Not that it told us much; nor did the pathologist's evidence or the girl's parents. It all just confirmed that the killer was in all probability the same as the one that had lured away and strangled four other girls: three in the Didcot area and one in Worcester. The real breakthrough came that afternoon when a fourteen-year-old and her father turned up at the police station in Shrewsbury with a story about another internet friendship that had culminated in a plan for the protagonists to meet.

'This girl – Jo, I think her name was – had got to know a boy online. She showed us a photo, which we eventually traced to a completely blameless lad in Minnesota who had uploaded his picture to Facebook with no intention of it being copied and used to trick girls into thinking they were talking to someone their own age.

'Anyway, she'd arranged to meet "Kevin" after school in Shrewsbury town centre, but he didn't turn up. Instead a woman arrived, who said that she was his mother and that Kevin had been involved in an accident and been taken to hospital. She said he'd asked her to come to tell Jo that he couldn't make it. Jo asked if she could go to see Kevin in hospital, but the woman said it would be better if she went home now and they'd be in touch later and she could visit once he was back home. Then the woman went off and that was the last Jo heard from either her or Kevin.'

****

'If *I* was a teenager in love,' Karen Evans said, as they sat in Jonah's hotel room after supper that evening, discussing the incident in Shrewsbury, 'I don't think I'd have been so easily put off. I'd probably have *insisted* on going to the hospital.'

'What are you saying?' Paul asked. 'Are you suggesting that you don't believe what Jo told us?'

'No. I just don't think that her behaviour was necessarily typical of a girl of her age in that situation. And maybe …' Karen thought for a moment. 'Maybe, her reaction wasn't what they were expecting. Think about it: you're intent on abducting a fit and healthy teenage girl. You've arranged to meet her in a public place where you know there are lots of CC TV cameras about and plenty of witnesses who might report it if you were seen taking her away against her will. So, you think up a story that will make *her* the one asking *you* to take her away. It's a question of psychology.'

'I like it.' Jonah said, causing Karen to blush with pride. 'You're suggesting that this *is* the same woman as approached Alice – the height and build were the same and her hair may well have been a wig in one or both cases – and that she could have spun a similar tale to Alice, who then went off with her, not merely willingly but positively *demanding* to be taken.'

'That's right,' Karen agreed. 'They miscalculated with Jo. Maybe the woman overdid the act of reluctance to take her to see the boy, or maybe Jo had enough sense not to get completely caught up in the drama of the moment and realised that it wasn't a particularly bright idea to go off with a total stranger, or-'

'And then she heard nothing from the mythical Kevin after that,' Jonah put in excitedly, 'because they decided to ditch her, rather than having another go at luring her away.'

'They?' queried Paul.

'I think that we probably have a man and a woman working together,' Jonah explained. 'This woman and the man who walked past our girl in Didcot. Perhaps he lives down there and the woman lives up here.'

'And they meet up for a bit of recreational strangulation?' ask Bernie. 'Or do you think they each kill their own victims and then boast about it to one another?'

'Or it could be like you said in the first place,' suggested Paul, 'a copycat murder. And then there's my original dead girl in Worcester. Is that also part of the same conspiracy or not?'

'I think it would probably have taken two people to strangle the girls,' Jonah said. 'I don't know about your Worcester girl, but the pathologist here said that Alice's bruises on her arms were consistent with her having been restrained by someone gripping her with their hands, but not with having been tied up. I don't see how one person could hold her arms and strangle her at the same time, and once they let go of her to apply the ligature, what's to stop her running away?'

Bernie caught Paul's eye and looked meaningfully at her watch.

'Well!' Paul said, getting up. 'I think it's time we wrapped up for the night. We'll all think better when we're fresh in the morning. I'm off to my room now. Let's reconvene after breakfast tomorrow.'

'OK.' Karen got up obediently and followed him out of the room and up to the first floor.

An hour or so later, Bernie also made her way upstairs.

She knocked at the door of room 114, which Paul had left on the latch, and then went in. As on the previous night, he was sitting up in bed. Bernie sat down on a chair next to him.

'Once upon a time,' she began, 'there was a Detective Constable by the name of Peter Johns who fell in love with a beautiful Jamaican nurse called Angie Wheeler. By great good fortune, she fell in love with him too and, in due course, they were married and had two children. Their long and happy marriage was marred only by the presence of Angie's best friend Bernadette, who constantly turned up like the proverbial bad penny to disrupt their lives.

'After nearly twenty-five years of wedded bliss, Peter's life was shattered when Angie was stabbed to death in her own kitchen. For six long years, he lived with the pain of not knowing who had done the dreadful deed. He moved away so that he wouldn't keep meeting the friends and neighbours with whom they had associated. This was because he could never be sure that any one of them might not be the murderer of his beloved wife. And he moved in with his wife's best friend who believed that she owed it to Angie to look after him, and whose daughter saw him as a father figure.

'Two years later they married and were very happy together, although they both knew that it would never be the same as when Angie was alive. And still Peter bore the pain of not knowing and of suspecting everyone and of blaming himself.'

Bernie paused dramatically before continuing with the story.

'But, in the fullness of time, this dread spell was broken by DCI Jonah Porter, who, while on enforced sick leave following having been shot in the neck, reopened the enquiry into Angie's murder and uncovered the perpetrators of the dreadful deed and brought them to justice. And so DI Johns was able once again to walk the streets of the neighbourhood where he and Angie had been so happy and to make friends again with their old neighbours and hold his head up high knowing that there was nothing that he could have done to prevent the attack.

'And, ever after, he was aware that he owed a great debt of gratitude to the man who had at last given him peace of mind. And he made it his business to learn, and encouraged his wife and daughter also to learn, everything that was needful to care for Jonah so that this duty might not fall solely on Jonah's wife, Margaret. And they all became as one big happy family from that day forth.'

She got up to go. 'So there you have it. Now snuggle down and I'll tuck you in.'

Paul obediently lay back and allowed Bernie to pull the covers over him. 'I think I understand,' he said.

'Good.' Bernie kissed him on the cheek and went out, almost bumping into Karen, who was loitering in the corridor outside. Bernie closed the door quietly and the two eyed each other. Bernie resisted the temptation to say, 'It's not what you think!' well aware that this would only confirm in Karen's mind that it was exactly what she thought.

'Were you wanting to speak to Paul?' she asked eventually. 'He's all ready for bed, but I'm sure he wouldn't mind, if it's something important.'

'No,' Karen answered. 'I was just on my way to my room.' She indicated the room next door.

'Oh! I see. I hadn't realised you were so close – I mean that your rooms were so close.'

'Evidently,' Karen said coldly.

'Oh Karen!' Bernie sighed, trying to think of a way of defusing the situation. 'My late husband was a Detective Superintendent,' she went on at last. 'He used to say that a good imagination was an essential quality for a detective. He also used to say that it was important that hypotheses that were arrived at through the exercise of imagination were thoroughly tested and only accepted if there was cast iron evidence.'

Karen looked puzzled. 'What are you getting at?' she asked.

Bernie raised her eyes to the ceiling and gave another sigh. 'Do I have to spell it out? Look. Read My Lips. I am not, I have not and I never will be, having it off with Paul Godwin. Is that clear enough for you? We've known each other for a long time and we've been talking about old times. That's all.'

'Oh. I see.' Karen looked uncomfortable. 'Good night then.' She turned to unlock the door of her own room.

'Karen,' Bernie called softly. Karen looked up. 'My late husband also used to say that it was a big mistake to have a relationship with someone at work.'

Karen looked sulky. She was about to tell Bernie to mind her own business when Bernie went on. 'But, since he remained a frustrated bachelor until he was fifty-seven, I wouldn't take his advice on affairs of the heart seriously if I were you.' She gave Karen a kindly smile. 'Good night. Sleep well.'

Bernie walked off towards the stairs. Karen stood looking after her for a few moments, uncertain what Bernie was trying to convey, before shrugging her shoulders and going into her room.

****

'To cut a long story short,' Jonah said to Bethan, 'which I'm sure you will be grateful for, the following day several missing pieces of the jig-saw turned up and the whole picture started to slot into place. We got confirmation from the team that was working on checking out the internet chat room where the girl Jo had met "Kevin" that it was the same place that Alice had started communicating with a boy called Angus; and it was also the place where the surviving girl from Didcot had found a boy called Marcus.

'A witness came forward who had seen Alice getting into a car with a woman in her forties and CCTV in the car park gave us the number. It was registered to a man from

Chipping Norton who worked as a software developer in Didcot. I got on to the team back in Thames Valley to check him out and Bernie and I got ready to return home. I was pretty pleased with myself. It was a good weekend's work, taking me from a total blank to the expectation that in a day or two we would be in a position to make an arrest.'

****

Bernie parked the car on the drive outside Jonah's house and went round to the back to help him out. He looked at her, bleary eyed from having fallen asleep during the journey.

'Margaret's bike's not here, so she can't be home yet,' she told him, peering under the canopy that sheltered Margaret's motorbike from the weather whenever it was parked at home. They had received a text message that morning letting them know that she had been called into work because of a major incident. The radio news had confirmed that there had been a serious accident on the M4, involving a coachload of elderly people on a day trip to Bath.

'You look all in,' Bernie said to Jonah, as she undid the straps securing his wheelchair so that he could descend from the car. 'I think a nap would be in order, while we wait for Margaret to get back.'

Jonah pulled a face. 'I'm fine. I've just had a nap in the car.'

'It's not the same.' Bernie frowned. 'I'm responsible for your welfare this weekend. Margaret won't lend you to me again if I don't return you in perfect condition.'

Jonah steered his chair down the ramp and towards the front door. Bernie followed him.

'Look Jonah,' she continued to argue. 'Margaret's been there in the hospital since this morning, saving lives. When she gets back after a long day, the last thing she'll need is to find a husband who's tired out. You owe it to her to get a good rest, so that you can support her when she gets home. Goodness knows what sorts of things she's been dealing with today.'

Jonah sighed dramatically. 'I hate it when you're right!' he declared.

'You ought to be used to it by now. Have you still not realised that I am *always* right?'

Some two and a half hours later, Margaret returned. She saw the car on the drive and hurried inside to relieve Bernie of her charge. The sitting room and kitchen were empty and the house was surprisingly quiet. She eventually tracked Bernie down in the utility room where she was emptying the washing machine.

'Bernie! You shouldn't be doing our washing.'

Bernie looked up. Today Margaret's hair was bright purple, as were her corduroy trousers. Her blouse was a lighter shade of the same colour and she had a silk scarf in a purple Paisley pattern around her neck.

'Wow!' Bernie said admiringly. 'When I am an old woman, I shall wear purple.'

Margaret looked puzzled.

'Sorry. It's a poem. "When I am an old woman, I shall wear purple, with a red hat that doesn't go, and doesn't suit me." We did it at school. It's about growing old disgracefully.'

'I'll bear it in mind if I ever get to be old.'

'About the washing,' Bernie smiled apologetically, 'We had a bit of an accident overnight and I didn't want to leave Jonah's pyjamas any longer, so I just popped them into the machine while we were waiting for you to get back. Oh! And you ought to know about the other consequence of Jonah's wet bed. I have to confess that it ended up with both of us sharing mine.'

'Obviously the only option available,' Margaret said mildly.

'On Friday night, yes,' Bernie agreed, 'but I wasn't quite so sure about the fact that, despite the hotel having very kindly provided clean sheets, we adopted the same arrangement last night as well.'

'It was a very cold night,' Margaret continued to be unperturbed, 'and it was probably even colder in rural Shropshire, so I think snuggling together for warmth was completely in order.'

'Now there's an idea!' Bernie laughed. 'We never thought of anything so eminently reasonable. Our excuse was saving the planet by leaving clean sheets on one bed to reduce the amount of laundry that our stay created. Jonah seemed to think that was a matter of principle with me, after something I said to him once.'

'And where *is* his nibs? I thought he'd be waiting to tell me all about how his old protégé is getting on up there in West Mercia.'

'He's in bed. All the rushing about, not to mention the excitement of making a breakthrough on this case that's been worrying him for weeks, really took it out of him. I managed to persuade him to have a rest, but I promised faithfully to wake him as soon as you got back.'

'Jonah? In bed? During the daytime?' Margaret opened her eyes wide in exaggerated amazement. 'How did you do it? You're a better man than I am to have pulled that one off!'

'I told him that it was his duty to get himself into a fit state to welcome you home properly after a hard day in theatre. How has it been, by the way?'

'Pretty gruelling,' Margaret admitted. 'But at least we were kept too busy to think about it too much. There are going to be a lot of families coming to terms with life-changing injuries over the next few weeks I'm afraid.'

'You go and put your feet up,' Bernie said solicitously. 'I'll go and get Jonah up and then we can all have a brew.'

'Can't you let him sleep on? It seems a pity to wake him if he's settled."

Bernie shook her head. 'I promised I'd get him up when you got back. But,' she went on seeing Margaret's tired expression. 'I'm sure that you couldn't be considered to be properly back until after I've made you a nice cup of tea to help you relax.'

They went into the kitchen and Bernie put the kettle on. Margaret sat down at the table. She looked exhausted.

'I can't say how grateful I am for you taking care of Jonah this weekend.' She said. 'He'd have been like a bear with a sore head if he hadn't been able to go.'

'Honestly, I really enjoyed it.' Bernie assured her. 'Actually, that was something I wanted to talk to you about. I know Jonah's planning to tell you, but I'd like you to hear it from me first so you know that it was my idea. We've hatched a plan for me to take him on full-time – while he's at work, I mean. I'm going to take early retirement at the end of Trinity Term and then I'll be free to become Jonah's personal assistant, or whatever you like to call it.'

'I think that's a wonderful idea!' Margaret's face lit up. 'But you must be paid – we can't let you do it for nothing.'

'Of course not. I'd expect the same as his professional carers are getting now – to supplement my pension.'

Bernie poured the tea and set a mug in front of Margaret. 'Now, drink this up while I go and keep my promise to Jonah to wake him up.'

'Thank you, Bernie.' Margaret called after her, as she walked towards the door. 'You've taken a big weight off my mind. It's so good to know that there's someone else who really understands Jonah and cares about him. I know I won't always be there for him.'

An hour or so later, Bernie pondered this statement as she drove home. It gave her a disturbing feeling in the pit of her stomach. Of course, Margaret often was not there to give Jonah the assistance that he needed for daily living. She had a demanding job, which they had both agreed she should not give up for his benefit. But surely a more natural form of words would have been 'I *can't* always be there for him' or 'I'm not always there for him'. 'I *won't* always be there for him' was more like what the parents of a disabled child might say when expressing concern about the likelihood that their offspring would outlive them. Bernie told herself severely that she was in all likelihood reading far too much into what was probably just a chance choice of words, but somehow she could not eradicate the grim surmise that had taken hold of her mind.

****

All praise to our redeeming Lord,
Who joins us by His grace;
And bids us, each to each restored,
Together seek His face.

He bids us build each other up;
And, gathered into one,
To our high calling's glorious hope,
We hand in hand go on.

The gift which He on one bestows,
We all delight to prove;
The grace through every vessel flows,
In purest streams of love.

E'en now we think and speak the same,
And cordially agree;
Concentered all, through Jesus' Name,
In perfect harmony.

We all partake the joy of one;
The common peace we feel;
A peace to sensual minds unknown,
A joy unspeakable.

231

And if our fellowship below
In Jesus be so sweet,
What height of rapture shall we know
When round His throne we meet!

Charles Wesley (1707-1788)

8 ABIDE WITH ME

'I, meanwhile, remained in blissful ignorance that there was anything wrong,' Jonah said, taking up the narrative. 'Margaret seemed rather drained, but I put that down to her having had a long and stressful day. And she seemed perhaps disproportionately pleased about the idea of Bernie giving up work and becoming my main daytime carer. Looking back, the conversation that we had in bed that night is a bit surreal.'

****

'Margaret?'

'Mmm?' Margaret murmured, resting her head against Jonah's shoulder as they lay next to one another.

'Bernie's thinking of taking early retirement in the summer.'

'Yes – she mentioned it to me.'

'We were thinking that then she could take on the job of being my support while I'm at work. She seems to think that it wouldn't be totally unbearable for her, and she'd certainly be more reliable than some of the people I've had recently. We haven't made any definite plans – I wanted to know what you think about it.'

'I think it's a great idea.'

They lay together in companionable silence for a few minutes.

'I think you ought to know,' Jonah said tentatively, 'that Bernie says she loves me.'

'I know she does.' Margaret sounded completely unsurprised. 'Didn't you?'

'I suppose I'd never really thought about it.'

'I would have thought it was obvious, but then I did have an advantage.'

'What's that then?'

'She told me. It was years ago, when you were still in hospital after the shooting. I thanked her for bringing Lucy to see you so often and she said – I remember the exact words – she said, "'I think you ought to be aware that Lucy and I are both totally in love with your husband.'"

'And what did you say?'

'I told her that, if she wasn't worried about this clear confirmation of hereditary madness in her family, I wasn't bothered either. We had a long chat about it and in the end we agreed to share you.'

'Share me? Like a bag of humbugs?'

'That's right – only we both hoped that you'd last a bit longer than they usually do.'

'I see. I'm not sure I'm keen on the idea of you treating me like – well like a commodity. I might not want to be shared round to all your friends.'

'You ought to be flattered to have women queuing up to get a part of you.'

Margaret put her arm round Jonah's shoulders and gave him a hug.

'What did you say to Bernie – when she told you?'

'Nothing much. She was rubbing moisturiser into my backside at the time, so I wasn't really in a good position to make conversation.'

'Presumably you did at least let her know that her feelings were reciprocated?'

'Well – no. I didn't quite like to say that. After all, I

promised to forsake all others when I married you, didn't I?' Jonah, usually completely self-assured, was feeling unusually discomfited.

'That doesn't mean you can't love members of your family. Bernie's family now. I think you ought to tell her.'

'Tell her I love her? Just like that?'

'Yes. Why not ring her tomorrow? You ought to thank her for going to Shropshire with you and you can sort out the business of her taking early retirement and becoming your right-hand woman. Then you could easily just throw it into the conversation. I mean – you do love her, don't you? And Peter and Lucy too – after all they've done for you, I mean for us? They *are* all family, aren't they? And I think Bernie would like to hear you say it.'

'Alright, I'll think about it.'

****

'At the time,' Jonah admitted, 'it all seemed quite bizarre. I couldn't work out why Margaret was suddenly so keen for me to declare love to another woman. But, looking back, I can see that it was all part of preparing me for losing her. I think she wanted me to realise that my life didn't have to revolve around her – that there were other people who could supply, not just my physical needs, but my emotional ones as well.

'I don't know whether this was a deliberate strategy on her part, or if she just said those things because in her own mind she was starting to imagine what it was going to be like for me when she was gone. But of course, that night I had no idea of the bombshell that was about to drop and shatter my life as I knew it.'

****

The phone rang in Bernie's college room. She shooed out her final tutorial pair of the morning and answered it. It was Jonah.

'I told Margaret about the plan for you to become my PA and she's all for it.'

'Good. I've written my letter of resignation. I'll drop it

in the Principal's pigeonhole on my way out today.'

'I'll talk to the Super about arrangements for you supporting me at work – you'll have to be vetted, since you'll have access to confidential information and police premises.'

They talked for some minutes about practicalities. Then the conversation stalled.

'Er …,' Jonah said hesitantly.

Bernie waited. It was unusual for Jonah to be lost for words.

'Bernie?'

'Yes?'

'Margaret said I ought to tell you …'

'Tell me what?' Bernie was instantly alert. Her heart started beating faster. All her worries of the evening before flooded back. Had Margaret broken some devastatingly bad news to Jonah after she had returned home – the news that she had started to suspect, following Margaret's cryptic remark the previous evening?

'Has something happened? Is she alright?'

'Yes, of course. What're you talking about?'

'Nothing. Sorry. Go on – I interrupted you.'

'We wanted you to know – that is I wanted to say,' Jonah struggled to force the words out, wishing he had never started this conversation. 'I love you, Bernie,' he muttered eventually.

There was a long silence. Jonah began to think that Bernie must have rung off. Then, at last, she spoke, in a strange, husky voice, very hesitant.

'Jonah?'

'Yes? Are you OK?'

'Yes, of course.'

There was another pause.

'Jonah? Are you at home?'

'Yes. Margaret's off duty today, after being on call all weekend, and I had some time owing, so we're having a lazy day at home.'

'Do you think I could come over?'

'Yes, of course. We'd love to see you.'

'Thanks. See you about two – and Jonah?'

'Yes?'

'I love you too.'

Bernie put the phone down and sat looking into space. Why had Jonah rung? Or, more to the point, why had Margaret instigated the call? Bernie felt more and more certain that something was wrong – something that Margaret had not yet told Jonah. Had she been there just now, in the room with Jonah, listening to their conversation? What would she have made of Jonah's diffident declaration and Bernie's stumbling response?

A new and terrible thought occurred to Bernie. Could it be that Margaret was planning to leave Jonah? Was *that* what she meant when she said that she would not always be there for him? Had caring for a severely disabled husband become just too much for her? Had she found someone else who could give her those things that Jonah could longer give? Surely not!

Nevertheless, it would all fit. An adulterous wife might well find it comforting to hear her husband declaring love for another woman – it would make her own infidelity seem less contemptible. Moreover, a wife who wanted to leave her husband with minimal hurt to him might take steps to ensure that he was surrounded by friends who would support him. But Margaret wasn't like that – was she?

Bernie pushed the thought to the back of her mind. She knew Margaret. Margaret would not do that. It was unworthy of her to think it. She went over to the small refrigerator in the corner of the room and got out the sandwiches that she had brought for her lunch. She ate them mechanically, threw the plastic bag away in the bin and set off for the Porters' house. More than anything else, she wanted to see Jonah face to face, to hold him in her arms, to comfort him if comfort were needed.

237

'Come in!' Jonah greeted her cheerily. 'Margaret will be back shortly. She had an appointment with the GP – just a routine screening test of some sort she said.'

'Oh! Right.' Bernie's mind and heart both raced at hearing this news. It sounded as if her initial suspicion might be correct: Margaret was ill, and was keeping it from Jonah. At least that removed the awful prospect that she was thinking of abandoning him. Bernie felt ashamed that she had ever suspected it. However, the alternative was not a pleasant prospect either. As they made their way into the sitting room, she became aware that Jonah was still speaking.

'But I can't help wondering,' Jonah went on, more serious now. 'She hasn't said anything, but I got the impression she was rather nervous about it – as if she was expecting them to find something. Has she said anything to you?'

'No.' Bernie tried to sound reassuring. She was not used to subterfuge. Her rule had always been to tell it as it is, but now she was not sure. Margaret had not said anything to her. All she had, upon which to base her suspicions, was a single throwaway remark. If Margaret was keeping something from Jonah then that was their business, not hers. And yet …

'Are you sure?' Jonah had detected the uncertainty in Bernie's voice.

'It was nothing really.' Bernie spoke earnestly, taking Jonah's left hand between her own two and looking directly into his eyes. 'I'm probably just imagining things, but she did say this rather weird thing about not always being there for you. I hoped that she just meant that she had other responsibilities and was grateful to me for taking over sometimes, but I did just wonder ...'

They sat there, neither knowing what to say. After a few minutes, there was the sound of a motorbike drawing up outside. Bernie came round behind Jonah's chair and put her arms round his neck. She kissed him on the cheek and spoke in a low voice.

'I do love you, Jonah. And whatever it is that's wrong we'll all be there for you both.'

Margaret came in and sat down. She smiled, perhaps rather weakly, at Bernie. 'I'm glad you're here,' she said. 'I've got something to say and I'd like you to hear it too.'

They sat expectantly while Margaret assembled her thoughts.

'It looks as if I have ovarian cancer.' She spoke calmly, but her eyes flickered anxiously from Jonah to Bernie and back again. They sat in silence, unable to think of anything to say.

'I've got a CT scan booked for Thursday morning,' she went on. 'That ought to confirm what stage it is. And then an appointment at the clinic in the afternoon to discuss treatment options.'

'I want to come with you.' Jonah said fervently.

'Thanks. I'd like you to be there.' Margaret took hold of his hand and squeezed it gently. 'I wanted you there before – when I went for the tests and when the results came back – but I didn't want to worry you, until I knew there was something to be worried *about*.'

She turned to Bernie.

'Do you think you could come too?' she asked. 'We may be there a long time and I'd like to know that there was someone else to see that Jonah's OK.'

'Of course. No problem. I'll come over here and drive you both to the hospital. Just let me know what time.'

'And what's the prognosis?' Jonah demanded suddenly. 'I mean, lots of cancers are curable these days, aren't they? Do they know what the chances are?'

Margaret fumbled in her handbag and brought out some leaflets. 'These are all available on the web,' she told Jonah. 'I'll give you the address so you can read about it. There's information about possible treatments and symptoms and side effects and everything too, but here are some statistics to give you an idea what we're up against.'

'Overall,' she went on, 'survival at one year is 72% and at five years it's 43%; but they think my cancer is stage two or three, which means that the five year survival rate could be as low as 20%. However, those figures mask a plethora of other factors that can affect the outcome. We'll have a better idea after the CT scan.'

Jonah shook his head in disbelief. 'And to think I always thought that if you predeceased me it would be as a result of an accident on that damn motorbike of yours!'

****

'It must have been a terrible blow,' Bethan said with feeling.

'Yes,' agreed Jonah. 'For all of us, but I think worst for the boys. Telling them was the worst thing I've ever had to do in my life – and I've had plenty of practice at breaking bad news. Looking back, I suppose they were still recovering from the shock of my injury and this was almost too much for them.'

'I think, feeling helpless to do anything made it worse for them,' Bernie added. 'Especially for Reuben – stuck up there in County Durham with a wife and two kids and another on the way. At least Nathan was only in London and could visit easily.'

'Not that having him faffing about was any help to Margaret,' Jonah remarked. 'He did his best, but he was too young. He didn't have the experience. He wanted to cheer us up by talking up the chances of a cure, instead of helping to work out ways of coping with the reality that there wasn't going to be one.'

'Margaret was incredible,' Lucy said in a rather awestruck tone. 'She wouldn't let it get her down. When her hair fell out because of the chemotherapy, she got seven wigs – one for each day of the week – all different colours. And she used to paint her nails to match each one.'

'The only thing that she really agonised over,' Bernie put in, 'was what was going to happen to Jonah after she died.'

'I remember her saying to me one night in bed,' Jonah agreed. 'She said she thought she could cope with everything if only she knew that I'd be able to carry on working for as long as I wanted and that I wouldn't have to go into a home unless I chose.'

'And did you manage to set her mind at rest?' Bethan asked.

'We called a family conference to discuss it. The idea was to enable Margaret to be included in the planning, so that she could feel that she had contributed to working out how to do it. Reuben and Anne came down for the weekend. Nathan was there of course and my sister, Sarah, from Kent. Peter and Bernie and Lucy came over to join us, and Sylvia offered to look after the grandchildren so that Reuben and Anne wouldn't be distracted while we talked.'

****

'I suppose we might as well get started,' Reuben said, putting down his after lunch cup of coffee and sitting back in his chair. 'Although I still think this is all a bit premature – no point dwelling on something that may be years off.'

'The evidence is that we're talking months rather than years.' Margaret answered bluntly. 'But we can't start yet – Bernie and Peter aren't here.'

'I thought this was supposed to be a *family* conference,' Reuben objected.

'They *are* family.' Margaret said firmly.

'Funny idea of family,' Sarah, Jonah's older sister, muttered. She had come up for the day from the house in Kent where she cared for their elderly parents. Their mother had debilitating arthritis and their father's dementia left him isolated in a world of his own. Sarah had felt obliged to attend, both to show that she was taking an interest in her brother's well-being and as her mother's representative, but she had her eye continually on her watch, anxious to get back to them to relieve the neighbour who had offered to keep an eye on her parents while she was away.

A car drew up outside and soon Reuben's children, George aged four and Carolyn aged two were in the kitchen with Sylvia, happily engaged in baking fairy cakes, which she told them they would all be able to share later. Bernie, Peter and Lucy joined the party in the sitting room. Everyone looked expectantly at Margaret.

'Thank you all for coming,' she said, rather formally. 'As you all know, it looks as if I am likely to pop my clogs before Jonah does – whether that's in a few months or several years off – and I asked you to come so that we could discuss how he's going to be supported after that happens.'

Nobody seemed keen to start the discussion, so Margaret went on, adopting the style that she used when chairing meetings of work colleagues. 'Maybe Jonah, you could start by outlining what your priorities are and what you see as the chief barriers to getting what you'd like.'

'OK.' Jonah thought for a moment. 'The main thing is that I want to carry on working at least until I'm sixty, maybe longer. Bernie here is going to be taking care of me while I'm at work; the problem will be finding people to be around outside working hours and particularly overnight when, at the moment, I rely on Margaret.'

'If you weren't so determined to keep on with the job,' Reuben said rather grumpily, 'the obvious solution would be for you to come and live with us.'

Lucy opened her mouth to protest, but closed it again when Peter put his hand on her arm and shook his head at her.

'Anne's going to be at home with the kids for a few more years yet,' Reuben went on, 'and there's a great day centre for people with spinal injuries just a couple of miles away.'

Jonah fought down the temptation to give his opinion of adult day care centres and forced himself to speak calmly.

'Thank you Reuben. It's very good of you to offer, but the job really is important.'

'I think Mum would be disappointed if you moved up north,' Sarah put in cautiously. 'I mean – at the moment it's only a couple of hours on the motorway for you to visit. If you were living with Reuben you wouldn't be able to go there and back in the day and we don't have the facilities for you to stay overnight.'

'I suppose,' Nathan said slowly, 'the obvious solution is for me to give up the flat in London and move back here. I could commute on the train every day – plenty of people do.'

'We could help!' Lucy chipped in eagerly. 'Couldn't we, Mam? We could come over sometimes – if you wanted to go out in the evening, or something.'

'I'll be taking Jonah to work and bringing him home each day,' Bernie said, 'So, if you didn't have time to get him up and dressed and everything, I could come earlier and do all that – and I could wait with him until you got back in the evening, if you had to stay late.'

'I'm not sure, Nathan love,' Margaret said doubtfully. 'It's a lot of commitment you'd be taking on. You mustn't jeopardise your Bar training. I don't like to think that I'm going to be offloading everything on you.'

She was partly motivated by concern for her younger son's career and wellbeing, but also mindful of the frustration that her husband often felt when Nathan had charge of his care. Nathan's over-solicitous attitude and tendency to put his perception of Jonah's safety and wellbeing ahead of his freedom were a constant source of annoyance. She very much doubted that Jonah would manage to keep his temper if he were subject to Nathan's ministrations on a permanent and daily basis.

'Oh Margaret!' Reuben's wife Anne spoke for the first time. 'You mustn't think like that. It isn't as if you *chose* to get cancer.'

'No, but it will make me feel a whole lot better about it if I know that I won't be leaving a whole lot of problems behind me. That's why I wanted us to talk it through together. I want to be able to help to work out some of the solutions, in a way that doesn't leave anyone doing more than their fair share.'

'I'm only talking about taking on what *you* do already,' Nathan pointed out. 'And you have a job too.'

'It's different when you're as senior as I am,' Margaret argued. '*You* still have to get your career established. You can't afford to appear unreliable. You need to be able to put in the extra hours to make yourself indispensable. And in a few years, you may be wanting to set up home for yourself and start a family. I don't want you committing yourself to living here with your Dad forever.'

'I agree with Mum,' Reuben said. 'It would be too much for Nathan, with his law studies as well. It won't do anyone any good if he tries to do too much and makes himself ill. I think we ought to look into care homes.'

'I think that's a very good idea,' Sarah agreed. 'If not for the immediate future, it would be a good idea to find out what's out there, so we don't have to do it in a rush later – just like we've done for Dad.'

'But Grandad Porter doesn't even know *where* he is most of the time!' Nathan protested. 'It isn't the same at all. Dad would never fit in in a home with a lot of old people!'

'There are lots of care homes for younger disabled people – including some people who hold down jobs.' Reuben assured him. 'I really think we oughtn't to rule it out – if only to provide respite care for you. *We* could help out financially. It would mean that Dad would have high quality professional care and Mum wouldn't need to worry that anyone was being overburdened.'

'No!'

Lucy had been becoming more and more agitated as the conversation progressed. She had been looking wildly from one adult to another, frantically hoping that someone would intervene to quash the suggestion of a care home as a suitable place for Jonah to live. At last, she could bear it no longer.

'Stop talking like that. You don't *need* to find a care home for Jonah. We *like* having him to stay – like we did when Margaret was in hospital. And it isn't far for us to come here, if he needs someone to look after him at home. Why do you keep going on about it as if … as if nobody *wanted* him?'

There was a stunned silence. Bernie put her arm round Lucy and pulled her gently towards her. Peter was the first to speak.

'I have a suggestion.' He said calmly. 'Why doesn't Jonah stay with us during the week and come home here at weekends? Then Nathan can live in his London flat on weekdays when he needs to be close to his work, and he can stay here with Jonah at the weekend.'

'If I may say so,' Jonah remarked, 'that is the most sensible thing that anyone has said all day.'

'I think that's a brilliant idea!' Lucy declared, flinging herself into Peter's arms and hugging him.

'Isn't he marvellous?' Bernie said to Jonah in a stage whisper. '*Now* do you see why I married him?' she added mischievously.

'I certainly do! I'd marry him myself if he wasn't already spoken for!'

'Watch it, you!' Margaret chortled, giving Jonah a playful dig in the ribs. 'Don't forget *you're* spoken for too – I'm not dead yet!'

Reuben and Anne looked round in bewilderment, unsure how to take this levity among the older generation. Nathan, having seen his parents relaxing with these friends of theirs before, was less surprised but, nevertheless, found the flippancy rather embarrassing.

'But seriously, Peter,' Jonah said, catching Reuben's eye and realising that his son did not consider jocularity to be appropriate. 'I am really grateful to you for offering to take me in. It's very generous of you.'

'Not at all,' Peter said dismissively. 'It's quite clear that, whatever I say, my wife and stepdaughter are determined to devote themselves to you. At least if you're living with us there's a chance that I might occasionally get a look in too!'

****

'And your wife died, when?' Bethan asked.

'Just over a year after her diagnosis: April 2014. It was the day after Passion Sunday. We buried her on Maundy Thursday.'

****

'Her husband is with her. He said for you to go straight in when you arrived. It won't be much longer now.' The hospice volunteer spoke softly as she led the way to Margaret's room.

Bernie went in and closed the door quietly behind her. Margaret lay on the bed looking very pale and drawn; her breathing was noisy in the silence. Jonah was sitting in his chair, facing her with his back to the door. At the sound of footsteps, he turned it round slightly to see who had come in.

'Bernie! Thank you for coming. Nathan's on his way, but I thought it was better not to tell Reuben until …,

'Yes. It's too far. No point just making him feel guilty.'

Margaret's eyelids fluttered briefly. Bernie walked over and took her hand.

'Hello Margaret. It's Bernie.'

Margaret gave a weak smile of acknowledgement.

Bernie looked at Jonah. 'Would you prefer to be alone?"

'No, no – please stay.'

Bernie drew up a chair and, for about ten minutes, they sat in silence.

'Bernie?'

'Mmm?' Bernie looked enquiringly at Jonah.

'I'd like to hold her hand. D'you think you could …?'

'Of course.'

Bernie gently lifted Jonah's left hand off the controls on the arm of his chair and placed it in Margaret's hand where it lay on the bed. He grasped it as best he could with his three working fingers. For a moment, nothing happened. Then he felt an answering squeeze and Margaret's eyes opened for a few seconds. She smiled.

They sat like that for perhaps half an hour before Margaret's grip slackened and her face became expressionless. Jonah waited for a few minutes then spoke softly to Bernie.

'I think she's gone. Can you check for me?'

Bernie felt for a pulse in Margaret's neck. She nodded to Jonah.

'Can you tell the staff?' he asked. 'I think I'll go out in the garden for a while.'

Bernie replaced Jonah's hand on the controls of his wheelchair and held the door open for him to go out. Then she went in search of someone from the hospice staff to inform them that one of their patients had died. She was standing at the reception desk when Nathan arrived.

'Am I too late?' he asked anxiously.

'Your mother's dead,' Bernie said baldly, with her usual aversion to euphemism, 'but your Dad was there with her. It was all very peaceful. You said your goodbye to her last week, so I wouldn't say you were too late.'

'Can I … can I see her?'

'Of course.' Bernie led the way to Margaret's room. Someone had been in and spread a thin white sheet over her body. Bernie stepped forward and carefully drew it back so that Nathan could see her face. He gazed down in silent thought.

'She's not there anymore, is she?' he said at last.

'No,' Bernie agreed. 'That's how I've always felt too.'

Nathan gently replaced the sheet over his mother's face

and stood there wondering what to do next.

'Your dad's in the garden. I think he'd like you to join him,' Bernie suggested gently.

'I don't know. He might like to be alone.'

'If that's what he wants, he'll be quite capable of telling you,' Bernie persisted. 'Go on. He'll be glad you've come.'

'OK. Will you come with me?'

Bernie shook her head. 'Better you do it on your own. I'll wait at Reception. Peter and Lucy will be along when she gets out of school.'

They walked down the corridor together.

'Bernie? I'm sure it'd be better if *you* went to Dad. I won't know what to say.'

'You don't need to *say* anything.'

'I don't know. I'll only make a mess of it.'

'My dad used to say, "if a job's worth doing it's worth doing badly," by which he meant that there are some things that a person has to do for himself, even if they know they won't do them very well.'

'I don't get it.'

They reached the reception area and Bernie pulled Nathan down into a seat. She spoke with quiet passion.

'Listen, Nathan! You're looking at this all the wrong way round. Of course, I'd love to go out there and give Jonah my sympathy. There's nothing I'd like more than to put my arms round him and tell him how much we all feel for him losing his wife. But you are the only one who can give him the chance to be a father to the boy who's just lost his mother. He doesn't need you to say the right things – he needs to be able to feel that he can still be a proper father to his sons, to be strong and support them. So please – just go out there and let him know you need him.'

Nathan nodded. 'OK.' He got up and moved towards the door that led out into the garden. Then he turned back for a moment. 'How do you know these things?'

'By being a whole lot older than you – that's all. Oh!

And by having made a whole lot more mistakes over the years.' Bernie smiled encouragingly. 'I'm hoping that I can force you to invent a whole lot of new ones instead of just repeating all the same ones I made when *my* mam died!'

Nathan walked briskly over to where his father was moving slowly along a path between rows of lavender bushes. Jonah stopped his chair and turned it towards the sound of footsteps. He looked up and Nathan could see that his eyes were red. All of a sudden, tears pricked the backs of his own eyes.

'Dad?'

'Nathan! I'm sorry I left it so late to phone you.'

'Don't worry. I expect it was better that way. I said goodbye to Mum last week. That's how I'll remember her – smiling while we all sang *Abide with Me*, with Reuben's kids crawling about under the bed.'

Jonah gave a weak smile. 'Yes. That was a good do wasn't it?'

****

'So now you divide your time between here and your own house in South Oxfordshire?' Bethan checked her notes. 'Would we be able to film there at all, do you think? Perhaps show the place where you were when you were shot?'

'I'm afraid not. We sold that house eighteen months ago. I live here permanently now. Things didn't really work out with Nathan taking over at weekends.'

'Nathan's a good lad,' Bernie said graciously. 'To give him his due, he tried his best.'

'But it would never have worked,' Jonah explained. 'I mean, he still helps out quite often, but it just doesn't feel right somehow having all my most intimate needs attended to by my own son. It seems only yesterday that I was wiping his nose and picking him up when he'd fallen off his swing. It's awkward for both of us now that *he* has to wipe *my* nose – and worse!'

'I think I understand,' Bethan said thoughtfully. 'I think

I'd feel awkward about looking after my mum – getting her undressed, taking her to the loo, that sort of thing.'

'And of course it did put a damper on Nathan's social life,' Jonah added, 'having to leave London every Friday, just when all the shows and parties were about to start. You can't blame him for feeling that he was missing out.'

'It wasn't just a matter of social life,' Peter pointed out fairly. 'As a trainee barrister, he had all sorts of evening and weekend events that he really had to attend for the sake of his career.'

'You're right,' admitted Jonah. 'And to be honest, I was usually only too pleased when he asked if I could come here at a weekend because he had something on. I always seemed to be missing out of the best bits by going home every Friday.'

'What were you missing out on?' Bethan enquired, intrigued.

'Well for a start, Lucy plays for a girls' football team on a Saturday afternoon and I always seemed to be hearing the post-mortem but never able to watch the match. Then, in the summer, everyone in Oxford goes messing about in boats at the weekend. And of course, we didn't get to go to church together. But the clincher was the Saturday evening cabaret.'

'What does that entail?' Bethan was curious.

'When I was a child there used to be some highbrow families who would say,' (at this point Jonah put on an accent reminiscent of a nineteen-fifties BBC radio announcer), '*We don't have a television set – we make our own entertainment.* I never believed them. I thought they were just being pretentious. But this lot really do gather round the piano on a Saturday evening and do their party pieces. That's after High Tea round the kitchen table with all sorts of interesting characters that they've picked up over the years.'

'Such as?'

'Sylvia and Stan, of course, and Wayne and Dean come

over quite often. Then there are a few university people and Peter's favourite forensic pathologist. Peter's daughter and her family come to stay sometimes and so do Reuben and Anne and the kids. All sorts.'

'Sylvia and Lucy both play the piano.' Bernie added. 'And most people end up contributing something – even if they start off swearing that they can't even join in singing the chorus!'

'So what do *you* do?' Bethan asked Jonah, wondering whether this would provide a good clip for inclusion in the programme.

'Jonah has a lovely singing voice,' Lucy said loyally.

'I can only sing a *comic* song,' Jonah said with a smile. The quotation from *Three Men in a Boat* was lost on Bethan, but the others laughed.

'You should hear him doing Gilbert and Sullivan,' Bernie said. 'He makes an excellent model of a modern major general or Lord High Executioner; and we all join in the chorus, "till now he is the ruler of the Queen's navee," and all that.'

'Not forgetting,' Peter added, 'a policeman's lot is not an 'appy one!'

'It sounds fun. That all takes place in this room, I assume?'

'That's right.' Bernie confirmed. 'The whole family lives in this room and the kitchen. Jonah has his own sitting room, bedroom and bathroom, which take up the rest of the ground floor, and there's plenty of space for the rest of us upstairs. It's a good thing Richard was an only child and his parents had such a big house. All we needed to do was to move some non-structural walls around so that the utility room, breakfast room and outside toilet became Jonah's bedroom and bathroom.

'When Jonah sold his own house, it gave us an excuse to get rid of the old dining room furniture and make that into a study-sitting room for him – where he could put some of the stuff from home and where he could get away from us if he wanted some peace and quiet, or to entertain guests in private. It all works remarkably well.'

'Do you think I could have a look?' Bethan asked. 'We'd like the viewers to get an idea of what life is actually like for you now. If possible we'd like to do some filming in the house – maybe show you in some everyday activities.'

'Follow me.' Jonah led the way out into the hall.

'This is what I call my study, but it's really more of a sitting room, I suppose. 'You've already been here. It used to be the dining room, as Bernie said. That door over there leads into my bedroom. We made that. Originally that was the breakfast room and it had doors into the hall and the kitchen.'

Bethan looked round the room. She walked over to some shelves on the wall opposite the door and pointed to the photographs arrayed there.

'This is your wedding?'

'Yes – thirty-five years ago now. The picture to the right of that is Margaret about two years before she died.'

Bethan picked up the photograph and looked down at a smiling woman, flame orange hair sticking up in spikes around her head, standing astride a powerful looking motorbike, with a crash helmet under her arm.

'That's how I like to remember her.'

Bethan replaced the photograph and looked along the shelf at the other pictures.

'That's quite a recent picture of Reuben and his three. That's Nathan's wedding. And that's the latest addition to the family: Nathan's first – little Rachel. So now I have four grandchildren.'

'And you don't think it would be nice to retire so that you could spend more time with them?'

'Certainly not! Now come through here and I'll show you where I sleep.'

The door to the bedroom opened automatically and Jonah led the way through.

'As you'll have noticed, the doors all have electric opening devices which I can control remotely from my chair. We've also widened the doorways so that the chair fits through more easily.'

'All these alterations must have been quite expensive,' Bethan commented.

'When my first husband was killed in the course of duty I got a lump sum in compensation,' Bernie explained. 'I didn't have anything to spend it on at the time so I put it in the building society and forgot about it. It came in very handy when we were getting the house ready for Jonah to move in, and I'm sure that Richard would be pleased to be helping one of his old colleagues.'

They went into the bedroom. Bethan was immediately struck by the array of equipment, which made it look like a hospital ward. Jonah explained how each item contributed to his daily life, enabling him to be moved between bed and chair, to take a bath or shower and to sit on the toilet. Bethan started to realise that the public image that Jonah managed to project, of a man whose disability had little impact on his life, concealed a very different reality.

'Do you think we could show you using some of this equipment on the programme?' Bethan asked. 'So that the viewers can get a picture of your everyday life.'

'Well, I don't want to inflict on your Sunday afternoon audience the sight of me being lowered into the bath!' laughed Jonah, 'but I suppose a transfer from chair to bed would be OK.'

'The thing you ought to try to get across to people,' Bernie suggested, 'that is, if you want them to understand what it's really like – is how *long* everything takes, compared with an able-bodied person. Getting dressed, for example. It's much more difficult to dress someone else than to dress yourself – especially when they can't do anything to help.'

Bethan nodded and wrote in her notebook. She looked round the room taking it all in. Jonah's hospital-style bed was central, leaving plenty of room for manoeuvre on either side. There was a second, narrower bed under the window.

'That's where whoever is on night duty sleeps,' Jonah told her. 'There's a baby alarm in this room so that I can call out to alert people in other rooms in the house if I need anything, but often it's less disruptive to have someone sleeping here.'

'We take it in turns,' Lucy explained, 'a week at a time.'

****

Peter was awakened by the sound of Jonah's voice coming through the baby alarm. The words were indistinct; with the only one that Peter could distinguish clearly being Margaret's name repeated over and over, but the distress was obvious. A nightmare, Peter correctly concluded. He slipped quickly out of bed, taking care not to wake Bernie, who was sleeping peacefully at his side. He hurried downstairs and into Jonah's room.

'Jonah,' he said quietly, kneeling down by the bed and putting his arm around his friend's shoulders. 'Wake up. It's alright.'

Jonah lay on his side, facing away from Peter. His shoulders trembled and he continued to shout out his dead wife's name. Peter shook him, gently at first then more vigorously. 'It's alright,' he repeated. 'It's just a dream.' He rolled him over so that he was lying on his back. His face was tear-stained. His eyes opened and he looked up dazedly at Peter.

'Margaret?'

'It's Peter. You were having a nightmare. It's all over now.'

'Margaret?' Jonah repeated as he gradually emerged from sleep. 'She gone, isn't she?'

'Yes. She's gone.' Peter agreed. 'But it won't always hurt quite so badly.'

'I dreamed that she was drowning,' Jonah explained. 'She kept going under and there was nothing I could do.'

Jonah blinked away the tears and looked up at Peter. Peter pulled a tissue from the box that lay next to the bed and wiped away the mucus from beneath Jonah's nose.

'Let's sit you up for a few minutes,' he said, lifting Jonah's upper body and carefully adjusting the backrest and pillows so that he was propped in a sitting position. 'I'll be in deep trouble with my women if I allow that to get on your chest.'

He helped Jonah to blow his nose and dried his face with another tissue.

'I'm sorry. I suppose I woke you.'

'Yes. But it's not far off being time for me to come and turn you anyway, so no harm done.'

'Did I wake Bernie too?'

'No. She's not on duty.'

'What d'you mean?'

'Angie and I used to call it "holding the baby syndrome",' Peter explained. 'All the time she was on maternity leave, after Hannah was born, I wouldn't wake up however much the baby screamed in the night. The first night that Angie was on duty at the hospital, after she went back to work, we were both worried that I'd sleep right through if Hannah cried. But when Angie wasn't there, I always woke up at the least little sound that the baby made. Somehow, subconsciously, I knew that it was my responsibility. Now tonight, it's my turn to see to you, so Bernie slept right through your frantic cries for help.'

He looked down at his bare feet. 'Do you mind if I get in with you?' He asked. 'I forgot to put on my slippers.'

'Be my guest.' Jonah smiled.

Peter lifted the duvet and carefully moved Jonah's left arm out of the way, giving his hand a friendly squeeze as he did so. He got in beside him and drew the duvet over them both.

'I reckon we ought to put another bed in here,' he said, pointing to a space on the other side of the room. 'There's plenty of room under the window. Then whoever's on duty could sleep here and it wouldn't be so far to come when you need them.'

'Wouldn't you rather be sharing a bed with Bernie?' Jonah asked dubiously. 'I wouldn't want to be keeping you apart.'

'Well, I wasn't necessarily thinking of the *whole* night – maybe I'd doss down here after coming to turn you over for the first time. Then I could still have my conjugal rights, if that's what you were worrying about.'

'Good. I wouldn't want to feel I was coming between husband and wife.'

They sat together in silence for a few minutes.

'I keep thinking she's going to come back.' Jonah said after a while. 'I keep expecting to see her sitting in her favourite chair or standing by the sink. The boy at the house opposite has got a motorbike and every time I hear it I think *that's Margaret coming home.*'

'Maybe it'll be better while you're here,' Peter suggested. 'Not so many associations.'

'That's how *I* came to move in after Angie died,' he went on. 'I couldn't stand being in the house on my own. Everywhere there were her things – things which I couldn't bear to see, but couldn't bear to get rid of. And every time I went in the kitchen I imagined her lying there.'

'I suppose it must be easier for me,' Jonah said thoughtfully, 'having time to prepare before it happened.'

'No,' Peter shook his head. 'I don't think there's any such thing as "easier".'

He got out of bed and leaned over to lie Jonah back down.

'And now, we'd better try to get a couple of hours more sleep before it's time to get you up again – that is if you're still determined to go back to work tomorrow. It might be too soon, you know. I took a month off when Angie died.'

'And did that help?'

'No.' Peter admitted. 'It just gave me more time to think about it all.'

'In that case, I think I'd rather have something to take my mind off things.'

Peter nodded. 'You're probably right. See you about six then.'

****

'So there you have it,' Jonah said to Bethan as he led the way back into the living room. 'This is my world – well this and the garden. The rest of the family also have the upstairs, which I haven't seen since I came visiting on Lucy's ninth birthday.'

'I must say, I'm very impressed at the way you've taken Jonah into your home,' Bethan said, turning to Bernie and Peter.

'No, but we don't see it that way,' Bernie replied. 'It's a privilege for us that he's chosen to come.'

'There's nothing special about us,' Peter insisted. 'It's just what anyone would do.'

'We *like* having Jonah living with us,' Lucy added vehemently.

'So you don't have any regrets? You never feel it's too big a commitment?'

'Absolutely not!'

'None at all!'

'Of course not!'

Bernie, Peter and Lucy all spoke at once.

'The way I see it,' Bernie added, 'is this. When a young couple has a baby, people may make all sorts of jokes about sleepless nights and changing nappies, but nobody would seriously suggest that they wish they didn't have their little bundle of joy. Everyone assumes that having a baby is a great blessing, even if it is hard work sometimes. A lot of what we have to do for Jonah is like having a baby – dressing and undressing, getting up in the night to turn him over, feeding him – and having him around the place is a lot more rewarding than having a baby, I can tell you!'

'Mind you,' Peter put in, 'it's a big responsibility. I remember, one night I was left holding the fort on my own. Bernie and Lucy had gone to Liverpool to her aunt's funeral. I remember lying in bed thinking, *suppose I forgot to go and get him up?* It suddenly dawned on me that if I didn't go into his room in the morning and get him out of bed and into his chair, there was nothing he could do about it. He was completely dependent on me.'

'But *I* know that you always *will* come.' Jonah put in. 'Being disabled has really brought home to me how much we all depend on one another. It's very obvious in my case, but we all depend on other people to do things for us. And, seeing as this is for your Sunday afternoon religious slot,' he added, 'you could also add that it has also brought home to me how much we all depend on God.

'I remember as a child being taught to pray when I went to bed, "Now I lay me down to sleep, I pray the Lord my soul will keep; if I should die before I wake, I pray the Lord my soul will take." *Now* when I lie in bed at night I know that if I wake up again Peter or Bernie or Lucy will come and get me up for a new day, and if I don't – well that's in God's hands. In both cases, it's a matter of trust.'

'Perhaps your next hymn ought to be *Trust and Obey*?' suggested Bernie.

'No. I know what I want for my next hymn, but it's a bit obvious. I expect everyone chooses it.'

'Go on,' Bethan encouraged.

'I'd like to have *Abide with Me*.'

'I don't see why you can't have that. Was there a particular reason?'

'Yes. We sang it for Margaret a couple of days before she died. She wanted to say goodbye to everyone while she was still fully conscious and not drugged up to the eyeballs. We knew there wasn't much longer to go, so we invited the whole family to the hospice where she was living and one of the things we did was to sing that together.'

****

Abide with me; fast falls the eventide;
The darkness deepens; Lord with me abide.
When other helpers fail and comforts flee,
Help of the helpless, O abide with me.

Swift to its close ebbs out life's little day;
Earth's joys grow dim; its glories pass away;
Change and decay in all around I see;
O Thou who changest not, abide with me.

I need Thy presence every passing hour.
What but Thy grace can foil the tempter's power?
Who, like Thyself, my guide and stay can be?
Through cloud and sunshine, Lord, abide with me.

I fear no foe, with Thee at hand to bless;
Ills have no weight, and tears no bitterness.
Where is death's sting? Where, grave, thy victory?
I triumph still, if Thou abide with me.

Hold Thou Thy cross before my closing eyes;
Shine through the gloom and point me to the skies.
Heaven's morning breaks, and earth's vain shadows
flee;
In life, in death, O Lord, abide with me.

Henry Francis Lyte (1793-1847)

9 IN HEAVENLY LOVE ABIDING

'Detective Chief Inspector Jonah Porter enjoys having his grandchildren to stay.' The television screen showed a happy picture of two children descending from a tree house and running across a lawn towards a group of adults sitting around a table. 'But he can't join in their games, ever since a bullet in the spine paralysed him eight years ago.'

A four-year-old boy appeared, climbing up into his grandfather's lap and opening a book, which they proceed to read together.

'This Sunday at 4.30 *Inspirational Lives* meets the detective who still solves crimes despite his disabilities and discusses what inspired *him* to overcome the odds.'

The camera zoomed in to show a close-up of Jonah's face.

'Taking your life over all, now,' the presenter said, 'would you say you're happy?'

'Yes. Yes I am – very happy.'

Lisa Price-Davies leapt to her feet and strode across the room to switch off the television set, which she had been watching with her father.

'What right has he got to be happy?' she demanded.

'He ruined your life! He killed Mum! He *can't* be happy! He *mustn't*! I won't allow him to be!'

'What d'you mean? What are you talking about?' Her father watched her, bewildered.

'Don't you recognise him? That's the policeman who put you in jail. He made up all those charges against you and told lies to get you put away. It's all his fault! You in prison. Mum killing herself. Me having to live with Gran. He *deserved* to be shot – I just wish he'd been killed. And now he has the nerve to go round saying that he's happy!'

Lisa pulled away from her father's hand, which he had put out to grasp her arm, and pushed past him out of the room. He heard her footsteps going upstairs. A few minutes later, she came down again and he heard the front door open and then bang shut. He ran to the window and looked out. Lisa was opening the door of her car. His heart gave a lurch as he saw that she was carrying her air pistol. He raced to the front door, but was only in time to see her putting the car into gear and moving off.

Merlin Price-Davies reached for his own car keys and gave chase. He managed to keep Lisa's car in view, as she left their small Buckinghamshire village. She seemed to be heading towards Oxford. What could she be intending to do? Surely, she wasn't planning to use the gun against a man in a wheelchair? Then an awful thought occurred to him. No! Surely not? But the more he thought, the more convinced he became. Eight years ago, while he was still trying to rebuild his life after coming out of prison, his daughter had gone out one day and shot a policemen in the back in cold blood.

He shivered as he peered ahead to see which road Lisa would take as they approached the ring road. She turned into one of the older residential areas of Headington. Then he lost her. Which road had she chosen? He looked round, frantically searching for her car. Then he spotted it, parked on the pavement outside a large house, set well back from the road. Just turning into the drive was a people carrier with a disabled sticker on the back warning drivers not to obstruct the rear doors by parking too close. He pulled up a few feet away, got out and ran towards the house. He called out to Jonah, who was descending from the back of the vehicle in his motorised chair.

'Don't go in! My daughter's there. She's got a gun! She wants to kill you!' Suddenly Merlin was out of breath. He struggled to continue, conscious that Bernie and Jonah were both looking at him in amazement.

'Really?' Jonah said with a slight air of amusement. 'You intrigue me. Who are you? Who is your daughter? And why would she want to kill me?'

'She thinks you got me convicted for a crime I didn't commit.'

'I see.' Jonah remained apparently calm. 'And did I?'

'No.' Now embarrassment was adding to Merlin's distress. 'I was guilty, but I told her I was innocent and she thinks it was all your fault. I think,' he went on, getting the words out with difficulty, 'that she tried to kill you before and now she's determined to finish the job. Look – let me go in and explain to her.'

'Oh, I think we can deal with this.' Jonah started his chair moving towards the house.

Bernie stepped forward and firmly moved his hand off the controlling joystick and on to his lap. 'No you don't! Stop trying to play the hero and listen to reason for a change.' She turned to face the stranger, who had appeared so unexpectedly.

'Can I get this straight?' Her tone was aggressive. 'You're telling me that there's a mad woman with a gun in there – in my house, with my husband and my daughter?'

Merlin nodded. 'If I could just talk to her?' he pleaded.

'Go ahead then.' Bernie stood back to let him pass. 'If you go through the back gate, you'll find the kitchen door open.'

Merlin entered the large kitchen and stared at the scene before him. At the far side of the room stood his daughter, her left arm around the chest of a fair-haired young woman to whose head she was holding her air pistol. A middle-aged man with greying red hair was seated at the table, his eyes fixed on Lisa and her hostage.

'Sit down, Dad,' Lisa ordered. 'He may be back any moment.'

Merlin stepped towards Lisa, his hand outstretched. 'Give me the gun, Lisa. Let's all sit down and talk about this.'

'Get back! There's nothing to talk about. I've got to do this – for you, Dad!'

'Lisa, listen to me. You've got it all wrong. It's all my fault – I lied to you. I was guilty.'

'No!' Lisa backed away, still gripping Lucy across the chest and holding the gun to her head. 'I don't believe you. You're just saying it to stop me killing him. But he deserves to die. I *won't* give up now.'

'Lisa, please!' her father moved towards her, still holding out his hand. 'You *have* to believe me. I'm telling you the truth now. I couldn't bear the idea of you thinking badly of me. You were so young – I thought you'd never understand how it happened, and I thought you might hate me if you thought I'd been dishonest. But it was all true – the police were only doing their job. I *deserved* to go to jail. Please! Put down the gun.'

Lisa gazed round wildly, seemingly unable to comprehend what she had just heard. Then she suddenly seemed to give way. Her right arm fell to her side and she loosened her grip on Lucy. Peter moved silently across the room and gently removed the gun from her hand. Lucy stumbled across to the table and sat down. Peter returned to his seat and carefully unloaded the pistol.

'Well, well! What have we here?' Jonah entered the room and was suddenly in charge. 'We've taken the precaution of calling for backup,' he went on, 'but while they get their arses into gear, I suggest that we all sit down and have a nice friendly chat.'

'I'll make a brew,' said Bernie predictably, picking up the kettle and heading for the sink.

Lisa continued to stare round, bewildered, until her father went over and, putting his arm around her, steered her to a seat. She slumped into the chair, resting her arms on the big kitchen table.

'Now young lady,' Jonah said brightly, 'We'll have to take you down to the station and get you to give a formal statement, but meanwhile, could you satisfy my considerable curiosity by explaining just exactly what you've been up to. Am I correct in thinking that it was you who took pot shots at me through the garden fence back in 2009?'

Lisa nodded miserably. 'I hated you – right from that morning when you came and took Dad away.'

'Oh yes!' Jonah cast his mind back to a cold November morning in 1998. 'You were there. I saw you looking through the bannisters in your pyjamas. You were scared.'

'And when Dad kept telling me that he hadn't done anything wrong, I was sure that you had framed him deliberately.'

'I'm sorry, Lisa,' her father put in. 'I was embarrassed. I couldn't bear to think of you thinking badly of me. You were so young. I never thought …'

'How old were you, Lisa – when I arrested your father?'

'Twelve. Dad had never been away from home before so it was awful not having him there anymore. And then he was let out on bail and I thought everything was going to be like it was before. But he and Mum kept arguing and Mum kept crying and then there was the trial and he was sent away and I didn't see him for *ages* and Mum got depressed and ….' The words suddenly came tumbling out as if a dam had broken, 'and then she took lots of sleeping pills and I tried and tried to wake her up and then they told me she was dead and Gran came and took me to live with her.'

'I never knew!' Merlin gasped, putting his arm round

his daughter's shoulder. 'I didn't realise that *you* had found her.'

'I made up my mind I was going to make you pay.' Lisa continued, becoming more animated as she recounted what she had done. 'I made a plan. As soon as I was old enough I joined a shooting club. I practised hard because I knew that I'd need to be sure of hitting you first shot. I got chosen to represent the club in competitions. I got good enough to be considered for the British team for the Beijing Olympics. Then I knew I was ready.'

Peter got up quietly and got a pad of paper and a pen out of a drawer. He sat down again and took notes as Lisa continued.

'I followed you in news reports on the internet and in the newspapers. And I found out which police station you were based at. Then I followed you home. It was good luck your house backing on to the golf course like that. I had the idea of putting the police off the scent by leaving footprints that would suggest that the killer was a large man. I got that from a children's book.'

'The Mystery of the Invisible Thief!' Lucy, Bernie and Jonah chorused.

'That's right.' Lisa continued. 'So I bought some big wellies at a market stall while I was on holiday in Cornwall one year and kept them in the bottom of my wardrobe until I was ready.'

'You must have waited a good long while,' Jonah commented. 'By the time we found the footprints they'd stopped making that type of boot.'

'It must have been five years,' Lisa agreed. 'It was the first holiday that I went on by myself. You see, it was all part of the plan that I'd made. I knew I'd have to be patient, because when you're twelve you can't do *anything*. So I planned everything to make sure you wouldn't be able to link me with the shooting.'

'Such as using a different rifle from the one we had on file as having been sold to you?' Jonah suggested.

'Yes. If you look back at your police files, you may find that I reported a burglary in January 2007, when a rifle was stolen. I faked the break-in and hid the rifle, so that I could use it to shoot you and it wouldn't be traced back to me.'

'And where is it now?' Peter asked.

'I was afraid that the police might get there before I could get away, so I wanted to get rid of everything, in case I was stopped and searched. I prepared hiding places for the gun and the boots. I think it was Baden-Powell who said that people never look up. There's a little copse on the golf course, about a hundred yards from the back of your garden, so I decided to hide them up in the trees.'

Bernie put a cup of tea in front of her. 'Sugar?' Lisa shook her head and continued with her narrative.

'I went there well in advance – about six months I suppose – and I found a tree that I could climb quite easily. Then I came back at night, when there was nobody about, and I climbed up and attached some straps to one of the branches. I used them to fasten the rifle to the upper side of the branch so it couldn't be seen from below, even if you knew where to look. I left it there, so that I could get it on whichever day I found an opportunity to do the shooting.

'And I fixed up a knotted rope on another tree – the sort of thing that children use to swing on – so that I could climb up and hide the wellies after I'd finished with them. They were more likely to be seen, so I wanted them to be separate from the gun. I wore a bright yellow tee-shirt and brought a dark-coloured jumper to put on top afterwards.' Lisa gave a smile of satisfaction with her own cleverness.

'I saw the appeals for people to report if they'd seen anyone on the golf course that afternoon wearing yellow. After I got home, I burned the tee-shirt on a bonfire in the garden. I thought of everything. The morning of the shooting, I practised on the rifle range for an hour so that if I was tested for gunshot residue the police would assume it had come from that. I joined a rambling club to show that I liked walking. I talked to them about how much I liked solitary walks, so that there would be witnesses to say that there was nothing unusual about me being on the golf course alone that day.'

'I have to say, I admire your meticulous planning,' Jonah commented. 'But it's a pity to devote your life to … to …'

'To revenge,' Lisa finished for him. 'I wanted you to pay. I wanted to kill you. At first, I was disappointed when I heard that you weren't dead. Then I started to think that maybe it was even better the way it was. I thought it must be like a sort of living death. My only regret was that you didn't know *why*. I would have liked you to know that it was for what you did to Dad … what I thought you'd done, I mean.'

'Armed Police!' The door slammed open and suddenly two police gunmen were there, weapons braced, eyes scanning the room.

'You took your time,' Jonah said scathingly. 'As you can see, we've managed without you. Now put those toys away and sit down while Lisa here finishes telling us her story.' He turned back to Lisa.

'So what made you change your mind? Why did you decide to kill me after all?'

Lisa did not reply, so Jonah looked towards her father.

'It was that television programme,' he explained. 'We saw a preview, where you said that you were leading a happy life.'

'It wasn't fair!' Lisa wailed. 'I thought, why should he be happy when Mum's dead and Dad can't get a decent job and …'

'It strikes me,' Peter put in, 'that if you'd spent more time working on how you could make a life for yourself and less on scheming and plotting to destroy Jonah's life *you* could have been happy too.'

'Never mind about that,' said Jonah in a business-like

tone. 'Time to get you two off to the police station, I think. Peter – can you go with them? And take those, no doubt excellent, notes that I see you've been making.'

****

Lisa was duly taken away for questioning and made her formal statement before being released on police bail. Over the following weeks, investigations produced further evidence of the truth of her story. A young police constable spent half a day climbing every climbable tree in the little wood before he found the rifle, still strapped to its branch. It took several days to locate the tree where the boots had been stowed, because the rope swing had long since disintegrated; only one boot could be found, the other presumably having fallen to the ground and become lost in the deep leaf litter. The case looked watertight and Lisa was almost certain, in any case, to plead guilty, but somehow Jonah managed to convince the Crown Prosecution Service that it would not be in the public interest to take her to court. She was, he argued, no threat to anyone else and it would be a waste of public money for her to serve the lengthy custodial sentence that would be inevitable were she to be convicted of attempted murder.

All this, however, was in the future. First, there was an important appointment at 4.30 p.m. on Sunday. Lisa and her father sat rather nervously in front of the television set, waiting for the start of the programme that they knew would only further increase their feelings of guilt and shame, but which they felt compelled to watch.

In County Durham, Reuben and Anne called the children to 'come and see Grandad on the television!'

In their cottage in Craven Arms, Paul and Karen set aside the guest list that they were preparing for their upcoming wedding and turned on the TV set in the corner of the room.

Jeanette was on duty at the hospital that day, but she gathered staff and patients from the unit into the day room to watch the success story of one of 'their' patients.

Jenny ushered members of the CU and the chapel choir and congregation into the room at the back of chapel where she had arranged for a television to be set up for the occasion.

Nathan and Georgia strapped the baby into her car seat and made the journey from their London flat out to Oxford to join in Sunday Lunch, preparatory to watching *Inspirational Lives* with the rest of Jonah's new extended family. Silvia and Stan came over as usual. Wayne and Dean were there, chattering eagerly about the new house that they were in the process of buying.

They all crowded into the living room. Wayne and Dean were squashed together at one end of the settee to make room for Nathan, Georgia and the baby at the other end. Sylvia and Stan occupied armchairs. Peter perched on the piano stool while Lucy and Bernie sat cross-legged on the floor in front of Jonah, whose chair was positioned centrally to give him the best view of the screen.

'Detective Chief Inspector Jonah Porter enjoys having his grandchildren to stay.' The television screen shows a happy picture of two children descending from a tree house and running across a lawn towards a group of adults sitting around a table. 'But he can't join in their games, ever since a bullet in the spine paralysed him eight years ago.'

Four-year-old Andrew comes running across the grass carrying *The Very Hungry Caterpillar* and climbs up into Jonah's lap. Andrew opens the book and they can be seen reading it together. The camera cleverly avoids showing the moment when Andrew dislodges Jonah's hand from the controls of his chair and Bernie sneaks up on all fours in order to replace it without getting in the picture.

'Andrew's very photogenic,' Sylvia commented. 'He has the making of a TV star when he grows up!'

'Today,' the presenter continues, a disembodied voice sounding over the idyllic family scene, 'I've come to Jonah's house to talk to him about his journey from devastating injury back into full-time police work, and to share some of his favourite hymns.'

The scene changes and Jonah is sitting in his chair the living room, with Bernie and Peter on the settee to his left and Lucy occupying a chair on his right. The presenter is sitting opposite them.

'Eight years ago you were paralysed by a bullet in the back of your neck,' he says. 'Now, most people would expect that such an injury would mark the end of your police career, but you were determined to get back to your work as a detective inspector. Can you tell me what motivated you to do that, instead of taking it easy?'

'Pig-headedness most likely,' Jonah replies with a laugh. 'I wasn't going to let some madman with a gun dictate the course of my life. And, of course, I had a lot of friends who supported me. I wouldn't have been able to do it without them."

'And foremost among them must be your late wife Margaret,' suggests the presenter. 'And it's in her memory that you've chosen your first hymn.'

They watched intently as the programme unfolded. It was remarkable the way that the director had managed to include so much within forty minutes. There was a shot of Wayne and Dean in their workshop (good publicity for the business). There were glimpses of Jonah at work, with Bernie ever-present in the background. One hymn was sung by the congregation at their church and showed the interior of the building off to good effect. As the programme drew near its end, everyone had a growing feeling of satisfaction.

'And now,' the presenter says to Jonah, who is sitting in the living room at home with Peter, Bernie and Lucy beside him. 'Can you tell me the single thing that you most miss as a result of your injury?'

'Being able to touch people,' Jonah replies, then with a small laugh, 'Oh dear! That sounds a bit sinister, doesn't it? I mean, for example, when my first grandchild was born, I wasn't able to hold him. And I can't give someone a pat on the back to say, "Well done!" or a hug to say, "Thank you."'

'But it's really good for us!' Lucy breaks in joyfully, hugging Jonah enthusiastically around the neck and shoulders from behind and kissing him on the cheek, 'because it gives us all an excuse to give him lots of hugs and kisses to make up for it!'

'Now, you tell me,' Jonah says, smiling broadly, 'how many men of my age can boast a seventeen year old girlfriend who can't keep her hands off them?'

There is general laughter and then the presenter says, 'You've chosen *In Heavenly Love Abiding* for your last hymn, 'Why's that?'

'I suppose because of its optimism,' Jonah replies, 'and you've just seen that I *am* surrounded by lots of love.'

'And if you could meet the person who shot you,' asks the presenter finally, 'what would you say to them?'

'I think,' Jonah replies, 'that I would say, "I bet *you* haven't had as much fun over the last eight years as *I* have!"'

****

In heavenly love abiding,
No change my heart shall fear;
And safe in such confiding,
For nothing changes here.
The storm may roar without me,
My heart may low be laid,
But God is round about me,
And can I be dismayed?

Wherever He may guide me,
No want shall turn me back;
My Shepherd is beside me,
And nothing can I lack.

His wisdom ever waketh,
His sight is never dim;
He knows the way He taketh,
And I will walk with Him.

Green pastures are before me,
Which yet I have not seen;
Bright skies will soon be o'er me,
Where darkest clouds have been.
My hope I cannot measure,
My path to life is free;
My Saviour has my treasure,
And He will walk with me.

Anna L. Waring (1823-1910)

THANK YOU

Thank you for taking the time to read Changing Scenes of Life. If you enjoyed it, please consider telling your friends or posting a short review. Word of mouth is an author's best friend and much appreciated.

Thank you,

Judy

MORE ABOUT BERNIE AND HER FRIENDS

Bernie features in four more books.

- **Awayday:** a traditional detective story set amongst the dons of an Oxford college.
- **Despise not your Mother:** the story of Bernie's quest to learn about her dead husband's past.
- **Two Little Dickie Birds:** a murder mystery for DI Peter Johns and his Sergeant, Paul Godwin.
- **Murder of a Martian:** a double murder for Peter and Jonah to solve.

You can find more information about some of the hymns featured in this book at:
http://www.singingthefaithplus.org.uk/.

Read more about Bernie Fazakerley and her friends and family at https://sites.google.com/site/llanwrdafamily/ or visit the Bernie Fazakerley Publications Facebook page here:
https://www.facebook.com/Bernie.Fazakerley.Publication s?fref=nf

Follow Bernie on Twitter: https://twitter.com/BernieFaz.

ABOUT THE AUTHOR

Like her main character, Bernie Fazakerley, Judy Ford is an Oxford graduate and a mathematician. Unlike Bernie, Judy grew up in a middle-class family in the South London stockbroker belt. After moving to the North West and working in Liverpool, Judy fell in love with the Scouse people and created Bernie to reflect their unique qualities.

As a Methodist Local Preacher, Judy often tells her congregation, "I see my role as asking the questions and leaving you to think out your own answers." She carries this philosophy forward into her writing and she hopes that readers will find themselves challenged to think as well as being entertained.